"Nickolas Cook has an eye for detail and an understanding of the horror genre. Cook writes with passion and skill and knows the biggest monster lies within the darkness of the human heart."

–Scott Nicholson, author of They Hunger, The Red Church and The Farm

"Black Beast is a deluge of atmospheric terror. I couldn't put it down."

–Ryan Thomas, author of Summer I Died and The Ratings Game

"Welcome to Poe country. Slime drips from the walls. Menacing occult powers fester, and a harsh landscape mirrors the turbulence of the characters inner lives. The Black Beast of Algernon Woods seethes with enough action and plot twists to fill a dozen horror novels–Nickolas Cook possesses a welcome appreciation for all the nearly forgotten traditions of dark literature. He evokes a creeping sense of dread, rife with unholy secrets and ancient curses. One hears echoes of Lovecraft...and Blackwood...and Machen. If only more of the new crop of horror authors displayed as much love for the language and the craft of writing."

–Robert Dunbar, author of The Pines and The Shores

THE BLACK BEAST OF ALGERNON WOOD

By

Nickolas Cook

THE BLACK BEAST OF ALGERNON WOOD

Copyright 2009
Nickolas Cook
All rights reserved
First Printing March 2009
ISBN978-0-9815845-4-6

Written by Nickolas Cook

Cover by Jose Pardo

Published by Dailey Swan Publishing, Inc

No part of this book may be copied
or duplicated except with written prior
permission of the publisher, Small
excerpts may be taken for review
purposes with proper credit given.

Dailey Swan Publishing, Inc
2644 Appain Way #101
Pinole Ca 94564
www.daileyswan publishing.com

Dedication

To my wife Kim. Patient as a saint, she's supported me even in my darkest moments. You are loved beyond words. Thank you for sharing your world with me, my dear.

To my mother, Martha, who always knew the value of imagination and encouraged my writing. She was my first reader and the one who expected better every time.

To my Great Grandmother, Annie May Cook, who taught me the power of the written word, of love, and nature. Your gentle wisdom is sorely missed.

To my brother Phillip, who always knew the coolest stuff to do when we were kids, and who loves horror movies as much as me. We will always share nightmares and dreamscapes, brother. (Do you still dream of the drive-in?)

To my father, Gene, who taught me the importance of hard work and perseverance, something that every child should be so lucky to learn–especially writers. There aren't enough words to thank you for the sacrifices you made for us.

To the gang at shocklines. You guys and gals have always welcomed newbies and shared your years of hard won industry wisdom. From the bottom of my heart, I thank each and every one of you for your generosity in sharing your wisdom, encouraging words, and sometimes hard truths.

CHAPTER -1-

The roiling funereal clouds bulleted rain down from the dark sky; violent wet shots that hammered the small slow moving car as it struggled along the sinuous mountain highway. Past the steeple-like crags of the surrounding rocky landscape, lightning flashed in telegraphic spasms. A harsh wind slammed into the mountains side- the voice of an unseen and angry God.

Conley Machen felt warm beads of fear sweat roll down his pale cheek, as he pushed the car for all it was worth, willing it up each steep climbing section of the road. He squinted through the storm in an effort to see the next turn in the roadway ahead. This was not the kind of car that could easily handle such inclement conditions. The engine was squealing for mercy each time he hit the gas to keep it climbing. The tires were old, too old for this kind of weather, and every second brought visions of the car slipping back down the steep hill, the wind throwing his vehicle headlong over the cliff on his right.

But, despite the dangerous weather, Conley was glad he had something to keep his mind occupied, anything to keep at bay the thoughts of his damned father.

Another sudden wind howled up from the mist-shrouded valley below and buffeted the car like an invisible linebacker, rocking it violently. He felt the involuntary clench in his abdomen, as he waited to see if the car was going to give up its tenuous hold sodden road.

Conley slowed the car, tried not to think about how far down it was to the bottom of the rock and pine lined valley below. He eased the small tired vehicle into another tight, rain-slicked mountain curve, and wound around the rock wall to his left. To his right there was only the flimsy excuse for a barrier between him and empty space- a joke on this road. Past the all-too thin metal was about a hundred and twenty feet of air, which ended abruptly in a rock littered forest basin. If he hit the metallic barrier doing even half of the legal speed limit, he knew he was going over the side. Gravity would take over from there; death would be a sure thing from that point.

Through the blinding rain, Conley tried to decipher road from a sure death over the side. The headlights weren't much help; the twin beams disintegrated a few feet beyond, impotent against the near-solid sheets of driven water. He had only vague shapes by which to navigate.

It was too dangerous to keep driving. He had to stop.

Another curve, the small car struggled. Tires slick, the back wheels slipped...slipped and then gripped the road again. His heart quickened, until he felt the car right itself once more.

He slowed down to a crawl, feeling the light shakiness of fear in his legs and arms.

Not one vehicle had passed him for almost thirty minutes. Swallowed by the fury of the storm, with its enforced early twilight, gave him as unsettling sensation of being the last person on earth. The isolation made the hairs on the back of his neck stand at chilly attention, and he shivered despite the warm air blowing from the car's vents.

He just needed to get home, off this road, out of this crazy rainstorm. Everything would be fine at home. Mary and Timmy were waiting in a nice warm trailer, eager to see him. At home, safe again, he could try to forget the call today. He could bury it safely under the happy routine of being a husband and a father. He could forget all about the call from his father, Stewart Machen.

Wiping a patina of chilled sweat from his forehead, he thought about how nice it would be to talk to Mary about it, let her reassure him that his past was of no consequence, that the Conleys were of no importance to their simple way of life.

But he didn't have the luxury of such reassurance. Mary knew nothing of his past. She didn't even know his family existed.

Maybe it was time, time to tell his wife the truth.

But the idea of finally telling Mary the truth and his thoughts inevitably went back to his damned father, and their conversation earlier that day.

The unwelcome phone call had come while he was at work. How his father had gotten his office number, Conley had no idea. But he suspected the old bastard had been keeping track of him all these years he'd fooled himself that escape was possible. Exactly the sort of underhanded, controlling behavior he would expect of Stewart Machen. It sure as hell wouldn't be the first time he had done so.

Conley could feel his temper flare like hot iron.

How dare he keep track of him? He wasn't his damned property to be watched.

Since walking away from the ancestral Machen Mansion, in Ellison County, Georgia, and out of the shadowy dark trees of Algernon Wood, nearly ten years ago, he hadn't seen or heard from his father. But there had never been much doubt that Stewart had been keeping tabs on him. Control was important to Stewart. It was power, and his father cared only for power. Money was only a means to an end towards having power over others. At twenty-one, Conley had left behind a legacy of a family worth millions and gone as far away from Stewart Machen as he could afford on the meager funds he could call his own. And he had been quite happy with being 'disowned', a threat that meant more to the old man than Conley. The money meant when he'd slammed the door behind him that day. All he wanted was to be left alone for the rest of his life, to be forgotten by the Machen family. He wanted nothing to do with the legacy of greed that his family propagated.

No appreciation for the values of our heritage, he could hear Stewart Machen shout. That sneering, cracking voice, a familiar, soul withering resonance, one he'd heard many times in the past as his father lectured him on one thing after another. *Your generation doesn't know what it means to carry on a tradition!*

Tradition... some words tasted like rusty metal on your tongue as you said them.

Being a Machen meant being part of a bloody custom, something from which Conley had decided at an early age to escape.

What made him more uncomfortable about the unwelcome intrusion of his father back into his life again was that he knew deep down the call had less to do with him and more to do with his own son, Timmy.

Sweet, innocent Timmy, with his concentrated frown and tousled curly black hair. A small version of himself, as Mary constantly reminded him. Six-years old and smart as anything. Full of character. Curious about anything he could get his hands on. The boy, his boy, had, in the past year, become like a little adult, a smiling, laughing entity that did more than watch TV and cry when he was unhappy. Every time Timmy gave him a curious stare, or a half-hidden smile, Conley was reminded of himself at that age. Sometimes Conley felt such an overwhelming happiness at being a father that he lost his breath when he looked at Timmy. Thankfully, so far, the kid was innocent of how shitty parents could be to their offspring. And Conley was going to make sure that he would always remain so. Conley was going to be different than his father. No trying to control every aspect of the kid's life. No pushing and prodding into uncomfortable discussions on the value of money and how to make people do what you wanted.

For the first time since the dread afternoon communiqué with his father, thoughts of Timmy drove out the familiar trapped feeling in his gut, a horrible sensation that had been cultivated during his childhood, and threatened to overwhelm him now, after all this time, just below the surface, that horrible feeling, waiting to boil up again at the slightest hint of his family. It snatched him unceremoniously back, like a sudden nauseating shift in time, to his childhood at Machen Mansion. The memories snipped at his emotions, like piranha, and he felt his cheeks burn with indignation.

The old bastard had no right to invade his life again.

There had to be some legal way to keep him from calling. First thing tomorrow morning, Conley would call around, seek some legal advice. It would be expensive, but he had to do something.

This afternoon, after the dreadful phone call had ended, Conley had sat behind his desk, wrestling with his emotions, trying to keep his mind on his work, until the claustrophobic feeling had finally driven him from his office. He hopped in his car and headed out of the city at an insane speed, racing foolishly down wet, gray streets. His mind had wandered through the bleak memory corridors like some angst ridden Poe character examining his own broken, cracked interior walls. Mindlessly, he had kept up the furious speed, until he reached the mountain pass that connected the city to his rural home set back in the woods high up the mountain. Then the rain clouds had burst again shortly after he'd turned onto the twisting, winding roadway. Up to now, the act of maneuvering his way home had kept him busy, so that he had momentarily forgotten his sensation of dread.

Against his will, Conley replayed the conversation in his mind. It had not been an overly long one; mostly consisting of Stewart making legal threats, something he did whenever faced with a situation in which he had no power, one he could not buy his way in or out. All the sneering threats, and snide comments, had come down to Stewart's demands to see his estranged grandson. When Conley laughed- actually laughed at the great Stewart Machen, a man who had made presidents and senators tremble with only a look- Stewart went into what Conley liked to think of as Tactic #2. Threats hadn't done any good against his son, so now it was time for bribery. His father had once told him that every person had their price; that even the most horrendous of acts could be paid for, if only you had enough money to pay for it. And that might be true for some people, but Conley was not to be bought.

Then the old man had reached into his grab bag for Tactic #3. He yelled and sobbed, pretending pity, guilt, and sympathy- unknown concepts to a lizard like Stewart Machen. If only he could just see his beloved grandson once, before he died. One visit. What son could refuse a man whom had given him life one visit with his grandson? And he was dying, for Christ's sake.

But Conley had stood his ground and told his father he was exactly that kind of man. Stewart Machen's tried and true Holy Trinity of power- legal threats, bribes, and guilt- had failed him miserably. In fact, the old man's manipulating attitude had only strengthened Conley's hatred for him. The Machens could go straight to Hell, as far as he was concerned. They would never get their greedy hands on his family as long as he lived.

And, in a way, that was exactly his crux. At the bottom of it all, what worried him most was who would fend for them against the Machens if he were to die right now? For all his father's talk of dying, Conley knew it was only a ploy: Stewart Conley, despite his agedness, had always been healthy, probably in better shape than Conley. He didn't know his father's exact age, for Stewart refused to discuss it. But Conley knew he had to be at least in his seventies by now- maybe older, so he didn't think the old bastard was going to outlive him. And his grandmother, the venerable family matriarch, Charlotte Machen, had been ancient even when he was a young boy. She must be at least twice as ninety by now. No way would she outlive him. As for his mother, Conley never knew her; she had died giving birth to him. Stewart had never bothered to remarry, so Conley was an only child.

Another gust of wind howled in from the right, braced the car. Conley fought the vehicle away from the high stone wall that suddenly leaped from out of the rain on his left.

Better keep your mind on road, he warned himself. Or you might just end up as road kill in this weather.

The fury of the driving rain seemed to double, and slammed against the windshield, heavier, more violent, a virtual curtain of water, shifting and dancing with the eddying winds, pulling and coercing patterns and shapes from the air before him. Conley slowed to almost a dead stop. He knew the road well enough to know he was about to hit a flat patch at the bottom of the hill. Only a few miles from home now, but as anxious as he was to see Mary and Timmy, to assure himself that his world was safe from his father, he knew that it was better not to chance it. Better to be late than dead.

The sodden highway curved and dipped, pulling the car along with it, and at the bottom of the next dip he could see the flat area. The perfect place to park and wait out the worst of the storm. He'd call Mary on his cell, let her know he was on his way. Besides he needed some time to think how he was going to finally tell her the truth.

Several times over the years he had been on the verge of telling her he'd lied about his family being dead. But something inside of him always held him back. Maybe it was the fact that after all these years of lying to her he was afraid that she it might create an emotional chasm between them. Oddly enough, it was the trust between them that he valued, as hypocritical as that sounded. And he knew how important trust was with his wife as well. Something like this...well, she might leave him. He could never live through that. He loved her more than life itself.

There was a lot about his family that he could never hope to explain to her. Hell, some of the things he had seen as a child in Algernon Wood he couldn't even explain to himself. The Machens weren't like other families. They never had been. How could he hope to tell her about the strange things that Stewart had told him as a child? She would think him insane if he told her of his fears, the unspoken things that he sensed about his father.

He could hear Mary now. Logical, grounded Mary. The supernatural did not exist. Then he would have to tell her about things he didn't want to ever remember again, horribly impossible things. The dark shapes at his window at night. The sounds in the depths of Algernon Wood that defied simple explanation. Then there were the stories the locals told about The Black Beast, an inhuman creature that called the woods home. And there were the stories they told about his family, terrible tales of ancient deviance, murder, sickness, and death.

No, he wasn't about to get into that with level headed Mary.

At the bottom of the hill, Conley gently brought the car to a stop in the deluge and shut down the engine. The noise of the rain increased, and the violent tattoo on the roof of the car gave the illusion that he was drowning in a vast, dimly lit sea. All sound but the din of the deluge, and the tiny sounds of his car squeaking back and forth in the playful hands of the wind, ceased. He was swallowed by the wet violence. The noisome cascade on the metal roof deafened him. For a few tense moments, he sat listening to the sounds around him, feeling his mouth pressed into a hard line, and tried to push away the ever-growing sense of dread that refused to go away.

He fumbled with the glove box and dug out his cell-phone...then he froze in mid motion. Had the car just moved?

Through the rain swept windshield, he could see no change- still the same underwater sensation as before. But he had felt the car move under him, hadn't he?

He waited, one hand holding the cell, the other clutching the dashboard with white knuckled intensity. His breath was caught in his throat, fluttering like a caged bird with every slam-thump of his heart.

The car began to slide across the wet ground. Mud crumbled in thick sodden layers, gave way, carrying the vehicle closer and closer to the edge of the embankment. Rain sluiced down the side of the cliff, fell into the vast emptiness beyond.

With the cell still clutched in one hand, Conley leaned toward the window and saw the mud slurping greedily at the front tires. He watched the mud sliding him closer to the edge as if he were in a dream.

The car shook as another gust of wind helped move it closer to the edge.

Conley snatched himself from his confused daze and made a move to open the door. In a handful of precious moments he would never get back, he forgot about the lock, fought vainly against the handle.

The deadly incline moved closer.

His hands shook as he pulled against the locked door. The doomed moan of a trapped animal caught in his throat.

The car gave a sudden lurch...

And then chaos took control as his world became a twirling, confusing unreality. He crashed back and forth from the seat to the roof of the car. Through the sound of his own grunting cries, he could hear trees snapping loudly all around him. Mud splattered across the scant view of his tumbling world. Metal screeched in agony, pierced and ripped apart by sharp pine tops and jagged rock fingers that gouged greedily at the contents of his falling coffin.

Conley slammed into the passenger side door. A hot, screaming pain tore through his arm, as it snapped at the elbow. Something warm and thick coated his tongue and knew that it was his own blood. Pain- a living monster bent on ripping him limb from limb- exploded across his body, a red-hot thing boiling to the surface from within. His neck slammed hard against the back of the seat. His body went numb below his knees, as if his body had disappeared. The cell-phone, still clutched desperately in his hand, cracked in two when he flew against the windshield like a crumpled doll. Something else hit his head and the tumbling world narrowed to black, then went away for good.

The car careened and bounced, rolling down the steep hill, hitting unforgiving ancient pine and rocks, tearing and driving huge chunks of sodden earth before its violent path. It only took a few moments for the twisted metal of the car to finally find rest at the bottom of the steep canyon. When it settled into a mass of steaming, torn metal, Conley Machen was nothing more than a broken frame of torn muscle and bone. Rain splashed through the cracks and tears, washed pink diluted tears along his still face.

For Conley Machen the nightmare was over.

But for his wife and child the nightmare was just about to begin.

CHAPTER -2-

Two hours into the party, as couples began to arrive by the carload, Mary Machen knew she was wrong to have come tonight. She hadn't been ready. She should have waited to try this on her own again. Mary stood against the wall, watching the ever-milling group of laughing partygoers talk animatedly to one another, carrying drinks from the porch to the living room, and back again, all the while she tried hard to pretend that Conley was somewhere in the room. That he was not dead. Only lost somewhere in the noisome crowd, maybe just across the room getting a drink at the bar, maybe obscured for a moment by the heads and shoulders of the crowd between them. But Mary knew no matter how much she played this stupid- and possibly mentally unhealthy- game with herself, Conley was dead, gone forever. He was not at the bar, or in the restroom, or on the balcony talking with their friends Tammy and Paul Barnett. Conley was not going to stroll in and catch her eye, smiling that boyish lopsided smile of his, walking a little too carefully because he might have had a few too many like he always did at these get-togethers. Conley, her husband, her only love, the father of her child, was gone from her life for good and she was left with nothing more than photos, memories, and this stupid game of hide and seek with a phantom in a crowded room of people she barely knew.

As she watched the crowd with a frown, a man, who looked to be around her own age, his early thirties, spotted Mary from across the room at the wet bar. He gave her an uncertain smile. Mary tried on an uncomfortable smile of her own, but it felt too fleeting and intangible; she could only claim it for a second or two before it fled. She could only imagine how false it looked to him.

As proof, the man's smile died, and he turned to a younger blonde woman that had moved to stand next to him. He promptly forgot about the woman with the sad smile across the room. Mary hung her head, embarrassed and ashamed that she had lost her ability to mix and be friendly.

Why had she agreed to come to this damned party tonight?

But she knew the answer. She had only agreed to come because of loyalty to her friends, friends who had supported her after Conley's death. Or was it, instead, some hidden desire to get out from under the pall of her husband's sudden death, a sign that she had been morning for too long?

She should've just stayed home with Timmy tonight. They could've microwaved some popcorn, curled up on the couch together, and watched an old movie, maybe played a game of Parcheesi. Instead, she was standing against a wall, in a borrowed blue dress, feeling lost and out of place in the midst of a laughing crowd.

Thoughts of Conley made her eyes tear up. She turned to face the wall to hide the fact that she was crying (again!), as the stinging tears rolled down her burning cheeks. The hostess, Tammy, suddenly appeared by her side and pulled her close, placed her forehead against her own. Mary could smell vodka on her friend's breath, yet another sign that everyone was getting into the swing of things but her. Tammy held drinks in both hands, passed one into Mary's shaking, grateful hand. The glass was icy cold and she gripped it as if it were her only lifeline at the moment. Embarrassed, she kept her back to the crowd, took two deep burning swallows of the vodka straight, wincing at the numbing strength of the alcohol as it coursed its fiery way down her throat and into her belly. She felt the crowd staring at her back, murmuring about the woman who was balling her eyes out in the corner. They probably thought she was some kind of maudlin drunk or something. Some of them knew her, knew what had happened to Conley; surely they could understand that she was still upset. Of course if they didn't, then they could go fuck themselves as far as she was concerned. Let anyone of them see how it felt to deal with losing your only true love. See how they did at parties full of drinking, happy couples, knowing that they would never again be among their numbers.

Tammy patted her shoulder, whispered, "It's okay, honey. I don't think anyone even noticed."

Mary smiled despite the miserable heavy sensation in her heart. "Thanks for lying."

Tammy snickered. "Well, if anyone did notice they'll be so drunk by the end of the night they'll never remember a thing. Right?"

Mary sniffled again, took a swipe at her face to keep more tears from spilling on her borrowed blue dress. Against her better judgment, she'd chosen to wear mascara tonight, and it was probably running all down her cheek by now. She shook her head and gave her friend an embarrassed shrug. "I don't know what caused it."

"It's only been four months, Mary," Tammy said, shaking her head. "No one expects you to be singing every morning, for God's sake. I'm sure about a million things could set you off these days."

Mary nodded. She knew she couldn't stay. She had to get the hell out of here. "Tammy..." she began, but before she could go on, Tammy hugged her and said, "I know, honey. It's okay. We'll both understand if you want to ditch the party. It probably wasn't the smartest thing in the world for me to bully you into coming tonight anyway." A laughing young woman bounced into them, excused herself with a tipsy giggle and moved on. "I'm sorry I made you come," Tammy continued. "I thought it might do you some good, that's all. You want me to drive you home? We'll drop your car off tomorrow afternoon."

"No, I can make it home," she said. "I'll be fine." She hugged her best friend once more, and gave her a quick kiss on the cheek. "Thanks again, Tammy." She handed her the half full glass of vodka. One thing she didn't need to do was drown her misery in alcohol.

On her way out, she found Paul surrounded by several younger men, as he went on about last week's baseball games. She felt she should at least say something. She thanked him and gave him a token hug, but Paul was on his way to being drunk. He gripped her shoulder, whispered in her ear that he was around if she needed someone to do anything at all. Rake leaves, do some repairs, just call me. Mary thanked him again, said she give him a call if she needed anything.

"You promise me?" he called loudly as she started away. "I mean anything. Maybe I'll swing by in a couple of days see if Timmy wants to go catch a few out at the park, okay?"

As she waved goodbye, leaving behind the loud crowd of men, she heard Paul telling the others how worried he and Tammy were about her.

Outside, the night was a welcome retreat. The sound of the party dimmed as she walked away. Above, a panorama of stars glittered down as she made her way past the shrubbery to her aged (but still running, thank you) compact car. Now that the sun had been down for a few hours, a chill had settled over the mountain top community, and she shivered. Inside the car, Mary got it going after the engine gave a couple of cold coughs, put the car in gear, and backed her way past a conglomeration of pick up trucks and mid size cars scattered across the yard. She followed the rutted old dirt road half a mile out of the woods to the ragged county asphalt roadway. She was in no hurry to get home, now that she was away from the party. She wanted to be less maudlin when she arrived. The last thing she needed was for Timmy to see her like this.

Mary turned on the heater, waited for the air to blow hot. After a few minutes, the vents began to spew a toasty stream of deliciously warm air that felt pleasant, almost erotic soft, against her face, like a lover's breath in her sleep.

Great. On top of everything else she was feeling physically dispirited, too. God, how could she even think about something so selfish right now?

It felt too much like a betrayal to Conley's

memory, so soon after his death, this sudden urge to be touched by another person. But underneath her emotional turmoil, she sensed the urge went much deeper than just a mere physical need. What she missed most was someone to talk to during those lonely moments. She needed that right now more than she needed a lover. Someone that wasn't a six-year old boy. As much as she loved Timmy, what she really wanted was some adult company. He was a great kid, but his topics for conversation didn't range much out of the cartoons he watched at home and the children's books he read at school.

Of course, the contradiction was that she had left a party full of adults a few minutes before. So if she needed to talk with someone so badly, why cop-out the first time she's around other people for any length of time since Conley's death? Why run away? She'd a chance to mingle and she'd thrown it away. But what the hell could she talk about with any of those people? What it felt like to raise a son alone because her husband was dead?

She had nothing in common with them. Surely, they were good people, but Mary couldn't force polite conversation right now; she felt too dislocated, still too damned angry that Conley had been taken from her and Timmy. She knew this was just a stage in the process of losing a loved one. But it didn't make her any less angry with God for taking him away.

Since the funeral, when she found herself cornered in a conversation with someone she knew, at the grocery store, or when she was picking up Timmy from school, she could see in their eyes what they really wanted to ask: How does it feel to lose someone you love? It was selfish and horrible, but she knew it was only human nature. She wasn't mad at them for it; she just didn't think she would be able to deal with it yet. She was still floundering with the hardest question of all these days: What was she going to do with herself now? How could she keep waking up everyday knowing that he was gone forever? She did not know; she had no answers. The soul-tearing ache was still too new, too horrible, to analyze with any perspective.

Even after four months, every book she read, every movie, every inner conversation she had with herself, she found herself wanting to share them all with Conley. No one else had had his sense of humor, his intelligence, his sense of purpose. No one could compare to him. Ever.

But Conley was gone.

She wasn't.

She had to keep reminding herself of that crucial fact.

She was still alive and kicking, and she had a son to raise. Though in the first two weeks, if it hadn't been for Timmy, she might have gladly joined Conley in some sad and bloody fashion. But there was Timmy to think of. She wasn't the only one to have felt the excruciating lose. The boy was good at hiding his sorrow, but she could tell losing his father had done him some serious damage. She had to make herself keep going each day, even if just for his sake.

As she ambled down the moonlit, deserted highway, Mary's memories of Conley and the life that they had shared together sat next to her on the way home. It was silent company, but comfortable. When she finally got home, and pulled into the driveway, she felt a little better, and even more relieved to be away from the party. Home was different without Conley, but it was still better than anywhere else.

In the splash of the headlights scraping across the front of the trailer she and Timmy shared, she could see her son standing in the front door, waving and grinning like a little maniac. He banged open the screen door, rushed headlong down the broken concrete steps to her. He latched onto her hips and she hugged him warmly, but didn't attempt hoisting him into her arms. She hadn't been able to do that since last year. She missed it. The kid was growing fast. He was jumping up and down, excited. She sure hoped it wasn't a Bugs Bunny marathon on Cartoon Network tonight; she didn't think she could take another cartoon marathon. Seeing Daffy Duck get his head blown off over and over again for the amusement of Bugs Bunny might wasn't her idea of entertainment.

"Mom! Mom! Granddaddy called!" he yelled, grabbing her hand and pulling her toward the door. Mary gave him a perplexed frown, as she allowed herself to be yanked up the broken cement steps. She needed to fix those soon. Before Timmy found a way to hurt himself on them.

Granddaddy?

Her father had been dead four years. Even though Timmy had been too young at the time to remember the funeral, he had been told about it more than once, so he knew her father was dead. Who could this 'granddaddy' person be?

Watching from behind the screen door, Mary saw Brenda, the babysitter. Brenda's eyes glittered with the kind of excitement only a sixteen-year-old girl, alone on a Saturday night, could muster. "How was the party?" she asked. Mary could hear the adoration in the young girl's voice, dreams of being adult, of going to adult parties. Then she frowned and looked at her watch. "You weren't gone very long, Mrs. Machen. Everything okay?"

"I'm fine. The party was fine," she replied in an offhand manner. She didn't even want to think about it right now, let alone talk about it. She still felt embarrassed about her crying jag in a room full of strangers. "Who called?" she asked the girl. "Timmy says someone called."

"Yeah," Brenda said. "Some guy called. He wanted to talk to you, but I told him that you were out, so he asked to speak with Timmy."

Mary felt her stomach clench with fear…and a little anger, too.

She tried to keep her voice even as she spoke. "And you let him?"

Jesus! Didn't this girl know what kind of world they lived in? Never tell a stranger you're alone in the house. Why did she bother having a babysitter if any freak could call on the phone and speak with her son?

Mary swallowed her anger. There was no sense in yelling at her. She was still technically a kid herself. Mary realized, too late, she didn't need to yell. Her anger was evident enough from the unintentional glare she was giving the girl.

Brenda backed away. "He said he knew you guys," she said, clearly rattled by Mary's unexpected anger. "I'm sorry, Mrs. Machen." She sounded close to tears.

Mary looked at the floor, ashamed at her reaction. She hugged her still bouncing son to her hip. "It's fine, Brenda. I'm sorry for being snippy. It's just been a hell of a night." She gently pushed Timmy aside and drew some money from her purse. "Thanks for keeping an eye on Timmy for us—" her voice caught in her throat, her heart thumped with the pain of realization. "I mean me." Again the sadness washed over her like cold water, startling her with its intensity. She closed her eyes, spoke quickly so as to have something else to concentrate on for the moment. "Do you want a ride home, honey?"

Brenda, still close to breaking into hurt tears, turned away. "No, I'll call my Dad. He's right down the road at his friend's house." She sidled past Mary and into the living room to use the phone by the couch- despite the one on the kitchen wall next to Mary.

Good going, Mary. You just made the one girl who needed no help feeling any lower, feel like a loser.

Between the girl's asshole drunk of a father, and dishcloth of a mother, she was going to have a hard enough time getting out of this shitty little hick town as it was.

Well, she'd just have to make it up to her next time. Maybe slip her an extra ten dollars. If she could afford it. Which wasn't likely these days. It was an indolent answer to the problem, but she was all out of ideas on how to help other people. These days she could barely help herself.

Since Conley's passing the bills had not stopped coming in, and her job as a waitress at the local greasy spoon wasn't doing much to keep up with them either. And, of course, there had been the final stab through her soul after her loss: The exorbitant cost to bury her husband. Even though she had used all of his company's insurance money (which had been little enough to begin with), it had covered only part of the expenses. The rest she had had to cover herself. If things didn't turn around soon, she and her son were going to be riding the infamous welfare train.

And if there was one thing she refused to do it was to go on the welfare wagon. She had promised herself after leaving the backwards little town where she'd grown up never to go on welfare like half of her family had been. It wasn't until she was in her teens that she figured out that living off the state was considered ignoble. She was reminded every day by mean spirited kids her own age how useless her drunken father was, and how weak and stupid her mother was for staying with him. She asked herself a million times why her mother wouldn't leave her father. Hell, it wasn't as if they could be any worse off without him. They lived on welfare, in a shack, ruled by a man who couldn't hold a job down for more than a few months at a time. Why had she stayed?

She would not let that happen to Timmy. She wanted him to have some pride in himself and his family- as diminished as that family was without Conley.

She didn't know what she would do. Maybe get a second job. Christ, it was bad enough since taking on a full time position; she hardly had enough time with Timmy these days. If she had to get another job...

She didn't even want to think about that tonight. There would be tomorrow to worry about it.

She gladly turned her attention to Timmy. "Okay, little sparkplug, you can stop jumping around now." In the living room, she could hear Brenda replacing the phone on the cradle. The girl came back to the kitchen and hesitantly handed Mary a scrap of torn yellow notepaper. Her dark circled eyes stayed on the floor, as if she were a bad puppy who had piddled on the carpet. Mary took the note, mentally kicking herself again.

Good job, Mary. Jesus...maybe you could go kick a kitten or something for an encore.

"I almost forgot, Mrs. Machen, that guy left his phone number for you to call him. He said to call him, no matter how late it was when you got home. He said please. He sounded like a nice guy to me." Brenda shrugged.

Mary stared at the scrap of paper in confusion. She didn't think it was routine for freaks or perverts to leave a return phone number. Which made this mystery even more mysterious. Who was this guy calling himself granddaddy?

She thanked Brenda and tried to apologize again, but the girl remained unresponsive and sullen. When she left to wait for her father at the end of the driveway, Mary knew that she had lost ground with the teenager this evening.

Back in the small cluttered living room, Timmy was watching TV, sitting about a foot from the screen, giggling at the escapades of some anime characters.

"Timmy, move back from the screen. You'll screw up your eyes sitting that close," she warned him for the millionth time. She grabbed the remote from the scarred coffee table, turned the volume down a few notches, and stood next to her son.

"Maaaaawwwm," Timmy whined.

"What did the man on the phone say to you earlier?" Looking at the piece of paper again, she didn't recognize the number. The area code didn't look like anything in North Carolina that she'd ever seen.

As if remembering he had a reason to rejoice once again, Timmy turned his attention to his mother, excited by the idea of telling her all about the man known as granddaddy. "Granddaddy wants us to come and visit him and grandmamma. He said he wants to give me something that belonged to Daddy. If I'm old enough, he said. Can I have it, Mom? Please? Can I?"

Mary's breath stopped in her chest as her son's hurried words finally began to penetrate her tired thoughts.

'Granddaddy' was Conley's father?

But that was impossible. Conley had told her that his family was dead. In fact, no matter how much she had pushed him to talk about them, Conley remained uncharacteristically tight lipped about them. It was only after Mary had backed him into a corner while they were dating that he would actually speak of them at all. And when he did, she could see a distance in his soft brown eyes, a distance that spoke of buried pain, a pain that he wasn't going to share with her. The only tangible information that she had ever gotten from him about his childhood was that he had grown up somewhere in Georgia and that he was an only child. Unlike other people, Conley had never been one to talk about family holidays and such. And the way he had been with Timmy around those special times, Mary could always tell he was trying to make up for them.

Timmy was still gazing up at her and she realized that he had something. She'd been too lost in her own thoughts and hadn't heard him. "What did you say, honey?"

Timmy rolled his eyes dramatically. "I said I'm old enough, ain't I?"

Mary grinned. "Ain't ain't a word, dear heart." Timmy giggled at her joke, as he always did. It was one of Conley's favorites, too.

Had been, she reminded herself.

Had Conley lied to her about his family? If so, why?

She decided there was only way to find out the truth. She reminded Timmy to scoot back from the screen again, and went to the phone by the couch. Mary picked up the phone with a tremor in her hand, dialed the unfamiliar number. She took a deep breath and waited. Shortly, there came a clicking sound and a static noise hissing menacingly along the distance between the connection. It was sound that she had come to associate with North Carolina's 'best' phone lines. When you lived in hill country, sometimes a good phone line was a luxury, not a privilege. After a few seconds of that sibilant hissing, the phone at the other end began to ring. She swallowed hard as it continued to ring away. Twice…three times…four times…

This had to be a colossal mix-up. Conley hadn't lied to her.

But she remembered that distant look in his eyes.

By the fifth ring, Mary wasn't sure she wanted to know the truth after all.

She began to move the receiver away from her ear.

Someone picked up. "Hello?"

It was an elderly woman's voice, near breathless, as if she had run to catch the line.

Now that she had a person on the other end of the line, Mary had no idea what she should say, or even how to begin the conversation.

"Hello?" the woman asked again, an irritated edge to her tone now.

"Hi," Mary finally made herself speak. "I'm sorry, but I'm trying to reach the person who called my son tonight. A man said he was my child's grandfather."

"Oh, my," the woman said. She sounded flustered. "This must be Mary, Timmy's mother. It's so good to finally hear from you after all these years. You have no idea how long I—well, I mean to say, we— have wanted to contact you and the boy. But Conley wouldn't have liked that at all. No, indeed, he would've been most displeased with Stewart and myself for talking with either of you."

Mary waited for a break in the old woman's onrush of words. "I'm sorry… whoever you are, but I was under the impression that all of Conley's family was dead."

The silence on the other end stretched on. "Hello?" Mary said.

The stunned silence was understandable. After all, who wouldn't be surprised to learn a family member had lied about their existence? Mary was still trying to come to grips with the fact Conley had lied to her. It was so unlike him not to have been honest and open with her. Had he been ashamed of his family? Were they poor Southern white trash? No, he had known about her own background; no way could his have been any worse than hers.

Finally, the old woman spoke again. "I can understand, Mary," she said. "He and Stewart had so many battles of will that Conley couldn't make himself stay. I suppose he could never forgive his father for certain episodes of temper. Certain words spoken in anger."

"Whom am I speaking with, please?" Mary asked, knowing how rude the question sounded, but unable to think clearly enough under the circumstances to keep a polite manner about her. The refined elderly voice was pleasant to listen to, a breathless, educated Southern drawl, but she still wasn't getting her anywhere near the truth of why they were calling her now. Her head was filled with half formed suspicions and thoughts. Conley had lied...but why? There had not been a cruel bone in her husband's body. He must have had a damned good reason for it.

"I'm so sorry, my dear," the old woman apologized with one a self-deprecating chuckle. "My name is Charlotte. Charlotte Machen. I'm Conley's grandmother; Stewart's mother."

"I'm sorry, Charlotte, I don't mean to sound rude, but I'm feeling a little off balance right now. I mean, it's a lot to find out that your husband didn't tell you the truth about his family."

"Yes, I would imagine that you're a bit uneasy about it, as well. I'm sure Conley never mentioned us to anyone. But let me assure you it would make us- Stewart and myself- so happy to finally meet Timmy." Then the old woman added hurriedly, almost as an afterthought. "And yourself, of course, my dear. Stewart says he sounds like a dear, sweet child."

"How do you mean, meet us?" Mary asked. She looked at her son. Timmy was turned away from the TV now, watching her conversation with Charlotte Machen. His bright, brown eyes were full of curiosity. He was a smart kid, able to catch on pretty quick to other peoples' moods and truths.

"We want you and the child to come here for a visit," Charlotte said, as if the concept should have been self evident to Mary. "It's only a few hundred miles away. Of course, we'll pay for the airline tickets and all other expenses."

"But I don't even know you people," she said. Again, she was keenly aware of how rude she must seem to someone who was trying to be generous. But the bottom line was she didn't know them. She needed to find some kind of solid ground here.

"Precisely, Mary," Charlotte replied. "And, sadly, we do not know you either. I think that it's time that we all rectify such a terrible wrong, my dear. And considering, now that Conley has passed away, your son is listed as sole heir to the Machen fortune, it seems to me that we have a number of things to speak about."

"W-what?" Mary stammered. She must have heard the woman wrong. "What fortune?"

When she answered, Mary didn't like the sense that there was the grinning arrogance of the rich in the tone of her voice. "He's to inherit twenty-six million dollars when Stewart passes on, Mary. Conley was Stewart's only child. Now that he is gone, that leaves Timmy next in line."

Mary couldn't speak; surely she was dreaming this whole episode. She was asleep. She would awake any second to find that it was all a dream brought on by the overwhelming grief of Conley's death.

She could only stare at her son, his grinning face the only thing that was real in this strange dream. But even in a state of silent shock, she wasn't too discombobulated to silently acknowledge that arrogant tone on the other end of the line. It sat in her gut like a burning stone of resentment- a poor person's reaction to a wealthy person's blatant disregard for the riches they took for granted.

"Now," Charlotte Machen's voice caressed from over the line, "don't you think we should get together and discuss this turn of events?"

Mary found herself agreeing for many reasons- some of which she was not in the least proud to call her own. Mostly, she agreed, because she needed to know why Conley had lied about his other family.

At least that was what she told herself.

CHAPTER -3-

Machen Mansion was a domicile with two faces.

For as long as the residents of Ellison, Georgia could remember, the house had squatted like some beast of prey in the tangled bosom of the dark forest. Set miles away from the small town, the house seemed to rise up like some elemental god of stone, glass, and wood from the mysterious sanctity of the wood. Its tall gothic spires stretched like thin talons into the sky; its dim windows stared blindly each day.

The daylight face of the house watched with indifference as, along the pristine rustic gables and turrets, a murder of loquacious crows roosted and watched the vast expanse of the emerald lawn for small creatures to pluck for sustenance. Once spotted, they spread midnight wings, fall like doomsday shadows, and snatch their prey from the ground. And then, with gleeful caws, they flew away to the forest darkness to rip apart their still squirming meals.

But when the moon reigned in her velveteen court, the night face seemed to draw back from the inexorable mystery of the forest, and no one whom dwelled within its ancient walls dared to venture forth. Beyond the high electric fence surrounding the property, the midnight forest seemed to thicken, take on new dimensions of shadow and menace.

As he did most nights, Stewart Machen stood before the great bay window that overlooked the back of the expansive property and stared glumly past the electric fence. He wondered what the inky darkness was hiding.

Was the creature watching him even now from those shadows?

Ridiculous theatrics, he chided himself with a weary sigh, and turned away, his blurry reflection pantomiming his movements. Most likely there was nothing beyond the security wall except for a few hungry raccoons, maybe an owl or two on the hunt for meat. At worst, a panther stalking the wetlands.

Nothing beyond his domain but the natural things of the world. Nothing to fear at all.

Stewart Machen swirled his evening brandy and tried to shake off the fear.

Why did he feel this unaccountable fear running up his spine with icy fingers? Why did he feel the same sensation every time he looked into the darkness of Algernon Wood?

But he already knew the answer.

Because it was almost time.

Soon, payment would be due and he nothing to exchange.

If he did not provide the payment…

Well, it was best not to think about the 'ifs' and 'maybes' at his age.

What was meant to be would be. Simple enough.

If he'd learned nothing else in his seventy-three years of life, he'd learned certain inevitabilities couldn't be escaped. One might forestall them, perhaps for a time persuade them in another direction, but they were always waiting for you at the end of the tunnel.

For Stewart Machen, the inevitable that occupied a great deal of his mind these days was the cessation of life, the end of his reign as the Machen master. It wasn't necessarily his own inevitable death that he feared, but what would be waiting for him on the other side of his soul, beyond that dark, obscuring veil. These days, the thought of it would nearly send him to gibbering screams in the wee hours of the night, when sleep refused him solace, and he had only 'visions' of his past to keep him company.

Of course, all of this fear and sleeplessness was Conley's fault. If he had only done what every Machen man had done in the name of the family, then none of this would be a problem. The hand would have been dealt in his favor. His life, and Conley's, would have been assured for a very long time to come. But Conley had chosen the coward's way out of the legacy. Had run away from his own 'inevitable'. And now Stewart was stuck having to live up to the infernal bargain made all those years ago.

Damn that infernal nuisance of a boy to Hell.
If there was such a thing as fiery damnation, he hoped that smug, self-righteous good fro nothing was burning in it right now.

What right did he think he had to change over a hundred years of family tradition? By his actions, he had destroyed all the Machens had worked for. He had belittled the very rooting out of the family's existence from the woods beyond.

But the bastard had gotten what was coming to him. Yes, the boy had paid for his desertion. And the laughable irony of it was that, no matter how hard he had tried to foil the family, he had gone out and done exactly what Stewart had asked him to do in the first place. He had gone and had a son of his own.

The sacred pact was broken.

The payment was soon due.

Stewart sighed and smiled, creasing his smooth tanned face into an old man's features for a brief moment. He didn't like the way it looked in the reflective window, so he let the smile go. Too many years had gone by. He could feel his age catching up. Yet another sign the time for payment was drawing nearer by the day.

No, one could not outrun the inevitable. Put it off for a short time, perhaps. But there it was waiting for you around the bend.

Outside, a familiar wispy, shadow shape flitted between two enormous sculpted hedges, and Stewart's heart skipped a beat, until he recognized it for one of his mother's servants. The shape disappeared around a bend in the foliage. Off on one of her missions, no doubt. What the mission might be was of little interest to Stewart. He was used to his mother's running the servants ragged for dubiously 'necessary' duties. But as it was one of the few joys left to the old dear he didn't interfere. Even when a servant disappeared from time to time. After all, it was the way of things.

Sleep.

He should try to make the effort. No sense in running himself down. He didn't want to be a cranky old man when the boy and his mother arrived. He needed the boy to trust him. It had been nearly thirty years since a child's footsteps had fallen in his home.

Not since Conley.

He hoped he could keep a civil tongue in his mouth while the boy's mother was around. He needed her to trust him as well, even if only for a short time. Then she could go and fuck herself for all he cared. In fact, she could disappear off the face of the planet.

He grinned archly. Of course, if she was worth a second look there was no reason to throw away good meat. Now was there?

With such thoughts to comfort him, Stewart turned down the lights in the giant room, until the only illumination came from the backyard of the estate, and made for his bed and the hope of sleep, if even for a few hours.

Outside the security fence, beneath the thick shadows of the trees, something black as night and full of hate watched Stewart Machen turn off the lights and disappear from view. For a moment the forest seemed to hold its collective breath, as the thing hunched down in the chill night, and glared peered past the electric fence and manicured topiary to the very spot where Stewart Machen had stood only seconds before.

It gave a low growl and stepped back into deeper darkness, until it was one with the black forest once again.

CHAPTER -4-

By the time Mary Machen found Ellison, twilight was beginning to gather in seeping increments. But there was enough daylight to show her Ellison was a lot like her own hometown deep in the hills of North Carolina. Like many rural towns in the South, Ellison was nothing more than lonely stretches of 'undeveloped' shadow laden forests, broken sporadically by a cluster of trailers or rundown houses. The road into the town was a long gray two lane- ragged and broken, fighting to stay alive in the overgrown culvert weeds and spreading cancerous potholes. On either side, a dark held sway. She supposed all forests had their own personalities. This one didn't strike her as very amiable. In fact, the apathetic face of all that darkness gave her the creeps to stare at it for too long, so she kept her eyes on the road.

The few houses she and Timmy passed along the way looked solitary and lost in the tall pines. On the way into town, she caught fleeting glimpses of the washed out gray faces that watched the strangers pass by with tired disinterest.

Next to her, Timmy watched the emptiness go by with his usual characteristic curiosity, peering at the small forlorn houses along the way.

The few signs they did see were hard to decipher. Years of harsh exposure to the elements had dulled the script to the point of obscurity; one had even been used as target practice for 'buckshot'. Past scores had left gaping rusty wounds behind. If Mary hadn't gotten specific instructions from Charlotte Machen on how to find Ellison, she surely would have gotten lost in this sprawling tangle of dismal Southern wilderness. The state map that she'd purchased at the beginning of their journey showed the town as a speck that might just as easily have been a printer's error instead of a geographical location.

Just before she had gotten off of I-95, she had stopped for gas, and when she had asked the gas station attendant about the town, he had given her a sullen smirk as if she were pulling some kind of big city joke on him. He'd never heard of Ellison, Georgia before. She didn't bother to point it out on the map. The lanky, grease-stained man didn't seem too interested in a geography lesson at the time.

Small wonder that he'd never heard of Ellison, she thought now, gazing past the bug-smeared windshield into the dark wood around them. So far, it wasn't anything to remember.

Insinuating its way through the skeletal pines, she saw felled, rust-ravaged barbed wire fencing snaking through the undergrowth. The sight reminded her Galvin, NC, and her own pitiful childhood. It depressed her to think back on it, even as an adult. There would always remain a seeping wound in her soul when it came to her childhood. She felt as if she had been running away from it all her life. But, even now, was she anything more than that ratty haired little girl with dirt on her tear stained cheeks and mud between her bare toes?

Timmy watched her. "What's wrong, Mama?" His voice cut through her glum thoughts. She forced a smile. No sense in trying to relate how that kind of existence had warped her. No good in explaining the black emotions it had caused deep down inside, how it had made her angry and resentful with her own parents for not having more.

She kept her eyes on the road, but she could feel Timmy still watching her with his sad brown eyes, trying to decipher her sudden depression. But as children do, after a moment he lost interest and went back to fumbling with the radio dials, vainly trying to find something to listen to that didn't involve ex-wives, beer drinking, and bars. Finally, giving it up, he shoved in a cassette tape that they had been listening off and on since the beginning of their long trip. 'The Sisters of Mercy', Andrew Eldritch's sonorously deep and spooky voice carrying the gothic banner high and proud, blasted out 'Dominion'. Timmy sang along. Mary doubted he knew half of what he was singing, but it made her smile anyway, watching him out of the corner of her eye.

The deeper they traveled into Ellison, the less Mary liked it. And she didn't like the way the last desperate rays of sunlight seemed to get tangled in the grasping claws of the forest beyond. Day was being dragged down the horizon, disappearing rapidly.

As she entered the town proper. More trucks than cars lined the curbs along the narrow, flat road. There were no stoplights, only a few leaning and faded pinkish stop signs to control the non-existent traffic. They cruised past a feed store/grocery store, a pawnshop, a small mom and pop style restaurant called Mamie's, and a Sheriff's office. Despite the fact there was still a light on inside the office, the anomalous sign of life on the dark street did little to dispel the sense of dilapidation that seemed to be rampant in Ellison. A single patrol car stood guard out front, parked askew against the curb. The dimly lighted window revealed nothing more than shadow shapes of office furniture huddled within.

After the town proper, the forest encroached by degrees towards the narrow roadway again, and the dark grew gloomier and thicker, blocking out the dying light of day, until she was finally forced to turn on her headlights to see the way. The twin beams provided scant comfort. In the cooling air, a peculiarly unpleasant scent drifted into the interior of the car. She recognized the rotten stink of swampy decay, the stench of wetlands that had boiled all day in the sun, dark water depths that refused light finding the sanctuary of night once more.

Timmy quietly continued to stare at the dark forest on the right of the constantly narrowing ragged road. Despite her feeling of foreboding that the streets of Ellison had left her with, Mary tried to get him to talk. But her efforts were wasted; Timmy would only respond with grunts and shakes of his tousled dark head. The darker the woods grew to either side, the smaller he seemed to sink into his seat, until she felt that he was becoming a mere shadow himself, watching the night coming on.

After a while, the woods became so dark that several times she convinced herself she had gone the wrong way, gotten them lost on some rarely used backwoods road, and best not traveled. But every time that she convinced herself of a wrong turn somewhere, she would see a wispy light bobbing in the distance, through the slate thin, gnarled pines. Then the road would twist off on some tangent of dirt and root, usher them past more gigantic trunks, claustrophobic bush, and the light would disappear. But it would soon beckon for them again, getting a little brighter each time. She decided the light must belong to a house out in all of this darkness; there was nothing else to explain it.

Timmy asked how big the house must be for so much light, but Mary shook her head, intent on keeping the car on the twisting road before them. The small car was taking a beating. She felt every jolt in her bones, knowing the thing wasn't meant for this kind of off road excursion.

Just as the road felt like it was about to finally give up the ghost of allowing them any further passage, the gray dirt made one last, desperate turn and deposited the car onto a sudden and unexpected straightaway. The straightaway led to a tall, imposing black iron and cement fence. The road was cut off by a looming slated black iron gate, but the gates were already open. Quelling her nerves, she gave her worried looking son a quick reassuring smile and drove inside. She could certainly sympathize; she wasn't so sure about this anymore. Maybe this had been a big mistake, coming this far to visit people she'd never heard of until a few days before. But she wanted to do what was best for Timmy. If he were due an inheritance, then she wanted to make sure he had a fair shot at it.

But always, at the back of her mind, like a whispering voice in the dark, she kept wondering why

Conley had lied about his family. What had he been trying to hide from her?

She drove onto a smoother expanse of stone bubbled road and a manicured property of lawn and topiary beyond. Silhouettes of spikes and intricate curlicues bedecked the imposing gate before them, giving it a medieval impression, as if a grand castle might lie behind the impregnable presence of the tall cement and steel wall.

"Are you excited about meeting your granddaddy?" she asked.

Timmy shrugged. "I guess so."

Mary frowned. His sudden pensive behavior was disconcerting. Her mother's instinct was to press her hand against his forehead to check for a fever, but she only gave him a worried glance. "What's wrong?"

For a moment, she didn't think he heard her. "It's so...so...", he started. But in the end he gave up and shook his head, as if he couldn't articulate his feelings.

Mary found herself speaking aloud the one word that came immediately to mind to describe the place. "Dark?"

And it was dark in this place. Despite the strong light that she could see blooming in a wide, bright cornea above the tall, sculpted hedges on either side of the car, it was pitch black all around them. And that blackness pressed heavily against her in a way that she hadn't known since childhood. She could definitely understand her young son's fear. It was scary enough being in the dark woods, but even more so when you were somewhere strange and unknown.

But when he spoke again she found that Timmy had a more prosaic fear in mind; more concrete than her own. "It's just so far from home," he said, quietly.

It felt like a long way from home to her; but to Timmy it probably felt like an interminable distance between him and his room back home. She thought about the eight-hour drive they'd endured to get here and felt the road weariness sapping her mental energy.

She smiled, ruffled his already tousled black hair. "Don't worry, kiddo. We'll stay a couple of days and then we'll be home before you know it. Alright?"

He gave her a sullen nod. "Can I turn the music back on now?"

"Sure," she said. And with a click the Sisters of Mercy again began to wax poetic about blood, love, and death.

The hedges leaned into the narrow dark asphalt driveway in several places. Thin, sharp protuberances caught in the head beams, giving Mary and Timmy the chance to see that the hedges were sculpted into various animal shapes. The animals towered and pranced above the grumbling vehicle, obscuring any view of the house from which the dazzlingly bright illumination emanated. At any given moment, only the next bend in the drive was evident beyond the frozen greenery. She had thought the road getting to Machen Mansion was claustrophobic, but it was nothing compared to this sensation of being absolutely boxed in by clutching animal vegetation.

Soon the animals grew smaller and finally fell to the wayside and the mansion, in its entire gloomy splendor, came into full view. Mary's eyes widened and she stepped on the brakes- a bit too hard- making them both bounce in their seats. She could not believe the size of the place. It was like a castle stolen from some European backcountry than a house, a dreamland hidden in the darkness of the forest.

How could Conley have given this up? What made him run away from such wealth? Sure they had been living comfortably enough, but this...this was magnificent beyond description.

For the first time since they had entered the forest, Timmy's attention was on something besides the darkness. Mary heard him give a stunned gasp of appreciation at the domicile's size and grandeur. She knew how he felt; she could barely take her on eyes from the sprawling structure towering before them, ablaze with lights. The dazzling display was like an oasis of illumination holding back the impinging forest.

"What a house," she murmured in awe. Timmy nodded beside her, still silently stunned.

But it was more than a house. A house was a place that people called home, where they rested after a hard day at work, a sanctuary of sorts that they could call their own. But this was a four-storey tall castle.

And this opulence, this obvious gesture of profound wealth, was like a slap in the dirty, slack faces of the people she had seen on the streets of Ellison. It made her angry for every one of those forlorn countenances, with their rust eaten, beat-up trucks, and ragged clothes.

How they must hate these people, she thought bitterly. God knows she would. It was little wonder they had to have all these black spiked gates and high walls.

Hold on. You don't even know these people yet and you're already jumping to the defense of the poor.

But she couldn't help feeling for the poor. She had grown up poor; she knew what living hand to mouth was like, not knowing how you were going to pay the next bill, knowing the next meal would be dictated by what could afford, not what you wanted. She had already decided she was more like the people she'd seen walking Ellison's cracked pavements than whom must reside here.

A pair of giant oak trees stood guard over the wide steps leading up to a roman columned porch. Thick beards of luminescent gray moss waved playfully at them in the night breeze from the stopping weight of the many branches clutching at the frame of the mansion. Along the walls and rooftop, more gray moss draped across the stonewalls, and brilliant purple trails of flowery vines- a reminder of the hungry natural world all around this white talisman of light and wealth.

As they sat in the still rumbling car, the front door opened, and an elderly woman peered out. She smiled, motioning for them to come up. But she didn't wait for them to exit, as she began to wobble her slow way down the stairs of the long porch to meet them.

"That's my great-grandmother?" Timmy asked, voice still hushed with awe.

"I guess so," she said. She turned the ignition off, wondering if this was a good place to leave their beat up old piece of crap, here, among the beautiful topiaries and perfectly paved stone road. Of course, it would make a great test as to how snobbish these new in-laws were. If they insisted she move the car then she would know how to react to all…well…all of this.

"Okay," she said, patting her son's small arm. "Let's get out. What do you say?"

Timmy gave a deep sigh, his mouth pressed into a firm frown, as if he had come to some decision. He gave her a solemn nod and reached for the door release.

She pasted on an uncertain smile of her own and got out to the wince-inducing squeak of the driver's door. Worse, she heard the distinct sound of the glass rattling when she closed it. She was going to have to think about maybe getting something a little less old than fifteen years soon.

Timmy waited for her to come around the car to meet him. He gathered her hand in his sweaty little palm. She propelled them both towards the grinning elderly woman waiting for them at the bottom of the steps. She was wringing her thin, wrinkled hands, and her cheeks were colored with excitement, plain enough even through the pasty powder which she wore. Mary was impressed to see she never once looked at the old car with a critical eye.

They stopped a few feet from Charlotte Machen, and Timmy staying huddled behind his mother's legs, peering up at the smiling old woman with big brown eyes. "I'm not sure if I should hug you all or shake hands," Charlotte Machen said in that near breathless tone that Mary recognized right away. "I'm not sure how to tell you all how glad we are to have you here at Machen Mansion." Then, as if on sudden impulse, she grabbed and pressed a quick hug on Mary. "There," she said with a self-deprecating smirk. "Now that's out of the way." Then she turned her rosy face to Timmy, stooped lower to see him past Mary's hip. "And you must be Timothy."

Timmy nodded, his lips pulled into a contemplative frown. Mary could almost feel the child's concentration on this new environment and this grinning new stranger in his life. His attention darted rabbit like from one detail to another, the house, the woods, the twin trees by the house, hulking like frozen gray giants. Charlotte waited for him to speak, the silence stretching on. Mary was about to reprimand him, but he moved from behind her hip, stuck out his hand stuck in a display of adult formality. "Hello, my name is Timmy. I like to be called Timmy, not Timothy."

Mary was well aware of her son's feelings about his name; he had always hated when anyone called him Timothy. She hoped that Charlotte wouldn't take the pronouncement as rudeness. After all, this visit all hinged on how Timmy reacted with these new people. For herself, she would rather not be here at all, but she needed to give her son every chance she could.

But she needn't have worried about Charlotte. The old woman took his little hand and gave it a polite shake. "Then Timmy it will be from now on, young sir. I'm very glad to meet you, Timmy. You have no idea what this means to Stewart and me that you all took the trouble to come to us." She turned back to Mary, but her glance took in the both of them. "Stewart will be so sorry he missed your arrival. He was pulled away into some unavoidable business late this evening. But he'll be back first thing tomorrow morning."

She cast a quick look over her shoulder at the house behind her, a sad frown on her aged face. "It'll be good to have some new people in this dreary old place again. It's been a long time since a little one's stepped through that front door."

Dreary, Mary thought. This woman doesn't have the least idea of what real dreary is. She doesn't live in the real world with the rest of us plebeians. She should take a drive through Ellison some time if she wants to see what dreary looks like.

"Let's get in before the mosquitoes remember their jobs," Charlotte said

"Okay," Mary said. "I'll just grab our bags."

"No need for that," Charlotte said, placing a withered hand on her arm. I'll have the servants fetch them in for you all."

Mary started to protest; she didn't like the idea of someone- even a paid someone- waiting on them; it didn't feel right. But Charlotte was already moving away from them, and she could feel Timmy trying to pull her along, eager to get inside and see the house.
Well, when in Rome.

She gave a mental shrug and allowed herself to pulled up the steps. Before entering the house, she took one last look at the wood surrounding the well-lighted estate. Mary couldn't shake the fear elicited by those dark trees. She'd never seen a forest that looked dark as the one that fought against the lights of Machen Mansion.

She gave the stooped old woman an uncertain smile and followed her inside. The door shut out the press of night beyond.

CHAPTER -5-

When Mary awoke, for a few confusing moments, she could not remember how she and Timmy had gotten in the large, musty smelling bed, wrapped up in faded blue and pink pastel sheets. Looking around, she saw that the bed was like an island in the midst of a vast room that was more chamber than sleeping quarters. After their arrival last night, the moments had passed like a parade of sketches; she and Timmy had been so exhausted from the drive and the emotions of the odd situation they'd both fallen quickly into slumber once Charlotte had left them alone.

Despite its expansiveness, the room was cluttered with mismatched furniture and shelves of knick-knacks. And, like the bed they found themselves in, it smelled of age and disuse. She wondered how long it had been since a person had actually seen the inside of the place.

She rubbed her hair, feeling her bleary thoughts coming together. Across the room, a dim early morning light swam through the double windows.

What time was it?

The stoic grandfather clock standing in one corner of the room read a little after 8:00 am. Well into the morning then. So why was it so dim outside?

She listened clock's steady ticking. The sound has lulled she and Timmy to sleep the night before. She remembered the look of awe on her son's face when Charlotte had shown them upstairs to the room. His eyes had alighted on the wonderful old clock. She could see he yearned to touch the gold gilded glass, the dark brown wood, and its shining silver pendulum swinging back and forth. Adults took such things for granted, but something like the ancient clock was a chunk of gold to a kid like Timmy.

Timmy was still asleep beside her, so she carefully sat up to take in all of the bric-a-brac that cluttered the various antique tables, dressers and glass showcases. She could see small items like crystal eggs, plates on stands, colored glasses. Some of them looked antique as well. It felt more like a museum than a bedroom and she was grateful Timmy had been unwilling to stray from her side last night. She would hate to see him accidentally break something that was more expensive than their car.

Her stomach grumbled. She hadn't realized how hungry she was; they had stopped for burgers and fries earlier in the afternoon, but neither had the energy to eat last night when they arrived. She hoped someone came up soon to show them to the kitchen. The place was enormous; she'd never have a chance finding her way around alone. She wasn't even sure she could find their way back down stairs. The trip through the halls last night had been confusing, so many twists and turns and dead end hallways. She'd lost count of the many doors they passed by as Charlotte escorted them. All the way up, Timmy had been reserved, unusually quiet, gazing around Mary's waist the whole time. And as much as Charlotte had tried to engage him in conversation, he only murmured his responses, too busy taking in details of the house.

Now that she was awake, her bladder screamed for relief. She pulled her arm from under Timmy's slumbering head, kissed the end of his nose, and rolled out of bed. She hoped he wouldn't wake up while she was gone. She could only imagine how frightening it would be for him to find himself alone in this sprawling room.

The floor was cold and she winced with every hurried mouse-step to the bathroom. She found the bathroom with no problem. It was as cold as a meat locker inside. She shuddered and locked the door behind her. For its size, the bathroom, unlike the bedroom, was quite utilitarian. A sink, bathtub, mirror, and two pink throw rugs. The walls were pink and white, with a cornflower blue tile floor. In the soap dish near the sparkling sink several pink and blue soaps in the shape of cartoon fish were piled high. She examined a pink one while finishing her business, sniffing it, turning it over and over to see the detail in the fins and bubbly cartoon eyes. There was no discernible scent, but her fingers came away with a film of sticky dust. How long had it been since someone had used this bathroom?

There was a movement outside the door. A quick shadow slithered at the bottom crack. Timmy must have woken up. She waited for him to begin calling out for her, but surprisingly there was only silence.

"Timmy," she said.

The stealthy shadow froze, as if listening.

She waited for Timmy to say something, but he didn't answer her.

"Timmy?"

The shadow shifted again. It grew larger, darker.

The doorknob began to turn slowly, as if someone were testing the lock.

"Timmy! Honey!" she called louder this time. "Don't open the door. Mama's using the toilet. Okay?"

Now the doorknob rattled harder, more insistent. She heard something sniffing next to the crack of the doorjamb, like an animal scenting out prey. The sound made her skin crawl. Had a dog gotten into their room somehow? She didn't remember seeing any animals last night.

The sniffer gave a high childlike giggle, and she sighed in relief. Just Timmy.

"Timmy? Is that you? You scared mama." Mary reached for tissue paper and quickly wiped. "I'll be right out." With half an eye, she continued to watch the shadow move back and forth under the door. The doorknob kept turning vainly in the frame, but there was no way he could get in. He was a little kid and the door was solid, a good heavy lock on the knob. "Wait a second, honey," she said. "I'm on my way out."

She pulled up her underwear and hurried to open the door, half expecting to see Timmy looking up at her with a frightened face, eyes swimming in tears. "Here I am—" she started, but the words died on her lips.

No one was at the door.

Across the room, she could clearly see Timmy's huddled form still beneath the blankets. She waited a few tense and confused moments for him to suddenly sit up in bed and start laughing at his gullible mother, but he didn't move. And the more she thought about it, the less sense it made. No way could he have moved that fast. No possible way. She had seen the shadow moving, and the doorknob had still been turning against the lock, even as she had grabbed it to open the door. So how could he have gotten from the bathroom door, clear across the room, and in the same position she'd let him, in the blink of an eye? She knew there was absolutely no physically possible way for him to have done so. Which left the only other solution. She must have imagined it. Not the greatest explanation, because it meant she was seeing and hearing things that were not there, a sure sign of mental fatigue, but the only one that made sense.

As she started for the bed again, Mary saw someone had delivered their three battered bags of luggage into the room and set them next to the bed.

They hadn't been there when she went to the bathroom. She was sure of it. She would've had to step over them.

Well, that cleared up the mystery, then, didn't it?

It must have been a servant, maybe one that was hard of hearing, and wanting to check the bathroom. But even with a ready explanation at hand, Mary still found herself shivering against a chill. The wavering shadow, the animal-like sniffing under the door, and the rattling doorknob. And the servant theory still didn't how anyone could move so fast. The movements, which she had attributed to Timmy, had, now, taken on a whole new deliberate meaning. Someone had been trying to scare her…or worse.

She hugged herself, looking around the room in dismay now. The clutter that had looked like a homey museum before, now gave the room a mazelike appearance. Anyone could be hiding in here and they'd never know it.

Don't be stupid. You're in a strange place. You're nervous. Just relax. Don't let Timmy see you getting freaked out because some half-deaf servant tried to open the door while you were taking a leak.

She went to the window nearest the bed and peeked out. Now she could see the reason for the dim light. Outside, the day was muddy and forlorn. Rain clouds roiled in the distant horizon. A bully wind careened through the trees and topiaries. And beyond the estate grounds, the forest stared back at her, bleak and menacing. She shuddered and pulled the curtains closed with a nervous twitch. How could it actually look darker in the daylight?

Mary decided she would avoid peering into the woods. There was an unhealthy sense in the way the trees clustered together, the way she felt as if someone were watching her from their depths.

A light tap at the bedroom door made her jump. She clutched at her throat, feeling a frightened pulse thumping against her palm. This place was making her skittish.

She crossed the room, and opened to door to find Charlotte wearing a blue sundress and two matching butterfly hairpins nearly hidden away in her wavy gray hair. "Good morning," she stage whispered, peering past Mary at the still sleeping Timmy. "I see our little man hasn't awoken yet. Poor boy must've been tuckered out from the drive." She patted Mary's arm. "Well, we can let him keep sleeping, if you'd care for some breakfast."

She considered the idea. She was hungry. In fact, now she was starving. But she didn't want to leave Timmy alone in a strange place "How about I meet you downstairs with Timmy in a few minutes," she said. "I need to make sure he gets a quick bath. After the drive, he needs one."

"Of course." Charlotte's smile withered away like a fallen over ripe flower. "I've forgotten about such things. It's been so long since I've had to worry about seeing to baths and dressings." For a moment, Mary saw the glitter in the old woman's eye, as she dredged through old memories. She felt sorry for her. All this palatial space, the money to keep her in comfort for the remainder of her years, and no grandchildren to fill her last days in this old house with laughter. "Children are such a blessing, aren't they?" Charlotte said. Her warm gaze fell on the sleeping form beyond. "I'll be waiting for you two, then."

"You don't have to wait for us, Charlotte," Mary said.

"Don't be ridiculous, dear," she said. "Our first breakfast together? I'll keep everything warm." With another soft pat on the arm, Charlotte moved back down the dimly lighted hallway, her stooped frame seeming to shrink under the power of the crouching corner shadows.

Once Charlotte turned a corner and disappeared, Mary went back across the cold wooden floor to the bed. Gently, she shook Timmy until his eyes fluttered open. Smiling at his long lashes, she could only think how much he looked like Conley. A miniature of Conley, really. Same light hazel eyes; same thick, dark black hair, a little curly, but getting straighter as he grew older; same grinning face, full of humor, but intensely serious at times, more so than other kids his own age.

Charlotte was right: Children were a blessing.

"Wake up, sleepy head," she said. "Charlotte- I mean, your grandmother- is waiting for us downstairs. She's got breakfast all ready. You're hungry, right?" Timmy yawned and nodded, still blinking himself to wakefulness. She went to the stacked suitcases and opened his, pulled out a few items of clean clothing, and sat the pile next to him on the bed. "First, we need to get you all cleaned up. The bathroom is over there." She nodded to the half open door across the room. "Do you want me to go with you, or do you think you can handle it alone, little buckaroo?"

"What's a buckaroo?" he asked, stifling another yawn.

She put a finger on the end of his small nose and made a honking sound. "That's you." He laughed, made a mock swipe at her retreating finger. "So do you need me to go with you?" she asked again.

He considered the question for a moment. "You'll be here when I get out?"

"Of course, sweetie. I won't leave you to wander around this big old house by yourself." Mary grinned. "Besides, you might scare the servants." At the mention of the servants, she remembered the incident earlier, but kept smiling. She didn't want to make him anymore nervous than he already felt. "Timmy," she said as nonchalantly as possible. "Did you hear anyone come in the room this morning?"

"No, ma'am," he answered as he began to gather up his pile of clean clothes. "I was sleeping."

"Right. Of course," she said.

Mary sent him off to the bathroom, waited until she heard the water running, and went to the bedroom door. She wondered if there were any servants upstairs? Maybe cleaning a room somewhere down the hall?

She looked back at the closed bathroom door. Maybe a quick peek down the hall would ease her anxiety.

But she had told Timmy she would be here when he got out. Besides, she wasn't sure if she got too far from their room she'd be able to find her way back without a map. Instead, she decided that if she saw any servants on their way downstairs she'd ask if anyone had been in the room.

She shook her head at her own trepidation. Of course it was a servant. Who the hell else could it have been? But it didn't much relieve the creeping sensation that had been with her since she'd seen that stealthy shadow beneath the bathroom door earlier.

Why was this place making her so jumpy? So far, Charlotte had been nothing but genial, soft spoken, and attentive- the perfect example of a charming woman of the Old South. It was if she had taken to them like old friends, and seemed to have no problem accepting the fact that Conley had kept them secret. She hadn't even asked about Conley, not even about his death. Nothing about Timmy's childhood or any other detail of her great grandson's life away from Machen Mansion.

So you're anxious because she hasn't asked you prying questions about your husband's death, the one thing you didn't want others to do?

Mary rolled her eyes at her own silly nerves and began to search through her own suitcase for something to wear.

A few minutes later, Timmy came from the bathroom fully dressed and ready to go. "I'm so hungry," he said in his best Johnny Carson impersonation, waiting for her to respond to his cue.

Of course, Mary had to reply. "How hungry are you?" she said with a comical roll of her eyes. It was an old joke between them, something that Conley used to do a lot. Timmy had picked it up from him.

"Why, I'm so hungry that I could eat a Brontosaurus burger with Tyrannosaurus-sauce." He let loose with a high-pitched cackle and Mary couldn't help but join in.

"Come on, my little comedian." She grabbed his hand and heading them towards the door. She had gotten much hungrier since Charlotte's visit, and thought she might just be able to eat a Brontosaurus burger with Tyrannosaurus-sauce, too.

As she was about to open the door, Mary stopped, her hand wavering over the doorknob. Coming from the other side of the door was another of those stealthy sounds. She gasped and snatched her hand back.

"What's wrong, Mama?" Timmy asked.

Mary shushed him and leaned forward. She placed an ear against the door and listened intently. There was a soft scratching against the wood, like fingernails. She waited, tension bunching in her shoulders.

Then the scratching stopped. She heard what sounded like shuffling feet on carpet moving away.

Feeling more anger than fear now, Mary jerked open the door.

But, again, there was no one there. The hallway was empty, no one in either direction. Mary thought she caught the tail end of a shadow fleeing at the distant left turn. How the hell anyone could move that fast? It was at least twenty feet away, and she'd just heard the shuffling outside the door only moments before.

Timmy tugged at her shirt. "What's wrong?" he asked again, his tension feeding off hers.

Mary shrugged off her unease and gave him a reassuring smile. "Nothing, honey." She hugged him against her protectively. "Let's hurry, before grandma eats all the food." All the while she was quelling the urge to chase the shadow, see who could possibly be screwing around with the doors. A confrontation to find a servant responsible for her fear of the unknown would do her good right now, but not with her son in tow.

After the first ninety-degree turn in the hallway, their bedroom disappeared behind them, and Mary felt as if she were in another house altogether. The walls felt somehow as if they had constricted around them, the dimness in the long, close corners, greater; though the sensation might be blamed on the riotous color scheme of the wallpaper, perhaps only an illusion created by the dark gold filigree running through the dried blood burgundy. The filigree seemed to squirm off the wall. In the swimming murk, the hall seemed to transform into an esophagus down which they were slowly descending, an unnerving illusion. Mary never considered herself a paragon of home design, but surely these colors weren't the most comforting. It made her cringe away from the closing sensation of the walls on either side.

At head level, several frosted glass lamps invaded their path; but to her eye, it seemed they cast more shadows than they dissipated. Pools of shadow, pools of light, fought the dread colors for domination of the hall.

After a few minutes of slipping nervously along the hall, she knew she would never find their room again. It was lost in the twist and shadows of Machen Mansion.

She heard Timmy's stomach gurgle into the stillness, and her own gut gave a sympathetic growl. She smiled down at him, squeezing his hand. The kid looked almost as nervous as she felt.

She kept them moving down the hall, took two more right turns, and just as her panic threatened to swallow her up, the long hall spit them out into a foyer-like staging area. She recognized the stairs from the night before, and felt the panic recede. She led Timmy down the beige and orange-carpeted steps. The stairway made a gentle spiral dive to the lower level, along white washed walls, and family. She felt the gaze of the ancient dead Machens following their descent with cold menace.

At the bottom, she glanced around until she saw Charlotte sitting and waiting for them in a dining area a few dozen yards to the right. Two large windows spilled the diluted storm light onto a black tile floor between the two areas, as they made their way to the dining area. Timmy pulled away at the welcome smell of bacon. Mary entered the room, silently marveling at the grandeur of it. The table where Charlotte waited was easily large enough to sit thirty people; above, the ceiling vaulted to a rounded conical shape. Mary was astounded to find a beautiful recreation of Da Vinci's 'God and Man' looking down. She smiled at the majestic sweep of the quiet colors. Suspended from the center of the painting, a hanging crystal chandelier, made the room feel more like a cathedral than a dining room.

Sitting next to the enormous table was an elegant wooden cart with half a dozen shining silver chaffing dishes waiting atop it. On the table, four place settings awaited. Timmy took a seat to Charlotte's left, his gaze darting from one detail to the next. The old woman motioned for Mary to take the seat on her right, her pale aged features seamed with an eager smile. "I hope you two are hungry enough to eat a horse," she said. "I wasn't sure what you all wanted, so I had the help prepare several different dishes. I hope we found something that you all like."

"Oh, Charlotte, we're not too picky," Mary assured, taking her place in the high backed, red cushioned seat. Charlotte reached to the serving cart next to her and began sweeping the lids from each dish, one by one, drawing grateful 'oohs' and 'ahs' from Timmy as each was revealed. Scrambled eggs, pancakes, waffles, poached eggs, biscuits- made with real buttermilk, sliced fruits, and to drink, coffee, orange and grapefruit juice, milk, and tea.

"Now, you all help yourselves to whatever you want." Charlotte nodded towards the cart of the steaming food. "I'm sure Stewart won't mind if we start without him. The poor dear seems always to be working. Never enough time for sleep, or even a decent meal, these days. He's like that when he's about to close a deal. It's so silly the way he goes on about making money. Of course, he got that from his own father- bless his soul. I'm always telling him that there are more important things in life than making money." Pausing, she looked to Mary with a slight arched eyebrow. "Don't you think so, dear?"

Mary blinked after the onrush of words, not sure how to respond. All she could think was that the old woman had probably never had to worry about having money; that was why she could say such things. Instead, she asked, "Mr. Machen will be joining us soon, then?"

Charlotte smiled as Timmy piled bacon, pancakes, and eggs on his plate, slathering the chaos with hot syrup from a serving tureen. "Of course, dear," she said. "He's so very excited about finally meeting Timmy. He even went so far as to make special arrangements for closing this particular deal so that he could spend more time with you all."

Well, I should hope the hell so, she thought, we only drove eight and half hours to get here, after all. And she had spent more money than she had right now to make this little reunion possible. Those kinds of things never entered the minds of people who had money, though. Scraping cash together for anything less than a new mansion never was a bother. "That's very good of him," she replied, putting on a grateful smile to hide her frustration.

She put some sliced fruit- pineapple, orange, grapes, and banana- on her plate and listened while Charlotte asked dozens of questions, mostly directed at Timmy. Despite his earlier reticence, it didn't take long for her son to open up to the old woman about school, his friends, his toys, and his favorite movies and songs. She listened raptly as he explained why he liked or disliked one thing after another. Charlotte laughed at his funny stories about teachers and friends. After a few minutes of this attention from the old woman, as she made the appropriate snickers and 'oohs' to his tales, he was chattering away like a noisy blue jay. Mary couldn't help giggling along with Charlotte, happy to see her son the center of attention. He seemed to have gotten over his case of nerves about meeting an unknown family. Mary wished she could do so. She was still bothered by Charlotte's lack of interest in Conley; she hadn't even discussed him since the night before. Of course, the old woman might be avoiding any discussion about the subject because Timmy was around, not wishing to upset him with talk about his dead father.

A voice from the entryway of the dining room startled them all. She saw Timmy's eyes bulge suddenly with something like surprised confusion. But when she turned to greet the man behind her, she understood. She felt as if her world had suddenly gone topsy-turvy.

The man she saw strolling casually through the dining room was Conley. A Conley thirty years older, but still with his same smirking, knowing smile on his handsome face. It was a vertiginous sensation seeing this duplicate of her dead husband standing before her. Stewart Machen was the spitting image of Conley, despite the age lines crisscrossing his cheeks and chin, and the tell-tale gray hairs mingled within his wavy, thick hair, the whitish curls blooming from the open V of his green silk shirt.

However, she could see some small, but important, differences between the two men. His features should have been warm with the smooth lines that Conley had worn so well. But this man's face did nothing warm with those lines. He wore them like chiseled stone. Now she thought she knew why her husband had left this house. If those frigid eyes had been inspecting her every day, she would have hit the road, too. Where Conley's eyes had always been soft with concern and empathy for others, this man's stare was colder, more clinical, as he looked them up and down.

Stewart Machen's chilly gaze barely brushed over her; his attention was for his grandson. Timmy's shyness returned as he watched the man's approach. As soon as the old stood over the boy, hands on his hips, his countenance came alive with some hidden reserve of warmth that she had first dismissed. Like sunshine on a cold winter field, now the old man's eyes sparkling with an uncanny glee. "My God, you are a handsome little devil," Stewart exclaimed. "Just like your father, son." He moved around the table lightly, his large, tanned hands reaching to touch Timmy. Mary felt a stab of territoriality, and she had to quell the sudden desire to leap from her seat to stop him. But the strangely expectant smile Timmy gave Stewart Machen reminded her why they had come so far from home.

Timmy stuck out his hand as he had with Charlotte the night before. "I like to be called Timmy, not Timothy, sir."

Stewart looked the boy up and down, smiling and shaking his head. He grabbed the small hand in both of his own larger hands and gave it a solemn shake. "Timmy it is, son. As long as you agree to call me granddaddy or grandfather. We got us a deal, Timmy?"

Timmy nodded. "Yes, sir- I mean, Granddaddy."

That settled, Stewart turned his attention to Mary. He took her limp hand between his long fingers, raised her hand, and, like some long lost Southern aristocrat, kissed her knuckles, flashing two perfect rows of white teeth at her stunned expression. "Absolutely beautiful," he declared. "My son always had very good taste in women." Stewart turned to his mother. "Isn't she beautiful, mother?" Charlotte nodded, chuckling along with Timmy at how embarrassed the compliment had made Mary. "I have waited so long to meet you both," he said.

Breakfast lasted another hour while the four of them sat and talked. Although no one brought up the fact that Conley had not told his wife and son about the two of them, Mary could still feel the uncomfortable ghost of the lie sitting between them, like a tense guest who was dumb with unanswered questions. She could sense the meandering tangents of conversation go on until the wall of Conley's lie stood before the continuation, and then the room would fall silent again. Someone else would start a new line of talk, but the unspoken tension was always there to meet each effort. Mary knew she had to get one of them alone if she ever hoped to get any answers about Conley's past.

Her chance came later. After the plates had grown cold with half eaten food, Stewart asked Timmy if he wanted to see the stallions in the estate's stables. Timmy's face lit up with excitement. He loved animals of all kinds. He was half out of his seat when he remembered that he needed permission first. Mary smiled and nodded at her son's desperate hopeful gaze. She was glad to see he seemed to have lost any nervousness about this strange visit. She watched the two of them, hand in hand, leave by the side door next to the dining area, Timmy almost constantly rattling in his excitement as the door closed behind them.

She turned see Charlotte was no longer smiling. "I suppose you felt it as well as I did," the old woman said, holding her coffee cup in a wrinkled grip.

Mary nodded; she didn't need to be told what the other woman meant. It was still wafting through the mid-morning air, like an odor that wouldn't be dissipated.

"I know Stewart wanted to explain about he and Conley's falling out, but he didn't want to say anything in front of the boy to make him think anything less of his father. After all, we never know what children will hold in their memories, do we?"

Mary shifted her chair closer to Charlotte. "So what did happen between them? Why did Conley lie about you and Stewart?"

Charlotte brought the cup to her pursed lips and swallowed a minute portion of cooling coffee before answering. "They were both to blame. Although, Stewart, being the adult of the two, should've seen what was going to happen before it did." The old woman shook her head. "The two of them were always arguing with one another. If Stewart said black, Conley would be convinced that it was really white. I've never seen two people so alike...or so very different as those two."

Charlotte got up and poured herself more coffee, turned to Mary and offered her more as well. Mary held up her cup, waiting for the older woman to finish. Charlotte sat back down, and gave a heavy sigh, looking into the dark liquid of her cup in quiet contemplation. "Conley left when he was barely eighteen. It was after an argument about- of all things- which college he'd attend. Stewart insisted, naturally, that Conley should attend his old alma mater, the University of Georgia. But Conley was head strong about attending Duke University at the end of the year." Charlotte stared up at the ceiling for a moment, as if a deluge of memories were subsuming her. "It was a silly argument, really. And it got out of control, as things always did with the two of them. Stewart threatened to disown Conley, to cut him out of the will altogether. Of course, Conley never cared about the money. You must know he was never money dependant, by nature. Nothing like Stewart at his age. The boy could always take it or leave it. He had something inside him that the other Machen men never had. An iron will live without depending on his father's money."

Mary felt sorry for the old woman, especially when she saw bright tears glistening in her eyes. Charlotte pulled a napkin from her lap, dabbed at the tears. "I tried to talk to Stewart. And to Conley. But, before I could persuade either of them to talk without shouting, Conley stormed out of the house with nothing more than the clothes on his back. Of course, once Stewart had thought it all over, he felt horrible about the whole dreadful incident, and tried his best to find the boy. He hired several private investigators. One was eventually able to track him down and Stewart contacted Conley by phone, hoping to patch things up, maybe to make amends for his past. But Conley was as bull-headed as his father. He refused to even discuss coming back home again. Of course, we couldn't very well make him do so. After all, he was an adult by then, able to make his own decisions." She suddenly smiled at Mary. "I suppose he made a few good ones, right? Or else there would never have been you and Timmy."

Mary felt terrible for the old woman. The sting of memories was obviously still too keen to ignore.

"Well, Timmy seems to have taken right to Stewart and you," she said, hoping to brighten the mood a little. The past was the past, after all. You couldn't change it by mulling it over. What was done was done.

"Yes," she agreed. "He is such a delightful boy. You know, he reminds me so much of Conley. And that smile of his...just like his father."

Mary needed to discuss the supposed inheritance. She didn't want to sound like a money grubbing ingrate, but was there any diplomatic way to bring it up?

"Charlotte, you mentioned something about an inheritance being willed to Timmy." Mary forged ahead, uncertain about decorum, but certain of her carefully chosen words. "I don't think we can accept something like that. I was raised that you didn't take anything you didn't earn."

Charlotte raised her gaze from the depths of coffee cup. Her mouth curled into an enigmatic smirk.

"Oh, you'll earn it, my dear." The expression on the old woman's face was no longer kind and gentile. It had been replaced by an icy hardness.

But before Mary could ask what she meant, a terrible beating, roaring sound rent the air like small explosions, echoing throughout the room. It was the nightmarish flapping of giant bird wings, slapping against the inside of her ears. Mary dropped cup and covered her ears. "What is that?" she shouted above the din.

Charlotte frowned, seemingly unconcerned with the hellish noise, and looked down at the small pearl band watch dangling from her thin wrist. "That must be Stewart's other guests."

"Guests?" The noise was deafening, painfully thumping inside her head now. "That noise…"

Charlotte stood and motioned for Mary to follow her to the side door where Timmy and Stewart had exited earlier. About a hundred feet away, a long red and blue helicopter was landing on the dark green of the front lawn.

CHAPTER -6-

Sully Borland waited for the helicopter to touch down in the middle of the Machen Estate before unlatching the side door. He turned to Garlen Winters, grabbed the handles of the heavy wheelchair, and pulled his boss towards the open door. He waited for the electric ramp to lower itself to the ground. The copter was still running and bouncing a little too much for Sully's taste, so he signaled for the pilot to stabilize the craft. He sure as hell didn't want to dump Garlen out on the grass- no matter how soft and perfect that grass might look. Not a good way to show up for a business appointment, squirming around on your ass as helpless as a stranded turtle on its back.

The craggy faced pilot turned and yelled above the deafening pitch of the air whipping blades. "Monday morning! 6:30 am!" Of course, the aged pilot knew the answer already. But like anyone that worked for Garlen, he wanted to make sure that it was still on before he left for his weekend at home. Garlen, the old coot, had been known more than once to change his mind mid-deal and leave his business acquaintances standing with their mouths open, wondering what had gone wrong. When you had as much money and power as Garlen, you could do such things with no crisis of conscience. Sully often thought it was sort of like living a second childhood, one in which others allowed you more liberality not because of your age, but because they wanted a percentage of your power.

Garlen sneered at the waiting pilot and snapped testily, "Of course, it is. Damn it! I say 6:30 am, I mean 6:30 am." The old man's shouts were barely audible above the blade noise, but the pilot got the gist and nodded. Sully rolled his eyes, smiled, and gave the pilot a 'thumbs up' over Garlen's shoulder. They both knew Sully would be the one to remember about Monday morning. Somewhere along the way Sully had become more than a bodyguard to the crippled industrialist tycoon. He had become his secretary, day planner, even times his good sense and conscience. Most importantly Sully Borland was his arms and legs.

"If you need to leave before then, you better call a taxi, fellas," warned the pilot. He jabbed a finger at the darkening skies. "Weather says ya'll are in for some wet weekend. Won't be able to fly in it."

"No problem," Sully said. "We'll be fine. See you Monday."

Sully wheeled Garlen down the ramp, careful to keep his head way down. Garlen continued to grumble about stupid pilot's and how much money he was paying these stupid pilots for them to keep asking what time he needed to be picked up on whatever morning it was he was to be picked up. Garlen was what Sully's father would have called 'a crusty old fart'. But once you got to know him, Garlen Winters was more than a paycheck. He was a strong little man made of wiry stuff that refused to give under pressure. Sully had seen the old man at his lowest, when he'd lost Susan and Richard. The business world had written him off after the funeral, but he had shown them he was strong, and had come back swinging away at the rest of the world like an aging prizefighter still trying to find that perfect round.

The chair rolled smoothly across the short emerald grass, as he moved Garlen safely out of the path of the blades. The wind whipped about them like angry banshees. Though a quick inspection of the cloudy sky made Sully wonder how much of it was due to the violence of the helicopter's powerful blades. The pilot was right. It looked like a nasty storm was moving in on Machen Estate. Dark clouds boiled across the pine-stitched horizon, making the wood look even more sinister than usual.

Across the expanse, near a long low building that could only be a stable, Sully saw Stewart Machen's gaunt form lurching towards them. Next to the tall man, a small boy hurried to keep up. Sully watched them approach with a quizzical frown. As far as he knew, Stewart Machen had no children.

Sully fought against the wind, back to the helicopter to retrieve their small collection of traveling bags. They had a case apiece, enough for their three-day layover. As usual, the older man's bag was twice as heavy as his own. Sully was a light traveler, never more than what he needed for survival for a few days at a time. No entanglements, no strings to tie him down, no material possessions beyond a few tattered copies of his favorite books, a few changes of clothes, underwear, socks, two pair of versatile shoes, his shaving kit, needle and thread, a couple of knives, a full medical kit for emergencies...and, of course, the guns. He and Garlen did not travel anywhere without the guns.

Sully did a visual audit of the house to acclimate himself to his surroundings. He wondered where that old bat Charlotte Machen was hiding? The last time he and Garlen had visited she had been less than happy with Stewart's fawning over Garlen's opinion and the hours long conversations about business. Sully she had barely looked at twice. In her eyes, bodyguard or not, he was only a servant.

As if called by his thoughts of her, Sully saw her exit the side door of the house, her long face pale and ghostly in the dark of the pre-storm air. Next to her was a younger woman. A very beautiful younger woman. Sully hefted the bags on each shoulder and started away from the helicopter. As soon as he was clear, the pilot lifted off, eager to beat the storm. Garlen had not waited for his return and was aiming his electric wheelchair to meet Stewart and the boy.

Sully couldn't stifle the twinge of worry as to how Garlen would react to the boy. It had been a long time since the old man had been near a child. Ever since the night...

No, he wasn't going to even think about that right now. Garlen's lose had been just as bad for him. He had loved Susan and Richard as if they had been his own family. After the attack, Sully had been the one to identify them because Garlen was in a coma.

Those were dark days for the both of them. The darkest. With his wife and child dead by a crazy political assassin's hand, death seemed like a better option than life for the old man. And then to wind up crippled for life because of it.

Shit. He was thinking about it anyway.

Sully was glad he still had on his shades. Stewart Machen seeing his eyes tear up with old painful memories wasn't going to help his own crappy mood any.

And his bad mood was because of Stewart Machen to begin with. Sully did not want to be here. He disliked the Machens, and he was sure the feeling was mutual. He was just a hired gun to Stewart, a servant to Charlotte, and it pissed them both off to have to allow him the same privileges as his boss when they stayed over. But even if they had not shown such an aristocratic attitude towards him, Sully wasn't sure he could have liked them any better. Usually his first reaction, his gut reaction, was on target. He had learned to trust his gut. Maybe it was because he could unconsciously read body language. Maybe it was only a low level psychic ability to read emotions. Didn't matter how it happened, he just knew his gut had been right more times than not when it came to dealing people. There was something about Stewart and Charlotte Machen, something their false smiles and Southern gentility was trying to hide.

As the craft disappeared up and into the distance, the wind died away and was replaced by a chill wind that spoke of the coming storm. The distant trees danced like skeletons in the cool breath of the dark clouds.

Sully hauled the bags behind Garlen's near silent electric chair. The old man whirred to a stop before a smirking Stewart Machen and the boy. The boy watched Sully's approach with wide, wary eyes. Sometimes Sully forgot how imposing his size could be for others. To a kid he probably looked like a giant. Standing 6'2", and weighing in at around 275 lbs., he was considered a rather large man, his frame accentuated by rippling muscles and hard angles. His size was usually enough to dissuade any problems from others; one look at his face did the rest. Sully wore an almost perpetual frown. Even with the shades off, his stare was like cold flint. He might be thinking of smashing your nose in, or he might be thinking about Eliot's poetry. It was enough to make strangers sweat when they were around him. Garlen told him he liked to bring Sully along if he felt that one of his business acquaintances might be trying to strong-arm him. Sully's massive frowning presence was a great deal negotiator.

Sully glanced down at the boy and tried to give him a slight smile, making sure not to show his discomfort around Stewart Machen.

And the forest. He could feel it behind him, wearing its own frown. He shrugged his rounded shoulders against the disconcerting sensation of being watched.

"Garlen, it's good to see you again," Stewart said. He thrust his hand forward and gave Garlen's hand a solid shake. Garlen eyed the quickly darkening sky. "Almost didn't see us at all with this crap." Not so far off, a rumble of thunder warned of the rain to come.

The boy suddenly stepped forward and stuck out his own small hand, startling Garlen. He frowned at the boy's hand, and looked up at Stewart. His astonished expression asked if this was a joke.

"My name's Timmy Machen, sir," the boy said.

Garlen stared at the earnest face for an uneasy moment more, and then to Sully's surprise, Garlen grabbed Timmy's hand and laughed aloud. "Well, it's wonderful to meet you, son. My name is Garlen Winters." He motioned over his shoulder. "And this guy is Sully Borland. A friend of mine." Sully nodded at the boy, hefting the bags, making his muscles jump like small angry animals beneath his tight shirt.

Garlen nodded towards Stewart. "This your grand dad, here?"

"Yes, sir," Timmy answered.

"I didn't know you had a grand son, Stewart," Garlen said, his shock evident. "In fact, I didn't even know you had any-"

Stewart interrupted Garlen. "Unfortunately, we had problems. Sometimes it's better to pretend. If you can understand…" He gave Garlen a meaningful look and shook his head. "An area that's not open for discussion, I'm afraid."

Garlen nodded. "I don't blame you," he replied. "Better to let the past go."

Stewart gave the bodyguard a nod, his first acknowledgement. "Sully, you can stow those bags in the same downstairs rooms as the last time. If you need a guide, I'm sure that Charlotte can find someone to show you the way." Stewart kneeled next to Timmy. "Timmy, I need to discuss some things with Mr. Winters for a while. Do you think you could follow Sully up to the house?"

Timmy gave Sully a nervous sidelong glance, but nodded. "Don't worry, son," Garlen said with a chuckle. "He hardly ever eats children anymore."

"Garlen," Sully growled. "You're not half as funny as you think you are sometimes." Shrugging the bags, sully turned to the boy. "Come on, kid. You lead the way."

The first few drops of rain began to fall as Sully followed the little boy. When he looked back, Garlen and Stewart were already gone, and only the forest gazed back.

CHAPTER -7-

The cabin on the edge of the swamp trembled as the departing helicopter raced overhead, dodging the low dark rain clouds- headers of the approaching storm. Ten-year old Jebediah Drury ran from the swamp shack cabin to watch the craft whiz by above. It wasn't the first time he'd seen a helicopter flying away from the old Machen place, but it certainly was the lowest flying one he'd ever seen. Couldn't have been more than a few dozen yards above the trees.

Jeb turned to the slate wooden door. He wanted to wake Daddy, so he could share his enthusiasm, but his father had come home late last night, and Jeb could still smell whiskey fumes wafting from him like swamp gas.

He decided instead to go check the traps, so Daddy wouldn't be mad. When he did eventually wake tonight, he would most likely still be drunk and hungry. There wasn't going to be anything to eat if he didn't check the traps. This time of the day there might be a turtle or two. A catfish, if he was lucky. Jeb didn't want to give him any reason to start hitting tonight. The last time had been bad enough. His left leg still hurt when he put all his weight on it. Daddy didn't know what he was doing when he was drinking. Mama had always told him that. Every time Daddy hit her until she couldn't move, she still told Jeb Daddy wasn't to blame. It was the devil's drink doing it, not the man she called husband. Sometimes he wondered if she was in heaven now. He hoped so. She had been good to him. He hoped Jesus had seen fit to bring her to him. He heard the mean things some of the people in church said about Mama when they thought he wasn't listening. That she had been weak and stupid for letting Daddy beat on her. If the church people didn't like her, did that mean Jesus didn't either?

Jeb stepped off the leaning porch as the helicopter finally disappeared past the towering tree line. Once off the shaky boards, his holey shoes immediately filled with chill dank swamp water. The ground was suppurating sympathetically for the coming rain, making the ground soft and wet, bubbling up dark moisture with every step. Leaving behind the three room ramshackle house he shared with his father, Jeb moved tired familiarity through the sodden surroundings. The shabby boy made his way to a set of long, thick boards extending out into the middle of the deeper waters of the swamp, his only way of getting to the traps, besides wading out in the swamp (which wasn't a good idea with all the gators that hung around). A veneer of slimy algae covered the boards, so Jeb had to watch his footing. He had fallen in the swamp a few times before. So far, he'd been lucky every time. There had been no gators to take advantage of his bad luck. Mama had been watching out for him those days, he figured. Her and Jesus.

The boards squeaked and bounced as he moved with care over the dark still waters to the first trap- a simple contraption of algae covered wire and wood. He got on all fours and pulled on the cold wet rope attached to the board and the trap emerged. Jeb's stomach was sorely disappointed to see that it was empty. Maybe the approaching storm was scaring all the swamp creatures off today. Although the frogs and whippoorwills didn't seem to be affected by it: Their raucous chorus echoed throughout the swamp, a comforting racket that had lulled Jeb asleep many nights. It was the kind of background noise that never stopped, but you noticed it the moment it was no longer present. When the swamp got quiet it was never a good thing.

The next trap held nothing as well, and he let it fall back in the water with a sigh. His stomach grumbled loudly. He was powerful hungry, and knew without looking that there was nothing in the house to eat. Daddy was not a big believer in buying groceries, unless you counted the kind that came in screw-capped bottles. If all the traps were empty, he figured he might be able to get something to eat from the Johnsons down the way. Mrs. Johnson always told him that if he needed anything to come by. But Jeb felt shame at the thought of asking for a hand out. His pride wouldn't let him go ask the Johnsons for food. He'd rather starve than beg. Besides, if Daddy got wind of it, he'd beat the hell out of him. No son of his was going to be a beggar, by God. They could do just fine without any help from the nosy neighbors, or the nosy church folks, or any nosy Sheriff, by God.

Jeb went on the next trap- his stomach feeling as hollowed out and empty as the trap when he finally pulled it to the surface. He would have to go deeper into the swamp, hunt down a snake or possum to fry up. Maybe he could pull up some palmetto roots for a stew.

It took him about another half-hour to check the remainder of the traps, and he found only two small turtles, far too small to bother with, so he tossed them back for another day. He figured he'd have better luck with the roots and possum today.

One look at the sky told him he had less than an hour before rain.

Jeb went to the end of the boardwalk, hopped off onto the squishy swamp ground, a spongy surface made up mostly of ancient tree roots, thick mud, and peat moss. He followed the winding animal trails deeper into the woods, past giant oak trees, over humped roots, past the green sprays of palmetto bush, until he found what he was looking for- a set of small pointed possum tracks.

A bone deep rumble of thunder sounded in the near distance, reminding Jeb hwo quickly storms moved in. The ambient light above had become a syrupy murk, as if the storm had gathered in the woods around him, and the nose tickling scent of ozone made him sniffle. The distant layers of trees and water had melted together to form one eternal shade of gloom ridden green and armies of shifting inhuman shapes. Bearded cypresses creaked in the wind, moaning their ancient aches. The Spanish moss swayed like waving fingers, signaling for him to enter the depths of their gray-green curtains.

The possum trail meandered further away from the house, and soon he lost sight of his home, continued to traipse warily after the tiny footsteps. Deeper and deeper into the swamp he went, his hunger driving him further despite the growing sense of trepidation in his shaking knees. The air grew colder, wetter, deep shadows shifted on every side. Jeb pretended not to notice. Everyone knew the Black Beast lived in the deepest parts of the swamp. He would have to stop before much longer.

Then Jeb did stop, his heart hammering in his chest.

So intent was he on following the possum trail he hadn't realized until now that the usual swamp noises had died. Not much would stop frogs from singing, especially with a storm coming on. The whippoorwills, maybe, but not the frogs. Stormy weather was a frog's favorite kind of weather; it was their time to sing.

He decided he'd rather be hungry than scared. He wanted to be back in the shack, even if his Daddy was asleep and drunk.

The trees seemed to close in around him. The usual harmless huddles of bush and indistinct gathering of trees took on frightening and bizarre shapes. Fear made the meager, but dependable, animal paths he used to navigate his way through the swamp seem like scattered leaves in his startled mind. Jeb moved back down the trail, eyes straight ahead. He refused to look into the trees. But the woods were in league with the shadows, and soon he felt as lost as the trails, stumbling breathlessly over roots, pushing frantically through cluttered palmetto bushes. Panic climbed up his chest like a thin-legged spider. He forced himself to calm down. He just needed to find one familiar stick trail and in no time he'd be home again.

Thunder erupted, followed by a brilliant crawling flash of lightning that made Jeb jump.

Something moved in the black thickness of the trees to his left, something that was following his every move. He didn't want to look, but something deep down, some insane need to see the shape of the thing, made his tearing eyes swivel to the darkness of the trees.

For a moment the shape looked like nothing more than a gnarled and ancient tree trunk. Jeb stared at it, praying it wouldn't move, so he could pretend it was only his imagination. But then it moved.

The thing was hulking and wide shouldered, standing no more than fifty feet away. It was patiently watching him. Maybe if he ignored the thing, it would leave him alone.

Jeb knew it was the Black Beast.

All the terrible tales he had heard throughout his childhood came rushing back at him like freezing cold river wave. As much as he did not want to think about them, the stories resurfaced like drowned leering corpses, reminding him of all the old folks' warnings of what the Black Beast did to those caught in its domain.

Somewhere to his right, Jeb heard a bull-gator hissing and grunting a warning that he was too close to his nest. Without thought, he edged away from the sound. If he were near a nest the gator would be on him so fast he'd never be able to outrun it. Gators could run short distances with staggering sprints of speed, almost as fast as a car. The only way to get away was to outrun one, or climb a tree and wait for the thing to go away. Jeb didn't think trapping himself in a tree with the Black Beast below was such a good idea. Everybody knew the Black Beast used the trees to get around the swamp, hiding in the high branches, until its prey passed below.

Jeb refused to let anymore of the stories the old folks told come to the surface- especially the one about a tribe of Indians that had been killed out in this swamp back in the old days.

The boy felt his chest heaving with stifled sobs. He just wanted to be home. But he couldn't decide what he should do. If he ran the Black Beast would be on him in a flash. And if he stayed where he was, waited for it to maybe lose interest in him, it might come for him anyway. As Jeb saw it, he had one chance.

He ran towards the sound of the bull-gator's warning grunts, hoping that he wasn't about to make an even worse decision. As he sprinted across the spongy wet ground, Jeb heard the crash of trees and palmettos as the Black Beast came for him. Another crashing tumult ahead guided him towards the nesting bull gator. There was a stand of tall green palmettos atop a muddy bank of moss and roots a few feet away, and beyond it he could see the telltale flattened weeds and trenches in the mud where the gator had moved to its nest. Jeb aimed for the area, his heart hammering like a small trembling gong.

Behind him, the sound of pursuit grew more violent, closer with every small leap he made toward his objective. The muddy, spongy ground sucked at his feet like a nightmare; but Jeb refused to slacken his pace.

As was about to enter the trampled copse of weeds and mud, the bull-gator suddenly erupted from the muddy bank. The creature was massive, a hundred years old at least. Its fat slithering bulk was covered in the grime and limp weeds for which it had used for its nest.

But it was only the male. Jeb didn't see any sign of the female and he felt an insane stab of disappointment. Two gators would have been better, even though he would've had to dodge the both of them.

With a cross between a cat's hiss and a dog's growl, the bull gator lurched towards him. His world became a yawning cave found only in nightmare, yellow teeth and pale gum line and cold reptilian eyes filled his vision.

Jeb jumped as high as his legs would thrust him, felt the snapping jaws of the bull pass just below his sneakers as he barely cleared the thrashing twenty-foot monster.

Jeb didn't spare a glance to see if it would intercept the Black Beast; he could only keep running forward, stumbling through the thick hindering mud, gasping for air, throwing himself over tripping, snagging roots which thrust from the quagmire of the swampy waters, intent on trapping him. Sounds of violence-the angry grunts and hisses of the bull-gator, the incoherent growls and roars of the unseen Black Beast-faded, and finally disappeared, lost in the tangle of trees and water behind him.

After what seemed like hours, he finally found a trail that looked familiar. He ran along the flat stick-path until he saw the shambling roof of his and Daddy's shack-house peering above the storm dark shadow of trees. With a grateful sob, he found the sagging boardwalk and scurried his way to the flat ground surrounding home.

Inside, Daddy was still snoring his way through whiskey sodden sleep. Jeb stumbled to find his own bed, fell into it, heedless of the mud and water, cold and terrified. Above him, the storm finally let loose. Soon, the usual whispering leaks spoke around the small dirty shack. Jeb closed his eyes and prayed to Jesus and Mama.

CHAPTER -8-

For the rest of the rainy afternoon Stewart and Garlen sequestered themselves in an office somewhere deep inside the confines of the awesome house, and Charlotte disappeared shortly after showing Sully to a pair of adjoining rooms where he and Garlen would be staying. She left Mary and Timmy alone in the entertainment room, begging off from watching TV, saying she had a headache and needed to lie down. The rain continued unabated into twilight, until a wet and chill night descended upon the land like a sodden blanket. Hours later, with night creeping through the windows across the room, the two of them were still snuggled deep in the leather softness of a giant cushioned couch in front of a wall sized television.

Darkness had triggered an automatic switch somewhere inside the vast mansion, so that dozens of strategically placed lights blazed along the rain drenched topiaries, lighting the perfectly manicured lawn, surrounding the large stone gargoyle fountain sitting in the center of the vast back grounds like angry villagers with purging torches. But the brilliance of the illumination that gave the lie of the wet night outside the windows stopped at the stone and metal security fencing at the edge of the property, refusing to penetrate the forest beyond. The rain, as if in rebellion against the light, seemed to redouble its efforts to drown the world. It slammed and careened against the windows like a liquid army.

Timmy had fallen asleep against her left shoulder while watching an old Harrison Ford film on one of the dozens of movie channels. The house felt silent as a tomb around her. She'd seen no servants, no Charlotte, and no Stewart for hours; the only evidence that she and Timmy weren't alone in the huge mansion was her occasional glimpse of the big man, the one who had been pushing the old man in the wheelchair, as he moved from the inside to the outside throughout the day. But she hadn't seen him in quite a while.

She tried to relax, but the profound quiet of the looming structure all around her, the new chill in the air because of the drop in temperature, brought about a sense of disquiet. And to make maters worse, the insistent sound of the pouring rain kept invading her thoughts, reminding her she needed to find a bathroom soon.

Mary leaned forward and gave Timmy a light kiss on his forehead. "I'm going to walk around for a few minutes, okay? You stay right here. I'll be right back." Timmy gave her a distracted, sleepy nod, and slid limply to the seat as she pulled herself from underneath his warm weight. She looked back at his sleeping form and left the lighted comfort of the entertainment room behind, and made her way to the dimness of the now familiar staging area for the stairs. She went past the stairway, to the left, and then even the ambient light of the staging area was gone. Bladder aching painfully now, she prayed a bathroom was around the next couple of turns. But she knew from experience, in this house, nothing was guaranteed. The next corner in the hall might be a dead end or a door for all the logic of Machen Mansion's architecture. The structure seemed to her more like a carnival funhouse than a sane abode, with its many hallways and corridors that seemed to turn and turn into themselves, and the sudden offshoots of stairs and doors that led to empty rooms, or even dead end passages. And so, despite Mary's careful insistence upon following the hall's disorder, it took only a few minutes for her to find that she was lost within this funhouse.

She paused before a red door on her right, wavering uncertainly between opening it or trying to backtrack to the staging area she had left behind. The dim yellow sconces spaced evenly along every hallway did little; behind her could have been a few dozen yards, or a half a mile, for all she was to discern by their meager offering. And where the hell were all the goddamned servants Charlotte talked about all the time? She'd think at least one would run across her in these halls.

Mary left the red door behind, turned back down the hall. She had to find her way back before she got hopelessly lost. The ludicrous notion that she might wander these halls forever, until she died of starvation, seemed less and less ridiculous with every passing second as made turn after turn to find dead ends and more hallways leading her deeper into the bowels of the mansion.

She rounded another sudden tight corner to find herself in the juxtaposition of an impossible three way split. Her rational mind screamed against it; there was no way that there could be a three-way split in this direction. She was positive she had just come this way and there had been no split. It had been a straightaway before. She was sure of it.

She must have taken a wrong turn. Unless she had made a wrong turn coming back. God! She was so confused. Maybe she was no longer in the same hallway. She must be in a new one.

She felt a combination of panic and disbelieving laughter flutter in her chest, certain now that she had managed to get herself lost.

At the end of the middle hall, Mary saw the shadows caused by the confusing flickers of the sconce lights deepen. The darkness slid along the far walls like inky night.

Someone was there. A quick movement, as of someone moving away from her, a stealthy shadow figure stretching, until it finally tapered into a massive liquid line of blackness and disappeared.

With a surge of relief, she shouted down the hall. "Hey! Wait up! Hold on, please!"

But the slippery shadow continued to flit away from her.

Mary ran down the hall, chasing after the elusive shape. She intended to force whoever it was to show her the way back, decided she wasn't going to go anywhere again without a guide, be it Charlotte, or a servant, that was for sure.

She hurried to turn down the hall, and rounded the corner, expecting to see someone. But the hall was empty- the only sign anyone might have been there a moment before the trembling flicker of the wall sconces. Mary hesitated, unsure if she should follow. The tight hall went on again for a few dozen yards before making another ninety-degree turn. Another impossibility, she knew, because if the hall actually turned that tightly in on itself there would have confronted the wall she had just gone past moments before. But she didn't have the mentality to concentrate on that mathematical paradox right now. The shadow was still moving away, making no sound at all in its swift retreat.

She had to catch up. Or else she'd never find her way out of here.

Mary ran along the red and gold carpet, feeling the squirming vertiginous wallpaper trying to throw her off balance. Another turn and the hall continued on.

She stopped. Beyond her tremulous breath, she could hear a quiet rustling sound from around the corner of the hall she had just left behind.

Someone was behind her now. Only a few feet away, just around the corner.

No way could they move fast enough to get away from her this time. She would tackle them, if she had to.

She whirled and jumped around the sharp turn in the hall. She wasn't surprised to see another empty hallway. The noise had stopped; but she caught the tail end of another departing shadow as it crept along the end of the hall again.

Then she heard something even more terrifying still.

Voices, low and muttering, from where she had just been.

Impossible. Her rational mind knew it was impossible. But, nonetheless, she heard a sibilant half whisper, half mutter, right around the corner she'd just left behind.

Rounding the corner once more, she saw that the hall was empty again.

The voices, speaking words too indistinct for her to understand, had dissipated as well. There was only the trembling sound of her own breath in her ears now.

Panic welled up within her. The walls felt as if they were closing in on her, ready to crush her in this damned shifting, crawling dimness. Hot uncontrollable tears suddenly flooded her eyes, more fear than frustration now. This was like being in a nightmare from which she couldn't awaken.

She swiped at the stupid tears dripping down her cheeks.

"God damn it! How the hell do you get out of here?"

"Are you okay?" a voice asked from behind.

The man's unexpected voice made her yelp and nearly jump out of her skin. She stumbled around in a panic to find the big bodyguard gazing at her with concerned bemusement. He moved forward slowly, approaching Mary as if she were a startled bird that would fly away at the slightest provocation. His blocky face wore a disarming grin, and, despite her confusion and fear, she found herself appreciating how much that smile suddenly changed his features. The tough guy sneer gone, he looked like someone's concerned father. Mary giggled self-consciously at her own reaction, feeling herself relax, the panic easing from her fear clogged throat like a slow leak. She wiped more tears from her reddened cheeks. "Oh, my God, am I glad to see another person."

"What's wrong?" he asked

She shook her head, embarrassed now. "I thought I could find the bathroom. I guess I got lost." She chuckled. "I guess I was wrong, huh?"

"This place can get to you if you're not ready for it," he said. "I've gotten lost here before. It's a little creepy." He gave an unconcerned shrug of his massive shoulders, but she could see that he was anything but relaxed. He was poised like some great jungle cat, ready for danger. His eyes watched the leaping shadows warily, arms and legs tight with barely contained violence. His sense of watchful readiness did little to calm her nerves. The halls were empty. Just the two of them here. Right? He cocked his head with a frown, as if he were listening to something that she could not hear. His eyes narrowed, and his hands moved towards the inside of his suit jacket. They both waited. Mary was afraid to speak. His face was full of concentration. And then, he relaxed. He sighed and relaxed his arms. He tried a smile, but she wasn't buying it. What had made his react like that?

It scared her a little being around a man so obviously used to violence that his entire body was an extension of the desire to partake of it.

"It's easy to get lost in here," Sully said. Mary could hear the slight trace of a tremble, as if he too could feel the tight claws of the house closing around them. "But it gets a lot worse at night, as I remember."

He turned in the small hallway- quite a trick for someone his size- and pointed back down the way she had come what seemed like hours ago. "I think I saw a bathroom back down this way." He softly grabbed her hand to lead her, and gave another of his warm smiles, transforming his face once more. "Come on, I'll show you where it is," he said. "My name is Sully. I met your son this morning."

"Timmy," she reminded him. "His name is Timmy."

"Yeah," Sully said with an embarrassed grimace.

"Timmy. It's nice to meet someone who's raised such a well mannered kid."

She felt her hand in his. It was warm, huge as a frying pan. "I'm Mary Machen."

"Cute kid," Sully said.

Mary felt the explanation for why she was here at the mansion hanging in the air between them, but she didn't continue. She really didn't know him well enough to go into that kind of personal detail. Instead, she laughed and said, "Don't tell him that. He's already cocky enough for his age."

"I could tell," he joked, grinning at her again. She liked his smile, liked the way it changed his hard lines. His voice was deep and soothing, and his size somehow made her feel more comfortable in the claustrophobic passages. She wanted him to keep talking so that she could keep her mind off of the hall and the way she felt looking at the squirming wallpaper. "I saw you walking this afternoon," she said. "Why were you going from room to room?"

"I was trying to get my bearings," he said. "I was here once before," he said. "And I spent most of my time getting lost in this damned place. I don't intend to do so this time."

"You'd think that we would've seen at least one servant," she said.

Sully shook his head. "You know that's weird, too. I don't remember ever seeing any servants here. I've heard the Machens mention them, but I've never actually seen one." He glanced back at her, saw her worried frown. "I'm sure there here, though. After all, somebody sets the table, makes the meals, makes the beds, right?"

She nodded uncertainly. That was true enough. Somebody had hauled their baggage up the stairs this morning, and she sure couldn't see Charlotte dragging them up. The only sane explanation was that they were busy doing their work behind the scenes where no one could see them.

Sully suddenly stopped before a nondescript door and leaned against the wall. "This is it."

Mary looked at the door in utter confusion, her gaze going from the hallway to the door and back again. This door had not been here before, she was sure of it. She wanted to protest its existence, but what could she say? It was right there in front of her. Wasn't that proof enough of its existence? Besides, her bladder hadn't stopped hurting any less for her fear. She was lucky she hadn't yet wet her pants. She looked uncertainly at Sully's as he leaned his heavy body against the frame. "Look, I know we don't know each other very well, but would you mind very much waiting for me out here until I'm done." She gave him a self-deprecating grin. "I wouldn't want to get lost again."

"No problem, Mrs. Machen," Sully said.

"Call me Mary, Sully," she said and brushed past

him to close the bathroom behind herself. She wasn't ready to dole out her personal history yet, but she couldn't stand being called Mrs. anything by someone her own age or older.

When she finished, and opened to door again, Sully was waiting. Their eyes met for a moment, and she suddenly felt like a speechless schoolgirl all over again. His gaze glittered with unspoken attraction, and she had to admit, she found his rugged features appealing. There was a solidity about him that comforted her. And she sensed layers beneath his tough guy exterior, a challenge for any woman.

She followed his lead again, as he made his way through the labyrinthine passages, back to the room where she had left Timmy. The boy was still fast asleep and she hugged his lightly snoring frame close to her as she scooted to sit next to him.

Sully waved at her. "See you at dinner, I guess."

She yawned and shrugged an apology. "Sorry. I'm pretty worn out from being lost. I- we'll both see you at dinner. It was nice to meet you, Sully. And thanks a lot for helping me out."

She saw him pause at the entrance for a moment, as if he would turn and speak, but then he moved away with that graceful gait of his. Mary found herself heaving a sigh and her thoughts slipped back to his smile and the secure warmth of his hand in hers, as she allowed her eyes to close.

CHAPTER -9-

Dinner was served at seven p.m. that evening in the same massive cathedral dining room that she and Timmy had eaten breakfast that morning. After she and Sully had parted ways, Mary had fallen into an exhausted, but troubled, sleep next to her son, curling up fitfully next to his warm little body. When she wanted them to be of warm hands and transmogrifying smiles on rugged faces, they were instead about hallways that kept going on and on, while she ran along them on exhausted and trembling legs; there were voices that whispered in the flickering murk behind her; the speakers always unseen. It was the voices she feared most. She knew to finally gaze upon the murmurers beyond the pall of the meager light would be to lose her mind with terror.

Even before Charlotte came to wake them for dinner, the smell of food had insinuated itself into her dreams, and she woke with the queer sensation of having eaten already although her stomach was growling with hunger.

Beyond the light of the room, sinuous rivulets of rain still bedecked the windows, and the night crowded against the wet glass like a secret watcher.

As she led them into the dining room, Charlotte kept up a continuous conversation about the dreadful weather. Mary followed sluggishly without adding much to the talk. Timmy no longer clung to her hip and asked his great grandmother questions about the horses and the house. The two of them got along fine without her, as she tried to brush away the clinging sense of dislocation the dreams had left her with. The bright lights of the dining room helped. She winced against their glare.

On the table, a long red tablecloth had been spread; silver capped dishes sat upon it, awaiting the diners. Mary and Timmy sat at one end of the table, next to the head where Charlotte had sat that morning. Soon, Garlen and Sully joined them, the big man pushing his boss' wheelchair. Rolling the chair to Mary's right, he removed the heavy, ornate dining chair, placed Garlen's legs beneath the table. Mary gave the old man a friendly smile and introduced herself- since Charlotte seemed too preoccupied with checking and re-checking the covered dishes to notice that no one had done so as of yet. Garlen removed his hands from beneath the red and black flannel blanket tucked around his withered lap, grabbed her hand in both of his steady, dry palms.

"It is a distinct pleasure to know you, Mary," Garlen said. "Stewart told me all about you and Timmy. I'm sorry about Conley."

Sully moved to sit across from Garlen, and she saw his curious glance. "Thank you, Mr. Winters," she said.

Well, the cat was out of the bag on that point, anyway

"I would much prefer if you'd just call me Garlen, Mary," the older man said, still holding her hand in his warm grip. "I'm not one to stand on formality."

"Then, Garlen, it is," she replied with a playful grin.

Charlotte's eyes lit up as her son made an appearance. Stewart chose a seat next to Sully and sat down. "Mother, I don't believe we've had this many people in here for ten years."

Charlotte chortled and nodded. "Not since that darling reverend from Atlanta visited with his colored entourage." She put a hand to her throat, as if she were having trouble not choking on the memory of it. "I don't know why he had to have so many colored folk with him. I don't mind saying it scared me having them running around the house like that. All of our belongings, you know."

"Mother…" Stewart frowned at her, shaking his head.

Timmy looked first at his mother, confused. She had taught him well, so before she could stop him, he spoke up to his great grandmother. "Why would you be afraid, grandma? Just 'cause they were black didn't mean they were going to steal anything."

The room grew quiet and tense. Charlotte's eyes narrowed, but she managed to keep a smile on her mouth, even though it thinned visibly at the boy's reprimand. Garlen snorted and tried to excuse it as a cough. Mary had the feeling he was trying hard not to laugh at the matriarch being called out by a six-year old. Across the table, Sully cleared his throat uncomfortably. Stewart kept his eyes on his plate.

Mary was proud of her son, no matter how ill timed his comment might have been. No way was she going to discipline him for speaking against such racist trash. But she wanted to make sure her new in-laws knew where she, and her son, stood when it came such comments. "Timmy," she said. "I don't think grandma meant they would try to steal anything, because that would be small minded and ignorant. And she certainly isn't that. Right?" She gave Charlotte a pointed look, daring her to disagree.

Timmy gave his mother a dubious stare and shrugged. "I guess not."

Charlotte's face blanched; she knew she was trapped. If she argued against the insult, then she would be as good as admitting to being a bigot. Stewart glanced between the two women as if he were enjoying a good chess match. Across the table, Mary caught Sully's eye, saw a smile creep onto his lips. And if Garlen wasn't quaking with pent-up laughter next to her, then he needed to see a doctor for the shakes.

The tension continued, until Stewart finally made a decisive move and removed a silver lid from the nearest dish. Aromatic steam wafted, exposing a platter of collard greens, slabs of boiled bacon fat sitting atop the dark green pile. Garlen gasped at the sight of the first dish and exclaimed, "Oh, my, Stewart how did you know I hadn't had any collard greens in forever?"

"Lucky guess, Garlen," Stewart said. "I don't suppose they have much call for them in New York City, eh?"

Stewart continued to reveal the dishes, exposing even more good down home Southern food. Corn bread, buttermilk biscuits, fried shrimp, fried catfish, corn on the cob, and fried chicken. With the food sitting before them, the awkward situation dissipated like the vaporous clouds from the dishes, leaving a quietly embarrassed Charlotte pursing her lips sullenly at the end of the table.

Mary didn't know if she had done the right thing or not, but she was not going to tell her son that it was okay to make a derogatory remark about someone because of the color of their skin. Just because it was an old person saying it didn't make it right- great grandmother or not. Why couldn't the older generation see how stupid and useless being prejudice was? What an enormous waste of emotional energy it was to upkeep that kind of hatred? She was glad she had had people of different races and backgrounds in her school to teach her that none of the surface things mattered. It was what a person was made of that mattered. Good was good, no matter what color your skin was.

Apparently everyone was as hungry as Mary, because plates were loaded with food, and the room got quiet again; this time because eating took precedence over conversation for a while. Garlen finished his first plate in record time, and went back for seconds of everything. Mary wondered where the little old man put it all. With almost every bite, and more for Timmy's benefit she was sure than was his natural inclination, he made a big show of rolling his eyes in near orgasmic pleasure, moaning every few bites. Timmy giggled in appreciation, and even Sully cracked an uncharacteristic grin, shaking his head at Garlen's act for the boy.

For her part, Mary ate with gusto, going back for seconds herself. She especially enjoyed the biscuits; they were perfectly moist and light, with just enough butter on the top crust to make them melt in her mouth. She was almost positive she could taste a hint of honey, too. Just like her own grandmother had made them years ago.

When conversation started up again, it was with a much lighter tone than the beginning of the meal. Soon, everyone was talking about how great the food was, and Garlen and Stewart were exchanging old business stories.

Once the meal was done, and no one could eat another bite, Stewart suggested that they all 'retire' to a smoking room, where everyone might enjoy an after dinner sherry. Mary wasn't even sure what an after dinner sherry was, but she supposed it couldn't be a bad thing to have a little drink. If they were going to brave those hallways again to go to bed, then a drink could only help.

They followed Stewart down a spacious ground level hallway, to a dark wooden door, bedecked with a silver door handle. The room was smaller than any other she had seen so far- only big enough for a small party of fifty or so. Ship paintings and darkly colored landscapes hung on the four dark wood panels walls. A small red lamp cast an ambient crimson glow across the room. In the corners, shadows played tag with the dull light, eluding pursuit. A low fire burned in the fireplace by the room's single window. A simple cherry wood desk took center stage on the room. A wheeled serving cart was already sitting next to the desk. Sitting in mute sparkling reflection upon the handsome cart was a finely cut crystal decanter filled with blood dark liquor and several tiny glittering crystal glasses. Next to the assortment of gleaming glassware was a silver tray heaped with an assortment of cookies and a glass of milk- presumably for Timmy.

Stewart began pouring the drinks, and Charlotte handed Timmy the silver tray of treats with a smile. Sully passed Mary a thimble-sized glass filled with the dark rosy rich smelling liquid. She found she liked it and sipped the smooth stinging drink with pleasure. Low talk ensued and she felt fatigue wrapping its insistent fingers in her thoughts, lulling her away from all worries and concerns. After a second glass of the strong liquor, even the hallways didn't seem as daunting.

Mary stared out the single window, at the obtuse view of the estate's lawn. The night world outside looked blurry and out of focus, a less-than-perfect illusion of reality. She moved slowly towards it, watching the slow drizzle of rain. Her grainy-tired eyes strayed to the stoic security fencing bordering the property, a black and white enigma, hardly visible at all from this distance, an abrupt cutoff from the rest of civilization.

She still didn't get it. Why the hell did they need something so enormous out here in the middle of the woods? An army would have a hard time storming that brace of metal and stone, so what exactly were the Machens trying to keep out? The bedraggled citizens of Ellison? Or were they just being paranoid? Mary again felt that familiar burning distrust of rich people, but pushed it aside with an angry sigh, knowing that it was a ridiculous reaction to something so innocuous as a security fence. They could do what they wanted on their own property, right? This old prejudice was something she was going to have to learn to quell, if even just for

Timmy's sake. There was no sense in passing on her paranoia to him.

Stewart's reflection suddenly swam into view behind her, startling her from her thoughts. "Quite beautiful, isn't it?" Mary frowned at the decidedly un-father-in-law-like roaming of his eyes along her back, a lascivious smirk lifting at the corners of his pale lips.

Uh-oh...looks like someone's had a little too much sherry tonight, she thought. Please, God, for Timmy's sake, don't let him make some clumsy drunken pass at me. Instead of speaking, Mary nodded, careful to keep her eyes on the reflective glass. She saw Sully watching her while he talked with Garlen and Timmy. His dark, mysterious eyes found hers and he gave her one of his uncomfortable smiles. Mary felt her stomach tremble and a slight blush colored her cheeks. God, he was so big, handsome in a thuggish kind of way, not in the conventional, pretty boy kind of way. His eyes, so striking, so inhabited by the dead, so tired; they were twin canticles of a secret pain. His dark stare was the closest thing to haunted she'd ever seen. And was she imagining the connection she felt between them? It was an odd, maybe even a forbidden feeling, given the death of her husband only a few months ago, but she couldn't ignore her attraction to him. She wasn't sure she wanted to.

"Did you know that these woods stretch for nearly ten miles in every direction around the estate?" Stewart startled her; she'd forgotten about him. His eyes still followed the curves of her back, and she felt herself tensing and shifting uncomfortably under his scrutiny.

"Really?" she said, throwing her voice up a pitch higher than needed for their intimate distance from one another. Thankfully, it had the intended effect: Sully started edging away from Garlen and Timmy, still talking, but making his way almost unconsciously to where she and Stewart stood.

Stewart leaned closer to her, his groin brushing against her lower torso. Mary's mouth tightened and she moved away as diplomatically as possible, smelling the sharp stench of alcohol on his breath. He moved closer again. "There's a swamp that even the natives that used to live here wouldn't go into in the old days." He rubbed his groin against her thigh. Mary decided she'd had enough of the window, and that she needed a chair between them before Stewart did something in his insobriety that would embarrass the both of them. She wasn't sure that his obvious come-on bothered her more because he was being rude, or because his glass muted reflection looked way too much like Conley for her comfort. Goose pimples danced along her arms at the almost unconscious feelings that seeing his pseudo-face did to her. She moved back to the center of the room, her father in-law.

Timmy's cookie garbled voice piped in, "Why wouldn't the Indians go into the swamp, Granddaddy?"

Stewart suddenly turned from Mary, reared over the boy's small frame, an alcohol induced grin smeared across his face. "Because they said that there was a horrible monster living in it." He gave a comical maniacal chuckle, his arms raised in a parody of menace. "Really?" Timmy's eyes went round with wonder...or fear.

Mary felt an unaccountable alarm at the image of Stewart Machen leering over her son, and she didn't care for the way this conversational tangent was going, either. In the past, she'd had too many nights staying up with her son because he couldn't get to sleep after watching a horror film. The night Conley had rented both Grizzly and Humanoids From The Deep had been one of the worst. Monsters seemed a lot more possible to a child who lived in the woods than to a city kid. Nighttime shadows and innocuous noises became evil creatures sneaking up on you, and your bed suddenly became a refuge for every creature of evil that could squeeze beneath it.

Recognizing his grand son's interest, Stewart's grin grew as he began to warm to his subject. Now even Garlen and Sully were listening, as well. Mary frowned in mild irritation. Despite her misgivings, she kept her mouth shut. She didn't want to come off sounding like one of those annoyingly over protective parents that she always thought were a pain in the ass, parents that didn't let their kids play in the mud after a rainstorm because they were afraid of ringworms or some such thing. She would just have to perform her motherly duty and stay up with her son, if need be.

"A real monster?" her son asked. Mary could hear a slight tremble in his voice now and his uneasy gaze at the night dark window gave away his growing trepidation. "Can it get in here?"

Stewart chuckled, rubbing Timmy's shoulder affectionately. "No, of course not, my boy. We wouldn't let that happen. If any monsters got in here, well, we'd just have to go outside and shoot them with one of my father's antique guns. Maybe tomorrow, I'll show you the guns. With your mother's permission, of course, that is." He gave Mary a bleary, irritated glance, as if it irked him to ask permission.

Mary tried to smile, but felt an instant tension in her gut at the thought of her son being around any guns- antique or otherwise. She shrugged uncomfortably, trying to find a diplomatic way to phrase her worry. "I don't know, Stewart. I don't think I like guns much. He's only six years old, after all."

Charlotte piped in from her chair. "Oh, I agree, Stewart. Those horrid things. And they stink, too. Showing off ugly weapons to a six-year old, why that's just dangerous."

Timmy rounded on his mother, his eyes narrowing in petulance. "I'm almost seven."

Mary rolled her eyes. His voice had taken on that special whiny quality that she hated to hear; it usually meant a tantrum was brewing. "Timmy, please," she said. "I just don't want you touching any guns. Maybe some other time, okay?"

"But you always say that and I never get to," he complained. Mary gave him one of those stern looks that only mother's seemed to be able to perfect, and Timmy crossed his arms across his chest, his lower lip already hitting the pout position.

Stewart watched the interplay with a strained smile, tousled the boy's dark hair. "I think your mother's right, Timmy. Some other time."

Garlen spoke into the tense silence. "So, Stewart, I'm curious. Is this monster some kind of legend?" He gave Mary a boyishly impish smile and a wink. "I'm interested in this thing. Tell us some more. I could use a good bedtime story."

Mary resisted the urge to frown. Just when she had dodged one bullet with Timmy, he was going to start up the horror stories again. Didn't any of these people know what it was like having a small child around for adult conversations? Didn't they remember what it was like to be six and afraid of the dark?

Pouting-Timmy vanished in a flash and cheering-Timmy suddenly reappeared. "Yeah! A bed time story, Granddaddy." Mary shook her head at how quickly the young forgot their complaints and troubles. Knowing her son as she did, she figured he'd never even mention the guns again, unless someone brought it up later. He only cared about them because Stewart had mentioned them first. One day around the old man and her son was already trying to please him. As much as she hated it, she didn't think it fair to blame Timmy. She knew he missed Conley as much as she did. His father had been his best friend. With him gone, it was a lonely time for the boy. In his needy eyes, Stewart probably seemed a likely replacement.

"Okay," Stewart said, moving to the fireplace and stirring the glowing embers; his short stabs chased dying sparks up the smoke blackened chimney. "A bedtime story you shall all have, then." His voice no longer held the tone of drunkenness. It had sunk to a deeper level, as if his voice were coming from a darker source. Replacing the fire poker in its rack with a soft rattle, he began. "There are lots of stories about this place- about this town and Algernon Wood. But the swamp seems to be the place from which most of the stories about the Black Beast originated."

Stewart's back was still to them. Mary looked at Sully with a half-amused smile. The old guy was really playing it up.

"And it's said that the swamp is where this thing- this Black Beast- was born." He turned, finally, to face them; the leaping flames back-lighting his features in to shadowy relief like dark water crawling in deep wells.

"Now, of course, I don't know if any of these stories are true—" His lips curled into mocking grin, as if to say he put not too much credence into what the locals said "—but something out there makes a habit of kills panthers, even occasionally, a bear. Or so say the local huntsmen. They find skeletal remains in the deeper parts of Algernon Woods from time to time."
Behind Stewart an ember popped loudly into the silence of the room. Timmy wasn't the only person with wide eyes now. Mary was sure her expression wasn't far from her son's wary stare. What could kill a panther or a bear? Of course, what could kill a panther or bear was old age or another panther or a bear. This was silly. It was the atmosphere making her feel nervous, the ambience of the dim room, the sense of story that made her cast her own uneasy glance at the window.

Stewart paced before the fire, his shadow looming large across the ceiling and walls. "Well, now…a story…let's see." He put a forefinger across his lips, deep in thought. "I seem to remember one told to me by my own father, many years ago." He gave Timmy a meaningful look. "I think I might have been about your age when I first heard it."

Timmy edged closer to Mary, nudging against her thigh. She wasn't sure how far this story session should go. He was going to be up all night if the story was too frightening, and, as everyone knew, once the story was told, there was no untelling it. But she could see the eagerness in Garlen's face, and even Sully was leaning intently forward in his chair with seeming interest, so she didn't want to ruin it for them. Again, she kept her mouth shut, convincing herself that maybe it wouldn't be so bad. Maybe like some bad campfire prank story, like The Hook.

The piled logs in the fire shifted with an unexpected crunch and fell into glowing embers; the room dimmed a little more, drawing the shadows from the corners into cold ash piles on the floor and ceiling. Stewart stared into the dying fire, his eyes distant. "The first white men who came here cut their very existence from the forest, helping to build towns all over the South. My great-great-grandfather Algernon Machen was one of the first lumberjacks to call this place home, way back in 1883. He was a bachelor then, living with the hard, violent men whom he'd traveled with from South Carolina. He was a kind of labor leader, the boss of the crew, making sure that the men were paid, that the housing was maintained by the company, and such things. It was a hard life, but great-great grandfather was a hard man. Young, then. Tough and mean. Had to be to keep in line the kind of men who worked the forest. He knew the forest could be tougher and meaner."

Stewart made his way to the drink decanter and poured another thimble glass of sherry. Once he had taken a noiseless sip, he returned to his story. "The woods...the woods..." His perfect teeth flashed a predatory smile into the dusky room. "Algernon had heard the strange stories about the woods from the native tribe. But he knew that there are always tales to be told whenever people are afraid, so he paid them no mind. The Indians, they called the woods Wend-o-Nagai, which, roughly translated, means 'the cursed land'. It's the area we call Ellison, now."

"I've seen Ellison," Garlen muttered with a sarcastic smirk, "and it still looks cursed."

Mary chuckled appreciatively. She was glad to hear that someone else in the room wasn't taking too seriously Stewart's attempt at scaring them. She gave her son a worried look. He was still pressed against her, but he looked up at her with a half smile, trying to put on a brave front. Sully shifted in his too-small seat, the wood creaking threateningly as he spoke, "So why did the natives stay?"

"Oh, they didn't live here," Stewart clarified. "They made their home all the way on the other side of the swamp. When the white men came to live here they tried to warn them. But, of course, no one believed them. After all, they were considered savages." Stewart swallowed more of the alcohol, his cheeks rosy with it now. "Algernon and his men were in the forest for about a month before the first of the men began to disappear. At first, it was thought that they had run off to drink away their first month's pay. Not terribly unusual for the type of men who worked lumber camps. Of course, the fact that the nearest town with a bar was over two days away didn't seem to impress anyone how unlikely that theory was. At least, not until it happened again…and again…and again."

"It didn't take long for the other loggers to suspect that there was something besides simple alcoholism at work in the forest. Many of them began to question what the natives had warned them about. Maybe those savages knew something they didn't."

"The disappearances were random. Sometimes, only one man went missing. Other times, it was three or four men who were mysteriously swallowed up by the forest. Gone forever, without a trace. Occasionally, the others would find a torn strip of clothing known to belong to one of the missing workmen. Algernon himself even found a skeleton that he was sure belonged to a man named Petey. Of course, it was so utterly decomposed that the only way he could say with any certainty that it indeed belonged to the man was the fact of its right clubfoot. No one but Petey had a clubfoot. And he had been one of the first men to disappear."

Stewart placed his glass on a side table and went to stand before the dying fire again. His lean body was silhouetted into a dark line, face invisible, hands clenched together at his sides.

Mary could see that Charlotte looked as if she wanted to stop the story there, but only pursed her lips and gave a minute shake of her head, and kept quiet.

Stewart didn't seem to notice her warning glare, as he continued his tale. "The men became frightened, and many refused to go out into the woods to work- even in large groups. Seeing that something had to be done, Algernon gathered them together, armed them, and put guards on all the workers round the clock. I guess he figured getting a quarter of the work done was better than no work getting done. Smart man, Algernon." He turned to look at Timmy. After all, this was all for him, wasn't it? "And do you know what happened, Timmy?"

Timmy shook his head, unable to form words. Stewart gave another of his shark smiles. "The disappearances stopped."

The room was quiet, and after a few moments, when Stewart didn't go on, Garlen spoke up. "So what happened then?"

"Nothing," Stewart shook his head. "They went back to work and that was that."

Garlen placed his fingers in a steeple under his thin, jutting chin. "Do you believe any of it, Stewart?"

Charlotte cleared her throat with an angry snort, "My great grand father wasn't in the habit of telling tall tales, Mr. Winters. He was as honest as the day is long and a God-fearing man."

Stewart ignored her outburst, looked at Garlen with an air of insouciance. "Well, something did happen to those men. The company paperwork concurs they did, indeed, disappear. None of them were heard from again. And the law, when it was brought to their attention, had nothing to add. The only theory that was even close to plausibility was that one of the loggers was responsible."

Mary shuddered. How horrible! To think, even so long ago, all those poor men going missing, and that it could have been someone they worked with the whole time. Timmy wasn't the only one who was going to have nightmares tonight. Despite that, however, she couldn't stifle the yawn that blindsided her. Next to her, Timmy gave a wide yawn of his own right after her. She was exhausted; they were both still trying to catch up from the long drive to get here. She didn't want to be rude, but she was going to fall asleep right here if she didn't get into a bed soon. Garlen stifled his own yawn.

Stewart nodded to Charlotte. "I think it's time for us to retire, eh, mother? I'm sure Timmy's quite ready."

Timmy protested, even as another yawn erupted. "I'm wide awake, Granddaddy."

"But I'm not," Stewart laughed. "You wore me out this morning. But tomorrow, barring any more of this bad weather, we'll go brush the horses down. If your mother doesn't mind." He cast a drunken smirk in Mary's direction. She nodded and smiled at Timmy's grinning expectant face. "That's sounds great. Maybe I'll help you guys."

"That would be wonderful," Stewart said. "Now off to bed with you, young man." He patted the boy's head and gave Mary another of those enigmatic smiles.

As Mary and Timmy moved past Charlotte the old woman leaned forward and tapped her wrinkled cheek. "Doesn't grandmother get a good night kiss, then?" Timmy giggled and gave her a quick smack of his lips. "Why, thank you, kind sir," she said. She pushed herself from the scarlet crushed velvet divan and shuffled after the two of them. "Perhaps I should show you the way. This old place can play tricks on you if you're not familiar with it."

No shit, Mary thought wryly. The house plays tricks? That was a good way to put it. Still, she was grateful for Charlotte's guidance. She'd not been looking forward to having to navigate the passages again. "I hadn't really noticed," she lied.

Behind her, Garlen and Sully both called out good night, and Mary gave them a weary sounding 'good night' of her own. Timmy and Charlotte were already getting away from her down the hall, Charlotte bustling unerringly along the passage. She hurried to catch up.

Sully was right: the halls had changed with the coming of night. And although the difference was subtle, it was there. The jaundiced sconce lights seemed dimmer now; the wallpaper squirmed a little more, and the cornered shadows danced a bit livelier. She felt as if the mansion had changed somehow. The floor seemed to vibrate with a low bone-deep sensation of power. As if it sat atop a hidden source of energy. It made her teeth ache slightly. She thought it could be her imagination, or a difference in sea level compared to home, that caused the subconscious discomfort. The walls played tricks with distance, so she could not convince herself that passages she remembered were, once again, impossibly different now.

Once they were in the bedroom again, she felt the darkness swell hungrily around them until Charlotte clicked on a corner table light. The air was permeated by a chill dampness- presumably a legacy of the still pouring rain- and Mary found herself shivering against it. Rainy weather did that to old places in the South, the dampness always called forth old memories of decay and death.

Charlotte made sure that they had everything they needed- blankets, more towels, and such- then wished them pleasant dreams and left. When she was gone, Mary got a bleary eyed Timmy into his favorite Hulk pajamas, changed herself into a flannel nightgown, and they both crawled wearily into bed, snuggling beneath the thick blankets. Together they fell into a deep sleep, hands entwined, quiet breaths intermingled in the night.

Sully watched Mary and Timmy leave, smiling to himself. She was beautiful as all hell in this muted light. The smile flittered from his face and immediately he quashed the thought of her beauty. Now what the hell was he doing? Sure, she was beautiful, but she was a Machen and that he didn't need. Besides, he and Garlen would be leaving in a few days and he'd most likely never see her again. What good could come of his attraction to this beautiful stranger? Best to let it go. He didn't need any complications in his life right now. His pondering mind would be better spent with his head in a book.

So why couldn't he stop thinking about Mary Machen's smile?

He turned to see Garlen giving him an impish smile of his own. Sully rolled his eyes, shook his head. "Not one word, you old coot," Sully said.

Garlen chuckled, but said nothing. Sully cast a glance at Machen; he was watching them. Sully had seen the way the old geezer had been eyeing Mary, with his drunken leers, and thrusting groin. He was like some kind of randy old dog sniffing around a bitch pup. One would think a man his age would have learned how to handle his alcohol by now.

Garlen looked exhausted. Sully wondered what the two elderly men had discussed all day, while he'd been roaming the halls of this damned place, looking in vain for any sign of the supposed servants that did everything behind the scenes to keep Machen Mansion running. As much as he had tried to play it off with Mary earlier that day, he did feel there was something odd about the fact that he had yet to see one damned servant.

Well, that wasn't entirely true.

He had seen one from a distance during Garlen's last visit. Man or woman, he hadn't been able to tell from his vantage point, as it scurried outside the house, into the twisted greenery of the topiaries. Nothing more than a vague impression, really. But he remembered how odd the shape had struck him, even from a distance. Something not natural about the way the person had moved so quickly through the garden.

He rolled his neck, feeling tension knotting his muscles into angry bunches. This place made him ready to smash things. He didn't like it; made his skin crawl, and he didn't know why. It bothered him how it sent his danger instinct into the red. It was crazy. It was only a house, right?

Mary. She was very beautiful, but she seemed sad, too. Withdrawn. She was still stinging from the loss of her husband, no doubt.

He knew about the stings of life, how they could warp your view of the world.

It had been a long time since he'd been forced to have a real conversation with a real woman, not one of Garlen's many social leeches. That was one of the reasons he enjoyed working for Garlen. He never had to worry much about meeting real people, or even the real world impinging on his own insulated solitude- a self devised world of guns, speed bags, weights and books. No one Garlen associated with in his business world could be much thought of as humane, let alone human. They were there for one thing and one thing only, a piece of Garlen's power and wealth. It was hard to like people who looked at their fellow beings as commodities and investments.

His mind drifted back to Mary. She had a nice smile. And her kid was a character. He had known right off the kid was scared shitless of him, but it hadn't stopped him from keeping up a chirpy conversation the whole time he'd been walking along with him this morning.

He decided he liked the boy. And Garlen seemed to be taken with him as well.

Again, he wondered what Garlen and Machen had been at all day.

Yours is not to question. That's not what the man pays you for. If he wanted you to know he would have told you before now. So just wheel him upstairs and get him into bed. Because that's what he pays you for.

Still, Sully couldn't help but wonder why Garlen had any kind of business relations with someone like Stewart Machen. Garlen himself had told him what kind of conniving and ruthless bastard was.

Did Mary know what kind of people her in-laws were?

"Sully," Garlen's weary voice murmured into the stillness, "if you don't mind, I believe I should get some sleep now. Not as hardy as I used to be, I'm afraid."

"None of us are, Garlen," Stewart said with his back to them. "We all grow older everyday." Stewart didn't turn as they left. He stood before the single rain painted window, a larger drink glass, half full of something amber without ice, in his hand, silently drinking and watching the night beyond.

Sully had a little trouble finding their room, but after some backtracking, he soon found the right door. Sully had the old man out of the chair and into his bed within ten minutes. The old man was asleep before Sully had even finished brushing his teeth.

Leaving the bathroom light on so that he could see his way to the bed, Sully pulled Garlen's blankets up around his neck, brushed gray hair from his forehead. The old guy was like a father to him, had been for a long time. Sully owed him more than he could ever repay him in one lifetime. There was nothing that he wouldn't do for Garlen. They shared a pain so acute that no one else could ever understand the terrible thing that held them together. A jigsaw of broken pieces of their hearts- intertwined forever.

Damn it! He was thinking about it again. All day his thoughts had been circling that past tragedy like hungry vultures, but he'd been able to fend them away with one distraction after another.

He was tired now and the battle had turned against him in his fatigued state of mind. Being in Mary

Machen's presence had called to the surface all the things that he had worked so hard to keep buried. The visible sadness in her face was a catalyst that revived his angst. But he wasn't alone. Sully knew Garlen well enough to know he'd probably be awakened at least once tonight by the old man's nightmares. Garlen was no more immune to the memories than himself.

Sully felt a yawn creeping up his throat, decided he should get some sleep. What sleep he could get, anyway. With a weary sigh, he left Garlen to his slumber, went to the door that connected their adjoining rooms. He crawled into the cold comfort of the dusty mattress and snuggled deep beneath the blankets to escape the chilly night. Sully fell asleep listening to the raindrops pelt the glass window across the room.

CHAPTER- 10-

A suffocating wet night held sway over Algernon Wood. Rain cascaded from high treetops to the sodden forest floor below. Night creatures waited out the bad weather with the impatient snarls of the hungry.

In town, Ellison's citizens did not venture forth to run 'stills', did not dare the dark of Algernon Wood. They knew what that deep darkness contained; the cautionary tales had been passed down through the generations, warnings for the curious. No wise person tempted the forces within Algernon Wood. The first people, the Seminoles, had known better. Now, after living in the forest's confines for centuries, the white man had learned better as well. The hours of darkness were the time of the Black Beast. Death stalked this forest.

By nine p.m., the streets were clear. No lights shone from the few ragged main street shops that were still prosperous enough to remain viable; the curbs were clear, excepting the bar, of course. The lights in McHughes would be on for another few hours, until Forty kicked everybody out for the night, so he could get home with the wife and the dog.

The sort of patrons that braved the dim smokiness of McHughes weren't worried too much with what lived in Algernon Wood. They were all too drunk to care about tales of ancient evil haints that their grandmamas had tried to scare them with as children. They were grown men. Nothing to be scared of in them woods. Ask any of the rugged men, downtrodden men of McHughes if they feared the night in Algernon Wood, and they would laugh in your face, or maybe smash your face in with a beer bottle. But if you asked any man to go walking in the woods once the sun was down, they would still most likely laugh in your face…though, it would be a nervous laughter, and they would find a reason to drink somewhere else. Even the most foolhardy of men know that some things should not be tested.

On the outskirts of Ellison, where the trailer people hunched down within rough circles of pine and oak, no one left their shack like dwellings to see why the dogs barked and howled this night. They kept their doors and windows barred, locked against the night. Wiser, more frightened, pets cringed beneath sagging porches. Some dogs might be missing by morning, but that was better than husbands or sons who would never come home again. Algernon Wood exacted a price from those who lived too close to it. Dogs and cats, even a goat sometimes, seemed little enough sacrifice to escape what lived in the haunted dark.

Past the scattered trailers, deeper within the forest, where the swamp held sway, the screams of hunting panthers could be heard, sometimes, the grunting territorial pronouncement of a bear, the deep throated grunting of a gator moving for night waters. But there were times when something that wasn't a natural part of the forest traveled the dark ways of Algernon Wood, something that was neither panther or bear, a thing that stamped through the underbrush with violence, something that howled with a horrible inhuman bloodlust. Ask anyone in Ellison what creature made such sounds at night, and there was only one answer: The Black Beast of Algernon Wood.

There were always those, of course, who had to challenge the danger, people who had to try the patience of the deep forest like a dark garrison stronghold. This was not to be confused with bravery. For, more times than not, these challenges were fueled by liquor and bar room bravado.

Sometimes the drunks at McHughes would drink and talk about the things that went bump in the night in Algernon Wood, until someone dared someone else to walk down such and such road with only a flashlight and shaking knees. Most times, these daredevils would grin lopsidedly and admit being a little scared of haints and such, and would chicken out long before they could be talked out of the comfort of the dank bar room.

Other times, there was the odd man who would not back down and admit his fear, and he would find himself dumped off by a chuckling, howling group of his drunk cohorts, watching the taillights trailing away, leaving him alone in the woods. Such 'brave' souls would run like the devil was on their tails. The lucky ones made it back to town, sobered by the experience.

The unlucky ones never made it back.

That was to be expected.

After all, the woods were dangerous at night; sometimes nature just swallowed someone up.

Everyone knew that.

Everyone in Ellison.

But there would always be disbelievers. No matter how many cautionary tales the old folks told, some people didn't take the legends seriously, refused to consider the strange number of chickens, goats, or cows that vanished during the lean months.

Frankie "Spud" Tucker (so nicknamed because he bore an uncanny resemblance to the dirty round root) was one of those souls who put no credence in his elders' warnings about Algernon Wood.

Although the four yowling teenagers who bounced and swayed drunkenly in the back of his new truck ranged from disbeliever to down right terrified of the woods.

Spud had just turned eighteen the week before, fresh out of high school, with a decent job alongside his Uncle Norrey in Waycross. Tonight, he was about as happy as he could ever remember being. After two years of driving a 'hand me down' truck that his Daddy had willed him when he died, Spud had finally gone out and gotten his own brand new cherry red Ford four by four, complete with roll bars, shiny chrome bumpers, dark brown leather interior, and some other fancy-smancy stuff that his Mama had hated.

And she made damn sure to tell him how much money he'd wasted on each and ever item. She didn't understand; Mama never would. As far as he could tell, she did nothing but nag about every expense- warranted or not. Probably had nagged Daddy to death. His Daddy had always said you only live once, and since you never know what's around the next turn, you better enjoy it while you got it. And Daddy had been a true-blue practitioner of his own philosophy. Only his idea of enjoying life was to flop dead of a heart attack in a cheap motel room a hundred miles from home with some woman he'd picked up hitching. Even after two years, Spud wasn't sure if he should be mad, or laugh at the absurdity. Of course, Mama had her own ideas about how he should feel about Daddy. When Spud thought about it he figured she might even hate him just a little for being Daddy's son. If that wasn't fucked up, he didn't know what was.

Spud caressed the leather seat next to him and smiled. Yeah, his baby was expensive, and he was going to have to stay with that stupid job with Uncle Norrey for at least five years just to pay off the enormous payments. But, hell, working in a box factory wasn't so bad. At least he and Uncle Norrey could talk about Daddy during the odd lunch hour, or over a secret beer in his uncle's small, hot office at the back of the plant, without his Mama going bat shit over it.

Spud looked in the rearview, saw his four friends getting comfortable with his slow-mo driving, about to come out of their squats again, blissfully drunk enough to feel confidence in standing. He gave a mean-spirited chortle and gunned the engine, sending them rolling and lurching all over the bed. Beer gushed in clumsy fountains and he shook his head. That was exactly why those assholes weren't sitting up front with him right now. No way was he going to let them ruin that wondrous new car smell with the sour stench of beer.

Spud had no illusions about how his life was laid out for him; he figured a man only got a few chances to enjoy that new car smell in his lifetime; better enjoy while he could. Despite the fact that his uncle was a big man at the plant, he couldn't see himself going too far with the job. And who knew what was coming around the next bend? Maybe a quick death in a stinking hotel room with a drugged girl young enough to be your daughter.

Spud lifted his own beer from between his legs and gave a silent toast to his dear old dead- but eternally wise- Daddy. He'd hit the nail on the fucking head with that one.

No beer and no food in his new baby...

Of course, he would be happy to make an exception for that fine-ass Clarke chick who lived down the road from him. She could eat a goddamned Happy-Meal off the seat if she wanted. Hell, if things worked out as he hoped, before too long she'd be doing a lot more in this seat than eating food. He'd seen the way she looked at him this afternoon when she saw him driving his big red truck up the driveway. She was hot for him; the kind of smile she had given him didn't tell lies, made promises whispered of only in high school locker rooms and Penthouse Forum Letters, two places that he'd learned that you could believe about half of what you heard; but, man, when they did come true...WOW!

He left off visions of fuck-play in his new truck and concentrated on the dark muddy dirt road ahead. Of course, it had to fucking rain the night he got his new baby. The headlights blazed through the wet night. The ubiquitous mud puddles threw back the light with a lackluster attempt at reflection.

Spud slowed for the next turn, hit a deep pothole, and heard his friends' slurred complaints and giddy laughter over his shoulder. Jeff, closest to his own age at seventeen, knocked on the sliding divider window. Spud reached back and opened it an inch or two. A cool breeze slip inside: a ghostly kiss that brushed along his cheeks. "What the hell ya' want?" he demanded, suddenly wishing that he had followed his first plan tonight, which was to go over and ask that Clarke girl out for a ride in his cherry baby.

"Man," Jeff said, "what the hell good is it to have a new truck like this if you gonna drive it like my goddamned grandma?"

The warm beer smell of Jeff's breath slithered past the cold breeze and wafted up his nose. He could see the beer sloshing from Jeff's can from the corner of his eye.

He better not spill that shit on the back of my seat, or, I swear, by God, I'll kick a new hole in his ass.

"Fuck you," he said. Screw them. So what if he was driving about twenty miles an hour? New shocks, man. He wanted them to last, right?

He reached behind him to close and lock the sliding glass again, but Jeff wasn't done yet. "And why the fuck we all the way out here near that bunch of crazy old Machens?"

"Cause you said you wasn't scared to come out here at night. Remember?"

The road narrowed ahead. He could see the bushes lean in, ready to scratch his cherry red baby. He slowed to a crawl as he gauged how close he could run to the left to miss the palmettos on the right.

Jeff pushed the window open more and leaned closer, whispering loudly in his ear. "Well, I ain't scared, but Petey is pissin' his pants back here. He's actin' like a fuckin' little baby, man. Looks like he's gonna cry any second."

From the bed of the truck he heard a defensive slur, "Fuck you! I ain't scared. I'm just cold, that's all. I just think we can drink at my house, where it's warm. My folks are out for the night. Nobody home to fuck with us. We could get shit faced, man."

Spud knew better. The tremble of fear running through his friend's protests was loud and clear. Pissin' in his pants was exactly what Petey was doing right now. He'd been listening to those old fucks that hung around J.J.'s General Store for too long. Probably believed all those crazy stories about the Black Beast.

Spud almost yelled over his shoulder to remind Petey what a pussy he was, but then he remembered Daddy telling him a tale or two about what the Machens did out here in the woods. Truthfully, Spud had been a little nervous about coming out to Algernon Wood, but he knew that if he admitted it now, he'd never hear the end of it from Jeff. No way could he turn around and go back to town under any other pretense than Jeff saying he was scared first. And, by God, they'd stay out here all night, if that's what it took. Spud had to prove, especially Jeff, that he was no chicken shit.

Tonight's festivities had all started as a stupid dare. Sitting around Petey's den, Jeff, already well into a twelve pack of Icehouse that he'd snatched from his old man's stash, dared Spud, in front of Petey, Danny, and that moron Richard, that he wouldn't drive all the way up Machen Road to the front gate and ring the buzzer on the security post. Ringing the security buzzer at the Machens' was Ellison's one true test of bravery which more than one teenage lad had used to pronounce his bravado, the game's innate challenge usually growing with every can of beer consumed.

Spud had laughed, tried to think of something to distract and reroute the conversation, but Jeff had seen it in his eye. The fear. And like a bulldog he had sunk his crooked teeth into the challenge, not allowing Spud any leeway. Even his claim that he didn't want to get mud all over his new baby didn't float him past the Jeff-shark hanging on his ass. Then that prick Richard had joined in, chanting 'faggot, faggot, faggot' over and over again, and Spud knew he was backed into a corner. There had been no choice at that point, so he piled his drunk-ass friends into his baby, drove down Main Street, while they had whooped and hollered like mad demons. Although, not so loud past the Sheriff's Office, of course. That fat fuck, Sheriff Lincoln, was always watching them; they'd all had run-ins with Lard-Ass Lincoln, every teenaged boy in Ellison did.

And, now, here they were, all the way through the goddamned mud, all the fuck way out here in the middle of Algernon Wood.

At first, Spud had been scared, like Petey, but now he just wanted to finish this stupid dare and get these goofy bastards out of his baby. Then he was going to go home (even though his Mama was home and she would grill him about where he was and what he had been up to) and he was going to get some sleep. But tomorrow, come hell or high water, he was going to go down to that Clarke chick's house and get himself a real date for once.

Petey was yelling for him to stop the truck, his voice strident with panic.

Spud slammed on the brakes, knocking his passengers down like bowling pins. His heart hammered in his chest, the warm beer bottle half off the seat between his legs. "What the fuck," he yelled, yanking open the divider window. "You scared the hell out of me!"

"Richard!" Jeff shouted, his voice just as panicked as Petey's. "He fell out of the truck, man!"

Spud felt a cold lump in his stomach, rising along his gorge like a chill, too-large stone.

Oh, man, that's all he needed was for one of these dumb asses to get himself killed while they were all drunk.

Petey leaped up and down, pointing off into the red tinged darkness behind them. "He didn't fall out of the truck, damn it. It was like he was pulled out!"

Jeff shook his head, his eyes wide and terrified. "No, man! He just fell out! That's all, man! Nothing pulled him out!" He made a clumsy punch at Petey, his legs shaking. "Stop saying that shit!"

"I don't know, man," Danny agreed, looking ready to piss his pants, too, more white than iris sprouting from the white oval of his face. "It was weird."

Spud felt it all going out of control, too fast for him to stop, as he twisted violently just in time to see Jeff jump out of the bed of the truck. "I'll show you," Jeff was yelling hysterically. "He's just back here. He just fell out. That's all, man." Spud thought he sounded past scared, more like fucking insane with fear.

Petey made a half-hearted grab for Jeff's sleeve, but the stumbling boy was already out and splashing back down the muddy road into the dark, yelling for Richard.

"Wait, man," Danny shouted at Jeff's dissolving crimson form. "Let's just drive back together. Wait!"

Jeff ignored him, continued to run down the throat of darkness stretching into the distance behind them. "Don't worry, Richard. I'm coming to get you."

Spud was trying to get the truck in gear, reverse it to keep up Jeff. His friend disappeared from the scant red radius of light.

Jeff's shouting abruptly stopped.

Spud heard only his own strangled breathing and the quiet rumble of the truck.

Petey was sitting now, his face as pale as Danny's, muttering between chattering teeth. "I don't know, man. I don't think he fell out. He just kind of jumped up and he was gone."

"Shut that shit up!" Spud screamed. His hands twisted the steering wheel like he was tearing off a limb, as he clumsily wheeled the big truck around to face the road where Richard and Jeff had gone. "I don't fucking need to hear that right now. Let's just find out what happened to Richard."

Four headlights peeled away the dark, making the trees and bushes jump in panic. Spud squeezed the steering wheel. He eased his foot on the gas, moving the truck back the way they had come. But there was no one in the road. No Jeff. No Richard. Just an impossibly empty road eating up the light.

Maybe Jeff had out run the truck. But Spud knew better. Jeff had been too drunk to do any fast running. And where was Richard?

They'd only gone a few yards before stopping, so if he'd fallen out they should be able to see him right now. Should be able to see the both of them. So where the hell were they?

Behind him, Petey started blubbering and he wanted to slap the shit out of the little cry-baby. He definitely didn't need that shit right now. Especially since he felt like blubbering himself. Actually, he felt like vomiting all over his new seat; his own sweat stank of fear and chased the new car smell out like a mugger in an alley.

But before he could say anything to Petey, Danny took things into his own hands. "Shut up, damn it!" Danny clutched Petey's collar and jerked him hard, once. Petey made some kind of sick sound and leaned over the side of the truck bed.

That was it for Spud.

He floored the gas, sending the truck sliding across the wet dirt road. He didn't even care when the truck sideswiped a stand of thin palmettos and his baby's cherry red paint job screamed in scarred agony. He just kept the truck sliding until he had it pointed more or less in a straight direction.

When he saw that Spud intended on leaving, Danny began banging on the divider window. "Stop! No, man! What are you doing?"

Spud didn't like to think about the pleading tone in his voice. The sound of it made him feel even sicker to his stomach.

"You can't leave them!"

The hell I can't, he thought, sweat rolling like clammy spit down his neck and face. He gritted his teeth so hard that his jaw ached, and muscles jumped in his neck. If Danny wanted to go back and look for them that was his lookout. Spud wished him all the luck, but he was going nowhere but back to town.

He pushed the truck to sixty-five down the road, uncaring of the shocks and paint job. Trees and bushes scraped and whizzed by; sweat and tears mixed, ran in his eyes, but he didn't dare remove his hand from the steering wheel. There were too many trees looming out at him. Too much darkness that the high beams never touched.

Spud saw something large move out of the road, just out of the range of his lights, and he blinked the sting from his eyes in an effort to see it better. But as suddenly as the thing was there it was gone again. And he wasn't about to stop the truck to find out what it had been. If it was his imagination, fine. If not...he didn't want to even think about that. Better to get home and forget all about this night.

The truck roared away, disappeared in the night, leaving the darkness as ruler once more. In that return of darkness, something large moved through the trees, humping away from the road. Behind it, the thing dragged two limp and torn bodies- lumps of meat that, in a few hours, would hardly resemble the boys they once had been.

CHAPTER -11-

Sully woke the next morning with a nose that felt like a piece of ice and toes that begged for warmth. The rest of him was fine, having been under the heavy blankets all night, but the room was cold as a crypt. He had set his travel alarm for 6:00 am, so that he could get Garlen ready for his morning. When the alarm went off, he pushed the covers away with a shiver and a sigh, forced himself into the damp chill of the morning. One would think, with all their money, the Machens could at least heat the damned mansion- even if it was huge.

When they traveled, Sully took over various other duties that would have normally been reserved for a nurse: bathing, shaving, and grooming Garlen. Sully didn't mind. In fact, it made him feel like he was doing something worthwhile for a change. Making his living as a gun-toting thug wasn't what he thought he'd be doing at thirty-five. No matter how much money Garlen paid to keep him around, it didn't change the fact that he was basically a hired thug.

Sully made his way to the other man's room and gave Garlen a gentle shake. The older man came awake groan. "Son of a bitch," he muttered. "It's colder than a house pecker in December."

Sully laughed. "What? No 'good morning, Sully'? How did you sleep, Sully?"

"How about 'piss off, Sully'?" Garlen replied. He began a coughing fit that lasted for a minute or so, and then motioned for Sully to settle him in his chair.

The coughing left him red-faced and weak. Being around Garlen was like watching a slow motion car crash. It was depressing, but there wasn't a damn thing he could do except make life easier for him. All the old man's money couldn't rebuild all his broken parts, and the complications because of them.

"Didn't sleep, too well?" he asked, as he lifted his frail body into the stoic cradle of his arms. He was as light as a bag of bones. Sully caught the faint glimmer of a bristling display of gray hair on his chin; he could remember a time not too long ago that there had been more brown than gray in that chin bristle.

"I can't sleep in this god damned place," Garlen said. "All the sounds and shit."

"What sounds?" asked Sully. He hadn't heard anything last night. In fact, he'd slept like a baby; the glass of sherry had been enough to put him out.

Garlen shook his head. "I thought someone—"

But Sully put his finger to his lips and leaned in close to whisper, "We'll talk about it outside."

Garlen's gray brows furrowed in aggravation, but he knew Sully well enough to keep his mouth shut until they got outside. For whatever reason, he did not want the sounds discussed inside Machen Mansion. He gave a silent nod of assent. Sully pushed him to the bathroom. "Now let's get you dressed for your nine a.m. appointment with Stewart."

"The last contract talk, before the lawyers get a hold of it," Garlen said. "The blood sucking bastards will be sure to dissect the hell out of anything I do here, anyway." He snickered humorlessly. "I swear to God, it gets harder to do anything without one of those bastards looking over your shoulder. Pretty soon I'll have to have one while I use the goddamned bathroom just to make sure I wipe my ass right."

By finished with Garlen's toiletries, and dressed in a white linen suit, powder blue silk shirt, and a matching pair of light tan loafers, sunlight was edging through the closed window, its muted warmth suffusing the chilly room. Sully wheeled Garlen out of the room, down the claustrophobic corridors, relying on his memory for guidance, until he found a doorway out of the house.

Shading his eyes, he got them into the warm, clean sunlight. After last night's rain, it was cold enough to make him shiver, but it still felt warmer outside, away from the mildew dampness of the mansion. White clouds moved like pale ships in the crystalline blue sky. The oak trees near the porch dripped glistening tears of dew onto the grass. In the gardens to their right, birds sang to the new day. The air smelled clean and fresh, despite slight swamp stench that wafted in from the woods.

Sully knew there was a swamp beyond the property. The Machens owned that as well. It was the same swamp Stewart had spoken about the night before. In the damp morning air, he could see a roiling bank of yellowish mist rising up through the skeletal trees beyond the security fence. Beyond the fog, he knew there was only wilderness, a no man's land of alligators and panthers and quick sand, oh my. He never understood, with all of their riches, the Machens chose to live next to this god-forsaken backwoods wilderness.

He wheeled Garlen out to the guardian oak trees and stopped.

"Let's make this fast, Sully," Garlen said. He tugged his blanket over is waist, stuck his thin hands beneath it for warmth. "I'll freeze my balls off out here. So what's going on? Why did you shut up back there?"

Sully's gazed towards the house. He watched the windows, but the early morning sun reflected only blue sky and grass. "Just a precaution. I get the feeling that nothing goes unwatched inside that house."

"Are you suggesting we're being watched?" Garlen asked incredulously.

Sully shrugged. "I don't know, Garlen. Maybe it's just my imagination. What about those sounds you mentioned?"

Garlen frowned, shook his head. "I could be wrong, but I think someone might have been in my room last night. And I know it wasn't you."

"Why do you say that?"

"Because this person was spindly-like. And kept whispering words I couldn't make out."

"What happened?"

"I was so exhausted that I closed my eyes, thinking it was only a dream. When I opened them again the person was gone."

"Maybe it was a servant who didn't know you had the room."

"Maybe," said Garlen. "But the whispering kept going after they left. I swear it sounded like..."

"Like what?"

"Who, Sully." Garlen's face was pale now, his

eyes watery and frightened. "The voice sounded like Susan."

Sully half smiled, then realized Garlen was serious. "Garlen, it had to be a dream."

The old man wiped at his eyes with the corner of the blanket. His voice turned to iron. "Jesus fucking Christ, Sully. Susan's dead. You think I don't know that? Of course it was a goddamned dream."

Sully didn't know what to say. Obviously, the man still suffered because of their deaths. A nightmare or two was common enough. But there was something about it having happened here in Machen Mansion that left him feeling dread.

Sully moved around the chair, crouched before Garlen, so that he could watch the property behind them. There was no one moving along the grounds this early in the morning. Crows exploded from a stand of pine beyond the security fence, like screaming demons, and then disappeared in the distance. He looked the old man in the eyes. "I don't like this place, Garlen. And I don't trust the Machens. I don't know what deal you've got going with the old man, but I think the sooner we finish up here, the better."

Giving Garlen a moment, he said, "You know, I don't like this. I felt uncomfortable as hell the last time we were here, but I didn't think I had the right to say anything."

Garlen smirked. "What makes you think you can now?"

"Because I think you know me well enough by now to know I'm trying to protect you. And that I have a pretty good instinct when it comes to assholes. And

I've go to tell you, I do not like Stewart Machen, Garlen."

"Neither do I," Garlen replied.

"So why the hell are you doing business with him? You've got enough money you don't have to do business with assholes you don't like, right?"

"True," he said. "But he has something that I need very badly, Sully."

"Like what?"

"You know Susan loved that little ranch we all stayed at a few year ago, right? Do you remember how she went on about how much she wanted to own it, make it into an animal reserve for endangered species? Well, I couldn't buy it for her then because one of Machen's rival companies owned the rights to it. Machen bought it. I found out a couple of weeks ago. That's why I came all this way to talk business with the son of a bitch. I want to buy that property. Turn it into the best goddamn animal reserve my useless money can buy. Susan deserves at least that as a legacy."

The silence hung between them. Sully watched the house again. When his eye strayed to the looming wood beyond, his lips tightened. "Well, we'll be gone in a couple of days, right?" he said. "I'll just keep my eyes and ears open. If someone is watching us…" He paused, unsure what he could do. "We'll just take it from there, eh?"

"Just remember," Garlen said. "I don't need any complications. I need this deal to come off, Sully."

"Look, I'm not worried about anything he'd to us, but…you know…" He was unable to finish, ashamed at how easily he'd appointed himself their unknown protector.

"You mean the widow Machen and her son?"

"Well, don't you think it's a little strange?"

"Sully, these folks are Southern," said Garlen. "I don't think you know what that really means. They do things a little different from the rest of the world. We're in Tennessee Williams territory here, my friend. This is none of our business what's going on here. I'd appreciate it if you kept out of it and let me finish this deal for the land."

Sully didn't much care for Garlen's lack of concern for Mary and Timmy, but he was right. It wasn't his business. Whatever was going on, the woman had obviously come here of her own free will. "I'll let it go for now," he told Garlen, "but I'm going to keep my eyes on them. You didn't see the way he was looking at her last night. It was pretty disgusting."

"Good to see that chivalry isn't dead," Garlen said, rubbing his hands together. "Now get me back inside the house." He gave Sully a dead-pan stare. "I'm so cold, I can't feel my legs."

Sully shook his head in mock disgust. "Very funny." The old man chuckled at his own joke as Sully wheeled him back through the chill morning and inside the waiting mansion.

CHAPTER -12-

It was barely six thirty in the morning and Sheriff Renny Lincoln was already losing his meager sense of humor. Lincoln liked his town to stay sleepy and peaceful. He spit on the cold, sodden ground in disgust. But there always had to be some smart ass that couldn't stay out of these woods at night and got hisself disappeared.

And, of course, now he had to deal with it.

He stood in the middle of the muddy road, peering down the tree-shrouded path.

Where the hell was that god damned Tucker kid?

He was supposed to have been here fifteen minutes ago, driving that brand new truck of his.

Damned asshole kid had come knocking on his office door at three am in the morning, him and two other peckerwoods, which he'd given stern warnings to more than once about drinking, hot-rodding down the back roads, even some small time vandalism, like painting underpasses and road signs. The three of them, blubbering like a bunch of scared little kids, claimed two of their friends had gone missing out here on Machen property. It had taken him an hour to get them calmed down enough to talk so that he could understand them. He didn't know what the hell was going on with his missing friends, but if this was the little peckerwoods idea of a joke...

Most likely they were sleeping off a nasty hangover somewhere around here. But having lived here his whole life, he knew there were certain things even the dumbest of shit heels like Spud and his bunch did not joke about. Algernon Wood and the Machens counted among them. Drunk or not, something sure got those three peckerwoods spooked, but good.

Lincoln burped and sighed in aggravation. Damn steak fries he'd had this morning at Mamey's were sticking at the back of his throat, sitting like rocks in his stomach. He ambled over to the patrol car, kicked angrily at rotted branches pulled from the high treetops night before by the storm. He was sure this was where the Tucker kid had said they had been earlier. He could clearly make out multiple big tire track marks, ripped all along the muddy dirt road. And he'd seen several empty beer cans on his way here, tossed by the side of the road. Drinking under age was a foregone conclusion, and he'd deal with that soon enough. But what had happened here last night?

He was going to have a long talk with those peckerwoods about their drinking. Spud Tucker could deny it all he wanted, but Lincoln knew beer when he smelled it. Tucker's buddies had smelled like open beer taps when they had been standing there shivering in their boots. The only sober one had been Tucker. Scared shitless, but definitely sober. He'd been Sheriff long enough to know drunk when he saw it.

As much as he wanted to scoff at the absurdity of the Black Beast having taken their friends, Lincoln had grown up in Ellison, and he had heard all the same stories as everyone else about the mysterious creature.

Ridiculous. There weren't no such thing.

He was forty-six years old; too damned old to believe in bogeymen. Something had scared them, but it could have been a panther or a bear.

Still, all the times by the fire when he was a little boy, his old Uncle Paul muttering about the people who had disappeared over the years, about the Indians who'd shunned the place long ago.

Lincoln snorted at the thought.

It was all nonsense, by God.

So why the hell did he suddenly feel a chill running up his spine?

He heard the sound of an engine. Coming down the road, he spied a red truck. That would be Tucker.

Spud Tucker pulled the truck up behind the patrol car and shut it down. Lincoln could see it was the worse for wear, scratched and dented along the fenders and left side panel. The boy had been in a hurry to get the hell out of the woods, just like he'd said.

When Tucker got out, Lincoln could see the kid was pale and still shaky. He didn't look much less deranged as he had a few hours before. The fat kid edged away from the truck with caution.

Lincoln eyed him impatiently and snapped, "Well, hurry the hell up, boy. I'm about to freeze my ass off out here waitin' for you. It ain't nice holdin' up the law. Some might even call it an obstruction of justice, if some had a mind to."

Spud was unfazed by the threat. He kept turning to look into the mist-shrouded forest. "Did you find anything yet, Sheriff?" he asked.

Lincoln looked at the empty truck. "Now where are those two little peckerwoods you came in with last night? Didn't I tell all three of you to come out here?"

Spud gave a sullen shrug. "It ain't my fault. I told 'em. They wouldn't come back out here."

"You little numbnuts get to drinkin' and you do stupid shit like this. And then you can't even be bothered to show up?" Lincoln's wide face was red with rage. " Now I got me two missing idiots out here in the middle of Algernon- by God- fucking Woods." Lincoln stamped his feet in aggravation against the loamy cold, wet ground, pointed a stubby finger at the boy. "And when I said all three of you, I meant all god damned three of you, Tucker."

"Yes, sir," he mumbled.

Lincoln wiped his hair away from his forehead and spit once more. He gave a deep rumbling burp and looked off into the misty woods. "Alright, boy," he said more calmly. "Now show me where your friends disappeared at."

Spud kept his watering eyes on the ground. Starting off at a stiff walk, Lincoln behind him, burping and wheezing, Spud followed the tire digs in the road, until he found the spot where Jeff's footsteps disappeared. The Sheriff pulled at the tight legs of his uniform britches and crouched down, pants near splitting at their massive seams, knees cracking like small gunshots. He fingered the edge of the footprints. It had rained quite a bit the night before, and they were sure to get some more tonight by the looks of the weather report this morning, but the boy had said they were out here after the rain. The print was solid enough he could tell it was less than twelve hours old.

"Where'd the other boy fall off the back of truck?"

Spud sniffled and rubbed his nose. "I didn't see that, Sheriff," he said. "All I know is that the other guys in the back of the truck started yelling for me to stop."

"Your friend, Peter, said it looked like something pulled him out," Lincoln added, raising his eyebrow, waiting for the boy to go on. But Tucker only shrugged again. Lincoln felt like smacking him. Instead, he gave the boy a hard gaze, didn't say anything for a few moments, until he couldn't stand the sight of the trembling tub of shit. He looked back down at the footprints again, sighed and burped. No other prints to explain how the kid's prints could just disappear like that. Nothing around but some tear marks, but those could have been from the tires or low hanging branches from the side of the road.

Pushing himself up from his crouch with a groan and silent curse, Lincoln walked the area for a few yards in every direction, carefully looking for anything that even resembled a foot print- even animal pug tracks. He scanned the roadside bushes, peered up into the trees that lapped over the road high above, but he found nothing to tell him how the kid had disappeared. And as for that numbnut Richard there were no tracks at all, anywhere.

Behind him, Tucker stayed in the road looking scared and angry all at once, like some spoiled rotten little punk who'd found himself in way over his head.

Hope he's freezing his ass off, Lincoln thought moodily. Serve him right, if I just pistol whipped the little peckerwood.

By God, everybody knew you didn't come out to Algernon Wood at night. Tucker's old man, as goddamn stupid as he had been to get caught with his pants down in the worst kind of way, would never have let this kind of shit happen if he was still alive. He'd had the boy working with him, learning to sell groceries, not out here drinking under age and getting his ass in a fryer. Still, he knew the boy's Mama and she was about as looney as a Warner Brothers feature. Hell, he might even have done some heavy drinking, too, if he had to be around that crazy bitch all the time.

Congratulating himself that he had decided not to pistol whip the kid, and even finding it in his heart to feel a little sorry for the goddamn worthless peckerwood, he walked back to the boy. "You have your ass back in my office by 6 pm tonight, Tucker." He snagged the kid's lumpy shoulder, and added, "And you make damn sure that your numbnut buddies are there, too. Or I might just throw all your juvenile delinquent asses in jail for obstruction of justice. You got me?"

Spud swallowed hard, eyes full of fear.

Lincoln had found something the boy was more scared of than the woods.

Good.

He waved him away without waiting for an answer and went back to searching the area, wheezing and feeling a bad case of heartburn coming on.

The truck started up and Tucker took off down the road like the demons of hell were on his ass. But not too fast- no, sir, not too fast at all. Numbnut like that needed to be scared of the law.

Lincoln gave it another half-hour before giving it up. He knew where his next stop was going to be and he sure didn't relish the idea of being around the Machens. But he had to at least ask them if they had seen or heard anything of the two boys on their property.

First, though, as much as he didn't want to, he should go ahead and call in the State boys for this one. No way did he have the equipment or manpower to take care of this by himself. Hell, he wasn't even sure he could talk any of the local boys into coming out here to search. The State boys would probably want to get some dogs out here and go over the place. All thirty something, by God, square miles of it.

Suddenly he felt exhausted. This was going to be eating into his sleeping time for the next few weeks to come. Even with the hours and hours of searching ahead of him, he knew it was hopeless. He knew all they'd find- if they were lucky- would be bodies, mutilated remains. As his Uncle Paul surely would have told him, them boys was as good as dead, son.

Lincoln gave one more disgusted look at the footprints and spit off to the side. With a tired sigh, and another steamy steak fry burp, he went back to his patrol car to make the dreaded call to the State boys.

CHAPTER -13-

Mary woke the next morning with the mildew stink of the room sitting at the back of her throat like a nasty hangover. Her head swam with the damp stench of the place. Blinking against the light of morning through the curtains, her hands sought for the familiar shape of Timmy next to her. But she found only emptiness.

The sudden thump of adrenaline hit her system, like being doused in ice-cold water. She threw back the covers in a violent rush, started from the bed, panic stealing her breath.

Then she saw Timmy standing by the window opposite the bed, already dressed.

Mary slumped with relief, the sweat already drying to a pasty sheen on her neck. Of course, he had noticed none of her reaction, because he had his back to her, looking at something outside. Once her heart stopped hammering, she could see that, thankfully, today there was sunlight streaming into the room, a welcome illumination that brightened the dull furniture and dusty knick-knacks, colored the ancient throw rug at the foot of the bed. She smiled at her overreaction and staggered to stand beside him. She kissed the top of his head, murmured a good morning, and then went to the bathroom. As far as she was concerned, she wasn't going to try and go to any bathroom but this one. She wasn't about to brave the halls of Machen Mansion again- with or without Sully's help.

In the bathroom, Mary found herself smiling at the remembrance of the big man's eyes, and his fragile transforming smile, the way he moved so gracefully for someone of such girth. His presence was as large as his body and he exuded a sense of strength; not just physical, but emotional, a solidity she lacked right now. Maybe that was why she found him so appealing. She wished there was some way to find more time to get to know him. She thought he was probably worth it. But she had decided last night, inheritance or no, she and Timmy were getting the hell out of here. Tomorrow morning they were going home. She hadn't liked the way Stewart had come on to her so aggressively the night before, nor did she think his obvious effect on her son was something to be nurtured right now. It was too confusing for Timmy to fill the void with someone like Stewart, a man who so obviously used others' emotions to his own ends.

Mary took a few moments to scrub her face, looked at herself in the mirror. Despite the face washing, she still felt grungy. And her hair was a mess, too. She looked tired; her eyes had bags under them.

Oh, yeah, that's real attractive.

She pulled in disgust at the tangles of her morning hair with a brush, but the attempt seemed only to make it worse.

God, Sully must think she was ten years older at least.

No, she needed a shower.

Mary stuck her head outside the door and told Timmy not to leave the room for any reason; she made him promise before she was satisfied. Not bothering to turn, he just murmured his ascent and continued to stare glumly out the window.

Poor little guy. Some vacation for him, being stuck in a house most the time. Well, she'd have to find some way to get him smiling again. After breakfast, if the weather held out, they would take a long walk around the place today. That was if she could pry him away from his grand father.

The shower was perfectly hot and perfectly steamy. The water smashed delicately against her skin and made her relax more than she had since she had set foot in the place. Mary gratefully moved back and forth beneath the cascade of hot water, letting the massaging liquid hit every muscle in her shoulders and back, releasing her tension in an almost erotic wash of sensations.

She washed her hair with an apple scented shampoo and then stood under the water again for a few more minutes, until she reminded herself that Timmy was waiting. She toweled off with a thick, soft blue towel, running the warm fabric along her hot, pink skin in slow progressive revolutions across her body. Her nipples grew taut and hungry under the pressure of her own hands and she felt herself pushing against the towel as if it were someone's caressing hand. Mary closed her eyes, enjoying the sensation, wondering how Sully's hands would feel running slowly across her flesh. Would he like the shape of her breasts? Would he be an attentive lover?

Someone giggled like a child.

Mary's eyes sprang open; her hands, like startled birds, flew away from her excited caressing.

The sound had come from inside the room with her. She was sure of it.

Mary pulled the towel around her body, feeling unseen eyes watching her.

She searched the bathroom, behind the curtain (ridiculous, since she had just gotten out of the shower stall, but she was taking no chances0, she even searched the cabinet under the sink. No one.

She decided it had to be some weird acoustical phenomenon. There was no other logical explanation. She was the only person in the bathroom.

The memory of the childlike laughter caused her naked skin to break out in goose flesh. She dressed quickly and left the room.

Outside the steaming room Timmy still stood by the window. She stood next to him and ruffled his dark tangle of hair, kissed the top of his head. Her eyes shifted down to the sunny, green grounds outside. Inevitably, her gaze found the woods beyond. The sunlight seemed to fall into those shadowed depths and disappear, as if the place were some great arboreal black hole.

"Mama," Timmy suddenly interrupted her thoughts. "Where's our car?"

Mary smiled down at him in confusion. She scanned the driveway. Their car was gone. She had parked it in the middle of the circular driveway the night they arrived, and that's where she had seen last night before turning out the lights.

Her stomach lurched with panic. That car was their only way out of here.

She took a deep breath, forced herself to think about it logically. Obviously, the car was not gone. It had just been moved from where she had left it. Someone had moved it. That was all. Charlotte, perhaps? Stewart? After all, it *was* an eyesore. But if someone had moved it, they should've at least had the common decency to let her know. It was her car, after all. As ugly as the broken down piece of crap was, it was the only thing she could say that she and Conley had bought together.

Mary was seething, clenching her jaw, knowing she had no right to be angry. But, damn it, she was!

She grabbed Timmy's hand, careful not to let the anger show in her voice when she spoke. "Come on," she said. "Let's go downstairs and have breakfast. Then see what your granddaddy has planned for you today."

They left the room together, with Timmy keeping close to her hip as they waded through the murky hallways. She chose to ignore the voices she could hear in the passages behind her. Servants, she told herself. No way was she chasing sounds through the halls this morning.

When she found the staircase, she smiled, and considered it a small triumph. She might just be getting this house under her thumb after all. Strangely enough, Timmy seemed to have a better sense of direction in the depths of Machen Mansion than she. Twice he'd corrected her when she was about to take a wrong, or dead end, passage.

Downstairs, they found Charlotte waiting in the dining room again. The table was set as sumptuously as it had been the morning before; silver trays upon the serving cart, the smells inviting. Two more places had been set, presumably for Garlen and Sully. In a short time, the two men joined them, Sully wheeling Garlen into place near she and Timmy. Sully sat to her right. She tried not to stare at him, but gave him only a small smile.

"Good morning, pretty ladies," Garlen exclaimed.

As she looked down the table at Charlotte, Sully's eyes met hers, and she blushed at the thought she had been fantasizing about him only fifteen minutes ago. Flustered by her reaction, she made an effort to pay attention to Timmy as he talked. She was no longer sure how to carry herself around someone she found attractive. It had been a long time since she'd had to worry about such things. And riding a bicycle, this wasn't. As you got older, all sensibilities about such matters were shed like an unwelcome and unneeded second skin. Some things would have to be relearned if she hoped to survive this period in her life with any amount of emotional sanity.

"Good morning, Mr. Winter," she said.

"Garlen, Mama," Timmy corrected her.

She smirked at her son's earnest admonishment. "Yes, I forgot. Garlen."

Garlen settled himself into place next to her. "Did everyone sleep well?"

Giving Garlen a testy stare, Charlotte said, "I was just about to ask the same thing." She raised her eyebrows at Mary and Timmy, awaiting their answer so she could continue the conversation her way.

But Mary could see Garlen was no fool; he knew the old woman's game. He broke in before Mary could say anything, again stealing the old woman's thunder. "Colder than hell in those rooms, Charlotte. I about froze my—" he looked sidelong at Timmy and grinned sheepishly "My ears. I about froze my ears off."

Charlotte didn't crack a smile. "Yes, I've told Stewart we really should see about getting something done about the insulation in the old place. But with so few visitors, he doesn't see any point in it."

"Spoken like someone who's never frozen his—" he glanced at Timmy again; Mary smiled at his discretion "—his ears off." Then he brayed a throaty laughter, shoving the lines of his face into deep trenches of humor. Mary couldn't help but laugh with him; he seemed so in need of it.

"Perhaps you'd like to speak with Stewart about it," Charlotte offered through tight lips. "Or maybe we could find you another room. I really don't bother much about such things, you know. It's usually Stewart whom invites people to stay."

Mary cleared her throat and watched the two elderly people sparring in some tacit way she couldn't understand. It was obvious, even to her, that Garlen was pushing her because he knew she didn't like him.

Garlen pursed his lips and looked up at the ceiling painting as if he were pondering her suggestion. "No. I believe we'll just rough it, old darling." He batted his eyelashes at her benignly and gave her a genial smile. Then he returned his attention to Mary and Timmy, dismissing the old woman's stern glare as if Charlotte's opinion was beneath him.

Mary felt the tension in the air. She glanced at Sully, but he seemed to be taken with his spoon, and wouldn't meet her gaze. The old woman was pissed; she could see her teeth clenching as she chewed in silence at her rage. She leaned toward Garlen to put her face between he and Charlotte. "So how long will you be here," she asked, hoping the question would be diversion enough.

"Only a couple of days," Garlen replied. "We'll be leaving Monday morning. And you?"

This wasn't something she wanted to discuss yet, not without having told Timmy first. And there was Charlotte, too. "We're not sure yet," she said, which earned her a pleasant smile from the old woman.

Her pronouncement seemed to lighten and they removed the serving tray lids. Sparse conversation went around the table, most of it centered on the weather and Timmy's favorite superheroes in comics. Sully agreed Wolverine was the coolest, but they agreed the Hulk ran a close second.

Stewart Machen, much to Timmy's disappointment, did not show for breakfast. Mary thought it very rude of him to leave the boy waiting for his companionship like an eager puppy. Especially after all the trouble they'd taken to get here so he could spend time with him. When she finally asked Charlotte where he was, she gave a wistful smile and said that he had been up later than usual, that his work was so demanding she didn't have the heart to wake him when he could sleep for extended periods.

More like he's sleeping off a hangover from last night, she thought

Despite his happy chatter with Sully and Garlen Mary could tell granddaddy's no-show had upset her son. The incident only reaffirmed her decision to leave the next morning. Money or not, they weren't toys to be placed on a shelf when the rich folks got tired of playing grandparents.

Of course, first she had to find her car.

Breakfast came to an end, and Garlen asked Sully to wheel him outside for some fresh air. Over his shoulder, he asked Charlotte to send someone out to let him know when Stewart was ready to talk business. His tone said how he felt about having to wait. "Would you mind taking Timmy with you?" she asked the two men. "I need to speak with Charlotte alone for a few moments."

Timmy hesitated to leave her side with people who were still essentially strangers to him, but she gave him the look that meant there was to be no arguments. As consolation, Sully offered to teach him how to do one-armed push-ups. Timmy jumped from his chair and rushed to meet them at the end of the table.

"When have you ever done a one armed push up?" Garlen asked.

"Lots of times," Sully said. "When you're sleeping."

"Ha!"

Mary could hear their chatter fade away as they left by the side door.

She turned to Charlotte, cleared her throat nervously. "I don't want to sound rude or anything, Charlotte- to either you or Stewart- but where is my car?" She smiled, but it was to hide the fact she was gritting her teeth.

"Oh, dear." Charlotte put a blue veined, wrinkled hand to her mouth in, what seemed to Mary, mock surprise. "I thought Stewart told you."

"Told me what?"

She began to shift her utensils with great interest. "Well, we thought it would be a wonderful gesture of our appreciation for all the trouble you and the boy have gone through to get here if we had a few repairs made to the poor thing. We know how hard it is to worry about those kinds of things on a budget."

Mary shook her head in confusion, thinking how unlikely it was that this woman had ever been on a budget in her life, let alone to know the precarious nature of living within your means from month to month, when the world demanded more. "Well, that's nice of you both, but I really wish you had asked me first."

Charlotte gave her an uncertain lift of her lips- a chastened child seeking forgiveness. Mary's suspicions rankled at the upturned watery eyes. "Yes, yes, that's what I told Stewart, but he said he was going to tell you last night. I guess it slipped his mind."

Small wonder. It must be hard to remember much when you're drunk and busy leering at your dead son's widow.

"So where's my car," she asked again.

"We had it towed down to the local garage," said Charlotte. "A man Stewart trusts is looking it over."

"I see."

The room grew quiet with tension. A clock ticked somewhere nearby- a counterpoint to the angry pulse of the vein in Mary's neck. She held the old woman with a steady, hard gaze, unsure why she was so angry, beyond the fact that her new in-laws seemed to be usurping her authority. Charlotte's face crumpled and her sloughed shoulders began to shake. She brought her linen napkin to press against her tears, snuffling loudly, her eyes red and watery.

Mary sighed, releasing her anger. After all, they had only been trying to help.

She leaned forward and placed a hand over Charlotte's trembling, wrinkled fist clutching the crushed wet cloth. "Hey, it's okay," she said. "It's no big deal. Really."

The older woman shook her head. "No, it was wrong, my dear. We should have asked you first. No matter how noble our intentions. I'm so sorry, dear. We were just worried about you two."

Now Mary really felt horrible about the standoffish attitude she'd taken with the old woman (and her barely concealed suspicions as to the motives for the act of kindness). But, damn it, they didn't understand, didn't see this for what it was. Charity. She knew she should be grateful, not angry.

"Charlotte," she said. "I'm sorry. It's just that I was always poor growing up and I'm always afraid that people are feeling sorry for me. It's a vicious and prideful thing, and I should be very grateful to you both for thinking of us. For this visit, too. Timmy hasn't been this happy and laughed so much since…well, not since before Conley died."

Charlotte's face dabbed at the remaining tears. "No, you were right to be angry. But I know Stewart really meant to tell you last night. I suppose his business with Garlen has cluttered his thoughts." She reached forward and hugged Mary, tittering in that breathless old woman voice of hers. "My biggest regret about all this business so far has been all the wasted years, because of the silly feud between Stewart and Conley. But we're going to make up for all of that lost time, aren't we? Please, promise me that we will, Mary. Stewart isn't a young man, and he needs this time with the boy more than you could ever imagine."

Mary wanted to tell her that, despite Stewart's need, they would be leaving as soon as the car was back. But she kept her mouth shut. There would be time enough to discuss her plans later.

Charlotte's next statement threw her off her balance again. "Now, I think we should talk about the inheritance." She settled back in her chair once more, in control of her emotions. No more tears.

Mary felt lightheaded at the thought of all that money. It was like a dream, even thinking about it. She didn't believe Timmy even understood what the inheritance meant, or the concept of any number past his own age.

"I would much rather Stewart explain these things," Charlotte continued, "but it looks like he might be tied up with Garlen later, talking over contracts and such. So it looks like it falls to me to do so."

She got up and moved to the serving cart, poured herself a half a cup of coffee in a delicate blue china cup. Taking her seat again, she leaned forward, and whispered conspiratorially. "Stewart would raise the roof if he saw me drinking this." She winked and motioned to the cup. "The doctors have forbidden me pretty much everything but water and herbal teas. But how I do love a good strong cup of coffee."

Mary found that she could only give the other woman an uneasy smile, unsure how to engage in a conversation that involved her son and the millions he would eventually inherit. It was a subject she would have happily ignored until Stewart's eventual death; then the details would have been handled by lawyers. Talking about it now made her feel like a vulture awaiting his death. Especially since her decision to leave. It made her uncomfortable, but with her earlier reaction about the car, she felt she owed it to Charlotte to at least try.

"You know, of course," Charlotte said, "that the money is only part of the inheritance, Mary. Timmy, or I should more rightfully say, his guardian until he turns eighteen, will be the majority shareholder in all of Stewart's various business ventures around the world. Now, I won't bore you with all the names of those things right now. Mostly because I don't even know them all at this point. Stewart dabbles in so many different things. But most important to us are this house and the adjoining property, Algernon Wood. They've both been in the family for a very long time, my dear. For the Machen family this is where it all started."

Charlotte paused to sip at her coffee, a satisfied grunt as she swallowed. Quietly placing the cup down, she continued: "There is one special proviso to the inheritance, Mary. A very important one. No one may sale any part of the Machen Estate, or Algernon Wood. As long as they hold claim to the monies, they must keep these things intact."

The old woman shook her head. "And, may God forgive me for saying this, but that was something that Conley could never understand. Blood is all that matters in this world. Family. This land- this house itself- is the Machen heritage. That can never be forgotten. He could never grasp the meaning of what this family stands for. Nor the sacrifices made by past generations of Machen to keep this for all time."

Mary found herself nodding with perfect understanding. A lot of old Southern families felt the same way- money or not. To some families, the land was all they had to pass on to those they left behind. Generations had lived and died for the land, and it was all they had to show for their blood, sweat, and tears. She could live with that proviso. Didn't mean she was moving in here, but she could live with it.

The rest of the conversation was short; it was obvious Charlotte was tired, even though it was only a little after 10am, and that she badly needed a mid-morning nap. Mary offered to help clear the table, but Charlotte only tittered and told her the servants took care of such menial tasks- that's what they were for. Mary almost replied that she had yet to see any servants, but decided against it. No need to get into details about a place she was leaving soon. But she still found it strange that during this whole time, night and day, she had yet to actual see anyone else in the house. She'd heard what had to be the servants moving around upstairs at all hours. But she had yet to see them.

Mary left the dining room and took the side door to the cool air outside. She saw Timmy capering like a jester next to Sully and Garlen near one of the gigantic oak trees that arched over the front of the mansion. Garlen watched her approach with a concerned and wary expression. "Everything okay?" he asked.

She knelt next to Timmy and hugged him close. She gave Garlen a tight smile. "Yeah, everything's fine." She pulled Timmy's collar together, almost absentmindedly buttoning it; the day was blustery and, despite the bright sunlight, chilly. A mother's job was never done. "It's just our car's missing this morning and I was a little upset."

Sully caught Garlen's eye, a glum frown on his mouth.

"Your car?" Garlen asked.

"Yes. It seems Stewart and Charlotte wanted to do something nice, so they sent it to a mechanic for some repairs. I mean...well, I guess it needed some work, but they didn't ask me. They just did it. I guess I got a little paranoid." She looked at Sully's grim countenance, sensing his tension.

"Easy enough to do here," he said. "So you two are stuck here until the car comes back?"

She nodded, wanting to tell him all about her unaccountable fears for herself, for Timmy, about the sense of menace that seemed to her to pervade this place- the house, and the forest beyond- and the sense of stealthy danger whenever they were alone. But she knew how ridiculous it would sound. She didn't want to sound like a nutcase, talking about things she couldn't put her finger on. There was nothing to back any of her sub-level fears, but she felt them nonetheless, as if some horrible revelation was coming, like a thunder-storm on the horizon. But how could she explain such nebulous feelings?

Next to her, Garlen suddenly clapped his hands and laughed like a giddy child. "What an extraordinary coincidence. Sully and I were just discussing the idea of staying on a few more days. So I guess you two will have company." He leered a toothy grin at Timmy, who giggled at the old man's playfulness. "If that's okay with you and Timmy, here?"

She saw the look the two men traded, and she sensed there was more to it than a simple 'coincidence' as Garlen claimed. A tacit decision had been made without her knowledge. It was obvious it was for she and Timmy's benefit, but she couldn't help feeling relieved to know she wasn't going to be alone with the Machens, almost against her will at this point, with no way to leave, in this sprawling testament to Southern Gothic.

At the sound of an approaching car, everyone turned, the view almost impenetrable beyond the tall conical topiaries. A police cruiser rolled to a stop in the driveway.

"What's this, then?" Garlen said to no one in particular.

It took a few moments for the rotund man in a dark uniform, wearing a black plastic covered cowboy hat and a thick winter jacket, to pull his bulk from the confines of the vehicle. Giving the front door of the mansion a cursory glance, he caught a glimpse of their small group huddled near the oak tree and made his way towards them instead. He waddled with a rolling motion only very large men seemed able to master. The sun gleamed off a gigantic gun strapped in a creaking black leather holster that bounced on the man's right hip. When he got closer, he tipped his hat to Mary. "How you folks all doin' this mornin'? Name's Sheriff Lincoln."

Garlen rolled himself forward and took charge, giving the Sheriff a polite smile. "We're all doing alright, Sheriff. Little cold, but better than rain any day, eh?"

"Yes, sir," Sheriff Lincoln agreed, showing a mouth full of tobacco stained teeth. "Cain't argue with that, sir."

Everyone waited for him to continue, but he just sucked at his teeth looking from one to the other of them for a quiet moment.

"What can we do for you, Sheriff?" Garlen finally asked.

He motioned with his head toward the house behind them. "Well, I guess I need to have a talk with the Machens if they're around," he said. "And I guess if any of you folks were here last night, I'll probably need to gab with ya'll, too."

Garlen leaned forward. "Something we should know about?"

The big man sighed and nodded, still sucking at his teeth. "Well, now, I guess you could say that." He smiled down at Timmy. "How you doin' there, little buddy?" He took a moment to lean down, so as not to intimidate the child.

Timmy gave him a shy half smile and pointed at the gun on his hip. "Is that real?"

"You better believe it, little buddy," Lincoln said with a chuckle. "I'd be in some kind of trouble if it wasn't." He levered his bulk up again with a grunt and turned his attention back to the adults. "Got myself a couple of teenagers missing up around this area. They were out here last night, out on the road, and got lost in the woods. They were drinkin'." Lincoln rubbed his bulging stomach as if he felt uncomfortable and frowned.

"Ah, the folly of youth," Garlen interjected. "Bacchanal does have his due."

The Sheriff looked a little confused at the reference, but didn't let it slow him down much. "I suppose you might be right about that. Anyway, I was wonderin' if any of ya'll might've heard anything strange last night."

"Sorry, Sheriff," Garlen said. "Not a peep. I'm a heavy sleeper."

Lincoln nodded and turned to Sully, gave him a careful once over. Sully didn't seem to Mary to be fazed by the lawman's attention. She guessed he was probably used to getting the once over from most people, especially lawmen. He was big and looked dangerous. Cops always found that combination a challenge to their authority. Sully returned the fat sheriff's stare with a bored gaze.

"How about you?" Sheriff Lincoln asked him.

"Sorry," Sully answered. "Nothing."

Lincoln raised his eyebrow as he looked at Mary and Timmy. "How about you, ma'am?"

Mary shook her head as way of answer, still trying to wrap her thoughts around how two people could just get lost so close to a house with the kind of air stripe bright landing lights like the ones bedecking

Machen mansion. She had been able to see the lights for a mile or so before she even got close to the place. If she were lost, she would have made for any lights at all. How could locals get lost in their own woods?

"Did you hear anything strange last night, little buddy?" the Sheriff asked Timmy. But the boy was still too entranced with the silver pistol to pay any attention to what was being said.

"Answer the Sheriff, son," Mary said.

Timmy looked away from the gun grudgingly. "No, sir. I was pretty tired last night."

"Well, now ain't you a pistol, boy," Lincoln said. "I like a boy who knows his manners. Guess your mama and daddy taught you right, didn't they." He laid his hand on the pistol butt and nodded. "I can see you got a likin' for guns, huh?" He saw Mary frown at him. "Not to worry, ma'am," he said. "Most boys do. Part of our nature to like things that go boom." He chuckled. "My Daddy gave me this when I was a just little older than you," Lincoln told him. "He used to be Sheriff here, too. A long time ago."

Now that it had been breached again, Timmy warmed to the subject. "You ever shoot any bad guys with it?" he asked, eyes wide and excited.

Mary tried to shush him. "Timmy, don't be rude."

But Lincoln chuckled again and nodded. "A couple of times, little buddy. But I sure didn't want to do it. Nothing worse than having to kill a man, just so's you can live. Don't believe that's what God put us on this earth to do." Sensing that his philosophy might be a little heavy for polite company, he heaved a sigh and looked at the house again. "Well, you folks do me a favor, huh? Keep your eyes and ears open, and be sure to let me know if something comes up. I sure would appreciate it." He made his way back to his car and folded himself back inside, and with a toot of his horn for Timmy and a wave for the others, he drove away.

When the Sheriff's car disappeared behind the blinding stand of topiaries once more, Garlen wondered aloud: "Now why do you suppose he didn't talk with Charlotte or Stewart? It was obvious he wanted to."

"And that he should have," Sully added. "Two kids go missing on their land and he doesn't bother speaking with the Machens? Just some people he saw standing outside the house by a tree? Strange."

"Didn't seem to be trying very hard at that, did he?" Garlen agreed. "Maybe he knows something we don't."

A cold wind blew across the lawn, rustling the leaves overhead, making a sound like whispering voices. Mary shivered and crossed her arms across her chest. She looked to the sky and saw that rain clouds were already coming in again. Did it evr stop in this place, she wondered. If she and Timmy were going to take a walk, they'd better do it soon and they'd definitely need something heavier than the shirt she had on right now.

She told Timmy she was going to go inside and get jackets for them, but the boy begged to let him do it. He jumped up and down, begging in a high whiny voice, until she decided this would be the perfect opportunity to speak with Sully and Garlen alone. "You be careful," she said. "Go straight to the room and right back." She cast a wary eye at the huge domicile.

"Are you sure I shouldn't go with you?"

"No, Mama," Timmy said, giggling at her worried frown. "I can find my way through that stupid old house."

She made him promise again not to go into any other rooms but their bedroom. He took off in a freeform run that only children can make look effortless. Once he was out of hearing, she turned to the two men, put her hands on her hips. "Okay," she said, giving them a stern look that said she wasn't going to be excluded any longer. "What the hell is going on in this place?"

Garlen spread his hands, feigning confusion. "How do you mean, dear?"

"Cut the crap, Garlen," Sully muttered. "She needs to know the truth."

Sully turned his dark eyes on her, and she was surprised to see, past the haunted look, there was an unexpected tenderness reflected within. He was worried about her.

"So tell me what you know," she said, meeting his troubled gaze.

"I don't trust your in-laws, Mary. That's all," Sully replied.

"Not to be nosy, dear," Garlen broke in-assessing Sully was lost for a reasonable explanation as to why he felt the way he did. "But how did exactly did you come to find yourself in the company of said in-laws?"

"My husband Conley died four months ago. He was Stewart's son. I didn't even know he had a family, until they called me."

"You never knew?" Sully asked.

"Apparently Conley and Stewart didn't get along too well. They had a big fight when Conley was young. He left and I guess Stewart disowned him."

"How very Tennessee Williams of him," Garlen quipped.

Mary smirked at his comment and continued, "Conley never told me about them. Well, actually, that's not quite right. My husband out right lied to me. He said they were dead. I don't know why. But it wasn't like Conley to keep anything from me. He must have had a reason, but for the life of me, I can't fathom one".

She hugged herself again, feeling the chill biting at her arms and neck. "So, anyway, a few days ago, I get a call asking me and Timmy to come here for a visit. That there's some enormous inheritance that Timmy's going to get when Stewart dies."

Garlen rubbed his sagging cheeks in thought. "You know, it's strange, but I've known Stewart Machen for almost ten years and I never heard him mention a son at all. Not once."

"So what happened to cause them to spilt so irrevocably?" Sully asked, then added, "Of course, if you don't want to tell us, it really isn't any of our business."

"No, I don't mind. Actually, it feels good to talk to someone about all this," she said "Charlotte said they argued about what college he should go to. Stewart wanted him to go where he went. Conley had other plans."

"Wait a second," Garlen said. "As far as I know Stewart never went to college. He inherited his father's business concerns, even quit high school to do so. He got married, had a kid, and never finished school. Not that kind of thing means anything when you've got the money he's got."

Mary frowned. "Why would Charlotte lie about it?"

Sully moved closer to her. "I don't know. But this is starting to sound worse and worse. Are you sure you want to stay here?"

She shrugged. "Well, I don't have much choice. Like I said, my car's gone."

"Oh, we can get you guys out of here," Sully told her, looking to Garlen for support. "Garlen has a helicopter on call pretty much twenty four hours a day, Mary. You say the word and it's done."

"Sully's right," Garlen agreed. "Say the word and I can get the pilot here in an hour or two. We can get you home. Don't worry about that."

Thunder rumbled in the distance, as if to contradict his claim.

"That is if the weather holds out," he added.

"We can always call a car," Sully said. "Point is, we can and will get both of you out of here if that's what you want." His eyes bore into her like dark lights. She had no doubt he meant what he said. He would get them away, if she asked. But she didn't like walking away from the mystery. She needed to know why Conley had kept his family a secret. And now, if what Garlen said was true, Charlotte had lied to her as well. But why?

"No," she finally said. "I need to know what's going here. I want to know why they were so eager to get me and Timmy here. I need to know why Conley lied."

Timmy came trotting back from the house, two jackets wadded carelessly in his arms. When he stopped beside his mother, she helped him into his, gratefully pulling on her own jacket. "We'll talk more later," she said, her tone warning against any conversation in front of her son. "Maybe after dinner."

She thanked them both, but she couldn't help but keep shifting her gaze to Sully. When he caught her stare, she blushed again, sure that those brown eyes could penetrate her thoughts about him. She hurried Timmy away, leaving the two men standing by the tree.

Sully and Garlen watched them make their way around the side of the house, as Mary searched for the pathway which led to the garden. Garlen looked up at Sully, his face bland but for a small smile. "She's quite beautiful, don't you think?"

Sully shrugged. "She's okay."

Laughing, Garlen reached over and patted Sully's thigh. "Sully, you're an open book."

"Screw you," Sully said. "She's very beautiful. But she's also a widow, raising a kid on her own. She's got a lot of baggage. So sad. But being alone will do that."

Garlen nodded. "We all carry our baggage, my friend. We of all people know that, eh?"

Sully moved to the tree and ran a big finger along the gnarled trunk, thinking. After a moment, he turned back to Garlen. "Tonight I think should take a look around the house."

Garlen rolled his chair closer, peering intently at his large bodyguard. Sully knew he'd known him long enough to know his instincts were eating at him. There was some niggling little doubt about this place and he needed to uncover its secrets.

"Why? What do you hope to find?"

"I don't know," he muttered. "Maybe some skeletons. I just feel there's something happening underneath all this Southern Gothic bullshit. Something's not right with this place. Or the Machens."

"Be careful, my boy," Garlen said. "I get the feeling this place doesn't like to be fucked with."

"Neither do I," said Sully.

Tonight, he promised himself. *Be damned the Machens and their creepy ass mansion, he'd tear the place apart if need be to find out what kept sending his sense of danger into overdrive.*

CHAPTER -14-

Mary awoke to complete darkness; not even moonlight shone through the gauzy curtains across the room. It was as if all ambient light had been banished by some outside force, drawing the house, and its occupants, into a void of heavy soulless black.

Panic scurried from the depths of her belly. Breath caught in the hollow of her throat, fear clenched her spine in its icy fingers.

How could it be so dark? And so quiet...

A crash of thunder broke the oppressive silence, nearly eliciting a scream from her. The explosion faded to a wall-shaking rumble, and she understood why the world seemed so dark. While she and Timmy slept, yet another storm had rolled over the land like a juggernaut.

Across the room, a mischievous wind battered the window, rattling at the glass like a quiet burglar seeking egress. Tree limbs scraped against the house, making a sound like beetles scuttling across a moldy skeleton. Ancient wood creaked against the buffeting breath of the oncoming storm, lending the house a moaning voice of its own.

A blinding streak of lightning into pure white heat outside, giving the room a staccato life. Dressers and tables, overloaded with forgotten bric-a-brac objects, leered and jumped in the shadows. Then the world was just as suddenly thrust back into profound night once again.

Mary could feel Timmy's weight next to her. Thankfully, he was still asleep. Assured by his silence and the steady rhythm of his breathing, she pulled herself carefully from the tangle of blankets and sat on the edge of the bed for a moment until, the next flash of white light showed her the way to the window. She treaded softly, and peeling back the thin curtains, she peered outside to check the storm's progress. As she watched, the bombastic display of lightning transcended to rain, pouring down in curtains that obscured her view of the grounds beyond the foggy glass. The rain's chill penetrated the window and she was soon shivering, but unwilling to seek solace under the blankets; she was wide-awake now.

She turned to check the time on the grandfather clock, and caught a light out of the corner of her eye. There was an orange glow creeping beneath the door to the bedroom. Not a sudden light, it grew like an approaching spectral force, a building crescendo of silent illumination.

Brighter and brighter, until she was sure the source was just outside the bedroom's door.

A flickering quality about it, made her guess it must be someone with a candle. Was someone hesitating to wake them, or was it simply someone passing by on their way to some other mysterious room for a late hour rendezvous.

Footsteps on faded rug weave. Stealthy. Quiet.

She wanted to run to the door and jerk it open, confront the person, maybe the same person whom had tormented her before. Mary walked quietly to the door, put her ear against the cold, damp wood, and listened.

Sully waited until for the rain to fall before slipping from his room. He hoped the storm's noise would cover his movements through the house.

He'd retrieved one of his handguns, a Glok, fully loaded and ready for action. He grabbed an extra clip. He'd also picked out a small penlight, checked the power, and stuck it in his jean pocket. His watch read eleven p.m. The rain was coming down steady now. The house had been still for two hours, not a sound of anyone traveling the halls, above or below.

He waited at his door, listened for any movements. He heard Garlen's raucous snore from the adjoining room.

Sully took a deep steadying breath and moved along the empty corridor, using his mental map as guide, until he found a staircase that looked familiar. The stairs went both up and down. He chose to go down first, deciding to press the lower depths to reveal their secrets.

He kept close the wall, pausing frequently to listen for anything beyond the steady machine gun hammer of the rain. Several times, he thought he heard voices, sibilant whispers, below. But each time he reached the next floor, he found no one, only more of the same dimness and the inanimate shapes of furniture.

As he continued, certain that he was not imagining the sounds, Sully sniffed the air, but found no human odor wafting upon the dank ethereal night. He trusted his senses, but there was a menacing atmosphere in the tight, dark corridors. Although his instincts could not explain the feeling of trepidation, he couldn't convince himself it wasn't tangible. He sensed a presence in the darkness with him, a silent something that ghosted his movements. And, still, there were those whispering voices, always just beyond his present position, on the next level, beyond the next turn in the corridor.

Sully felt himself reacting to the sensation. He was letting his fears get the best of him. He had to stay loose. He took a deep breath, rolled his neck a couple of times. He fondled the reassuring weight of the Glok stuck between his tee-shirt and pants, flexed his fingers a few times, feeling the crack of muscle and bone beneath chilled skin.

Keep your fucking head on straight, man. There is no such thing as ghosts.

But the drill sergeant in his head did little to quiet the whispers down the way, or to keep him from feeling the weight of the enormous mansion sitting above his head. It was like being swallowed by a Behemoth.

The stairs ended and he found himself in a passage that stretched out before him for what seemed like half a mile. On the right side, a long line of tall rectangular windows allowed the sporadic lightning to cast jumping shadows of foliage across the floor. Their swaying thin black fingers grasped at the empty hall like ghostly skeleton hands. The rug pattern crawled in illusionary movement in the distance- an illusion of depth and feral antagonism.

He stopped to look out the windows at a vast atrium situated on the tail end of the fenced property, but gave the flowers and thin unrecognizable stalks of verdure only a cursory glance before moving on to the end of the passage.

Out of the atrium hall, Sully found doors on either side of another long hallway, and he gave the knobs a cautious turn. Locked, he dismissed them.

During his reconnaissance mission, he checked behind unlocked doors. Behind some he found huddled shadows of dusty furniture; behind others he found empty rooms, filled with dark and cobwebs. Some of the doors led him to other halls; some led to more stairs, both ascending and descending. He used the stairs as his guide, always taking them down to the next floor when he found them. Unavoidably, he found himself led astray more than once, to dead end walls, or more empty rooms that led to nothing.

He wanted to see how far down the stairways went. Would they continue under the visible construct of the mansion? If so, what, he wondered, could be below the superstructure?

Soon, the air grew damp, cooler, and he detected a stench that reminded him of cold meat gone bad. Sully felt safe enough to risk the penlight. He switched on the tight little beam, illuminating the silent, dank corridor.

This far down, the straight pristine papered walls above had given way to glistening, rough-hewn bricks. The gentile décor had fallen behind him somewhere and had been replaced with dirty, crumbling stonework, laid at least a hundred years or more ago. Even the steps had become heralds of the gradual change. Soft carpet became ancient, pale unpolished wood. The yellow sconces, which seemed to be the chief source of illumination in the house's many corridors, disappeared. Now only bare 40-watt bulbs, dangling from dusty lengths of wires, gave him light. Down here, in the depths, was the utilitarian nightmare of crudity and age, the true representation of Machen Mansion, the trappings of wealth above only a mask worn by this great old beast of a house. Beneath, the true face was decayed and crumbling.

He could feel a steady thrumming sense of power through the soles of his shoes. At first he had attributed it to the storm raging without, but the steady 'rum-rum-rum' beat was too much like some giant unseen machine grinding away for unknown purposes down here in the darkness.

Sully continued down the pitching uneven steps, until he reached a damp stone floor. There were no forked passages here, and a rusted metal door before him denoted that the trip to the very bowels of the house had come to an end. Huge, cast-iron bolts hinged the inscrutable doorway into a rough stone frame. It glistened in the sickly light with a thin film of slime.

To the right, sunken into the stone, chest height, he found a security keypad. Its presence gave him pause. He felt a soul deep chill he couldn't attribute only to the stinking, cold air. The door was hidden beneath the house and secured against trespass. What would the Machens need to hide all the way down here?

There was only way to find out. He had to get that door open.

The keypad was old and grimy, coagulated with ancient dust and dampness, a pasty kind of muddy composite. It was at least twenty-five years out of date with modern security technology. That was a good thing.

Someone had become complacent about its upkeep. He might have a shot at breaking in.

On his knees, Sully turned his head at an angle so he could see the keys on the keypad from a leveled view. It took only a moment to see that there was more wear and tear on the numbers 6,2,8, and 0, the only numbers on the pad that had been pressed since its installation. On a newer keypad, he wouldn't have been able to make out the wear and tear so easily.

Now came the tricky part. He was assuming that the code to get past the door was four numbers long; but that didn't mean it was. There could be numbers in a longer combination that weren't as worn as the four he could see. Even if the code were only four numbers long, how many different combinations could there be? Thousands? Tens of thousands? And what if one of the four was a repetitious one? How many then? Hundreds of thousands?

It only took him a disheartening moment to assess that his chances of breaking a four number code weren't very good. He would have nothing going for him but luck. It would be like winning a lottery, and Sully never trusted in luck.

Of course, there was another way to get past the door. He knew ways to bypass any code, especially in something as ancient as this old clunker of a system. But that would necessitate his taking off the faceplate. If he did, would it be noticed later? Or, perhaps, was this system hooked into another that would alarm someone that it had been finagled?

Sully faced the keypad for a moment of indecision. Then heaved a sigh and decided to fuck the consequences. One way or another he was going to know what was behind the door. His instincts were screaming now, and he felt it somehow imperative to Mary and Timmy's safety to get inside.

He stuck the penlight in his mouth so the light was on the keypad's faceplate. From another pocket he retrieved a small Swiss Army knife, something he never left home without. He picked at the various implements and blades and decided on a small knife from the assortment, ran it around the edge of the plate. He smiled when he felt no obstructions to impede the knife's progress around the rim of the faceplate. Undoing the four screws that held the faceplate in place, he placed them next to the door for later when he'd have to rebuild this thing. After the last screw had been set aside, he wrenched the stiff sticky metal from its mooring, revealing six wires of different colors dangling from the sunken wire pit. Sully chose two of the wires and carefully nicked them with the knife. He rubbed the wires together, 'sparking' them, forcing the electric impulse that keying in the correct number sequence would have provided. It took a couple of times, but soon he heard a muffled thump that he could feel in the floor and the door 'shinked' open like a lifting guillotine blade.

Sully put the faceplate back together, replaced the screws, locking it back in place. With a critical eye he surveyed his work. The screws were old and easily marked. If someone looked close enough, the silver marks where the knife had dug into the heads could be easily detected. Wasn't much he could do about that.

He just hoped the dim light of the surroundings would hide it.

Before crossing the threshold, he took another deep calming breath, and pulled the Glok from his improvised pant holster.

He pointed the penlight into the dark mouth of the door and walked inside.

Mary waited until the light under the door dimmed before she made up her mind to confront the light harbinger. The was falling away with a slow devolution; the hall outside their room was easily fifty feet in either direction, so she knew evasion was impossible.

One last look over her shoulder at Timmy's still slumbering form and then she twisted the cold iron knob of the door. It opened with a muted click. She slipped into the hall on silent feet, closing the door behind her quietly. Of course, just like the other times, she found only an empty hall. The storm beat against the house, gathering force, slamming into the jagged peaks and gables. She caught the tail end of the light as it disappeared around the far away left turn.

Mary hesitated, unsure about leaving Timmy alone to go chasing shadows again. But she needed to know what was going on in this house. The longer she stayed, the more convinced she became something was going on she couldn't yet fathom, things she wasn't being told, perhaps something deadly cloaked in these tight, dim halls. And as much as she feared the house, she feared the sense that this mystery held danger for them.

Perhaps, in discovery of that secret, a final answer would lead her to other answers about Conley as well. Sully's confession of his dislike for her new in-laws did nothing to quell her growing paranoia. Although she'd only just met the big man, Mary trusted his judgment. He seemed to her to be a man in touch with his senses- physical and emotional.

Another crash peal of thunder pummeled the house, shaking its very foundations- a sound that whispered release in ancient wood and crumbling stone like a forgotten promise of death.

As if the thunder were an antidote against her uncertainty, she hurried down the hall to catch the mysterious light bearer. Rounding the corner, Mary hoped to at least see a leg disappearing this time; but there was a shifting shadow dancing in the nimbus of orange light. And then it, too, was gone.

Practiced as she was now at the house's illusions of depth and brio, Mary was still surprised how closely this hallway resembled the one she'd left behind. To either side, rows of closed unmarked doors greeted her in a clone-like procession. She continued her pursuit of the will-o-the-wisp light, now running faster and faster, until she was gasping for air and her hammered in her chest.

Around the next corner, she finally found the carrier of illumination. Although the person had still managed to make it to the other end of the hallway with unreal speed, she could plainly see the figure now. Thin and stooping. A shadow silhouetted before the orange pulsing glow of the light, held closely against the figure's emaciated chest. She could not yet make out the person's face, but their was the suggestion of beldam to it.

"Hello?" she called. "Wait! Please!" Despite her shouts, the sound of her voice seemed strangely muted in the hall's throbbing confines, but the figure paused.

The person still had their back to Mary. The light pulsed. And pulsed. Pulsed. Like a slow heartbeat.

Then the figure slowly turned its bulbous head. The face seemed to rise from shadow and into the pulsing orange light. Mary's blood froze like mercury in her veins, as two glowing orange eyes stared back her. She stumbled to a clumsy halt, confused by the strange face.

She was dreaming. That was the only explanation, the only way to explain the eerie, sickly patch of light that radiated from the thing's emaciated chest. And this thing was not human. She didn't know what the hell it could be, but it was not human. The surreal rhythmic luminosity came from a black space, a soulless hole buried within insubstantial shadows of the figure's chest.

The light mirrored the beating of a heart.

Thump...thump...thump.

She watched, hypnotized by the steady rhythm, frozen by shock and terror.

If she was asleep, and this was all a nightmare, why could she feel so distinctly the cold of the floor on her bare feet? Why could she feel the tremble of her own breath stuck in the catch of her throat? Or the niggling tickle of a cold rill of sweat as it glided down her cheek? But she had to be, because moving shadows with pulsing orange lights for hearts did not exist in the waking world.

To compound her terror, a sibilant whisper sounded from behind her. It was the same strange half-heard, half-understood voice that she had heard on that first day in these passages, as the words were just under the threshold of hearing and comprehension, a familiar cadence spoken heard from deep waters.

The nightmare escalated as the glowing shadow thing began to move towards her, gliding ghost-like down the hall, a black vaporous insubstantiality, its eerie light pulsing steadily. The sickly glow illuminated the crawling patterns on the wall and rugs, reflected in the dusty sconces.

Dream or not, in this hall, or in bed, fast asleep, the reflected sickly light on the curve of the sconces was too much for Mary to keep the flimsy illusion afloat that this might all be some strange vision and not reality. The detail of that twisted reflection killed it.

She backpedaled, turned and fled back down the hallway. Yes, she was going in the direction of the ambiguous whispering voice, but she had no choice. Better the thing she did not see, than the thing coming for her. The light blossomed in her periphery vision as the light bearer gained on her.

She stumbled round the corner, leaving the insubstantial glow of the thing behind, and ran as fast as she could, her heart beating in a tarantella of terror.

She turned another corner and followed yet another corridor. It seemed to stretch out forever.

She raced by the closed doors. She didn't know where she was. Nothing looked familiar. She took turn after turn to elude the nightmarish figure of dark light and shadow. They all looked the same now, familiar in their ambiguity.

She hesitated before a closed door, grasped the knob, turned to see the pulsing light growing again, heralding the creature's approach. She twisted the knob it in a shaking grasp.

It was locked.

She mewled in terror, as she pulled in vain at the closed door.

She left it, scurried to the next door.

The glow flickered brighter and brighter, the pulse stronger with every passing second.

She pulled at the knob.

Locked!

The whispering sounded again, louder than before, slipping and sliding down the dimness of the next turn of the hallway ahead.

Mary sobbed and ran to the next door, but it was as unwilling as the others to grant her ingress. She pulled at it in frustration, tears dripping down her cheeks.

She ran further down the hall, towards the whispering voice. The words were growing more definable now; she could almost understand the terrible, hungry secret the speaker in the dark wanted to give her.

Death…agony…never ending darkness…soul screams…never ending servitude…birth…light…never ending nothingness…useless…

Mary refused to let the words find purchase in her thoughts. To do so would be to invite the same sort of paralysis she'd experienced with the glowing thing's pulsing chest light.

The next hallway engulfed her like a constricted throat eager to swallow her; the carpet and walls crawled in the dim yellow light, adding to the illusion that she was no longer running down a hall, but sliding along a vast gullet into the bowels of the mansion.

She grabbed at the next door, jerked at the knob, a scream, part terror and part frustration, welling up in her chest.

The door flew open as she shoved against it. Mary scampered inside, slinging the door closed again with a crash. She locked it, hearing the security of metal click into place. She had forgotten how blessed a sense of security could feel.

Pressing against the cold door, she could hear the stuttering noise of her own breath rasping in and out. She slid to the floor, her legs slipping from beneath her like unhinged taffy.

Nothing could get her now.

Let the whisperer speak its obscene secrets. Let the light thing pulse against the walls and floors without. She was safe by God and she wasn't testing this place again.

Never.

She looked down between her trembling legs and saw the orange light growing and spreading beneath her.

It was right outside the door!

Stealthy movements, the same sounds she had attributed to some unseen servant the first day when she had been in the bathroom, sounded from the other side of the door.

Then the whispers changed. The almost subconscious volume of the voice altered. It had had no sex before. Now she knew it was a man.

It called her name in a low, eager whisper.

She knew that voice.

It was his voice.

Conley.

Her dead husband called her name again, and she felt her senses reel in a spasm of horror at the garbled, muddy voice.

"No...no...no...no," she whimpered. "You're dead. Dead. Dead. No, Conley, no."

The knob above her head began to rattle, an unseen hand testing the lock.

Her eyes swiveled up like hot marbles in a frying pan. In the dark she could just make out the worn golden circle slowly moving back and forth.

"Let me iiiinnn," the muddy voice begged. "Myyyyy sweeet."

Soft fingers scraped against the wood, clawing in entreaty.

God. No. This was too much. She couldn't take it. The gliding shadow thing... the whispered words she could not understand...anything but this. Not Conley, dear Lord.

She clamped her ears with her shaking hands to cut off the begging endearments; but she could still hear them. She was going to scream. She was going to lose her mind. The nightmare was beating her down, stealing her reason, tearing at the fibrous threads of her sanity.

The voice stopped.

The scraping fingers skittered away.

The doorknob stopped turning.

The pulsing glow under the door faded, until it was gone.

Drawing sobbing breaths, she waited, sure that this was just some kind of cruel break in the terror, a pause for the crescendo of horrors to come.

After a few moments of silence, Mary put her ear against the door. She heard nothing.

"Mama?"

Mary nearly screamed at the sound of her son's voice, sure it was yet another assault on her sanity, the thing posing as Timmy.

But Timmy's voice was coming from the darkness on the other side of the room.

It was inside with her.

A sudden movement of someone moving in the dark...

And then Timmy thrust into silhouette against the gray light of the window, sitting up in bed.

He called her name again, this time more strident and scared.

She realized she'd somehow found her way back to their room.

The frantic tone of her son's voice pulled her from stupor and she threw herself from the floor, hurried to the bed. Timmy's frightened sobs pushed aside her own fears. She would think about what she had seen, what she had heard, later. For now, she hugged him tightly, whispering that everything was okay, she was here, ssshhh...

In his mother's trembling arms, Timmy fell almost immediately back to sleep, his breath warm and wet against her cheek. She put him back under the blankets, and forced herself to lay down next to him. But she did not sleep the rest of the night. Her eyes refused to close, her thoughts refused to allow anything but the horrible sound of Conley's voice echo in her head.

Beneath the ancient floors of Machen Mansion, Sully stood in stunned disbelief at the faintly lighted chamber he'd just entered.

The room was conical shaped, like an upended egg, as if it had been carved from the stone that made up its curved walls and ceiling. Sully saw several glittering points that could only be some kind of polished metal inlaid in the stone. The lines and circles of dark metal ran from the smooth gray floor to the round tapering ceiling heights. The inlays seemed to hint at some kind of esoteric pattern, perhaps a written language that he could not read. Each cut and slash of the hieroglyphics reflected in the yellow sickly light from a number of recessed bulbs set half way up the round room's smooth unbroken wall.

A pedestal of rough stone rose up from the floor in the middle of the room. Long, flat steps led up to its round, flat expanse. Another set of indecipherable metallic inlays followed the pedestal's natural curve, the letters seeming more like knife slashes and sudden gouges in the stone.

The patterns made his eyes slip and slide across the designs as if they were oiled unrealities. He had trouble keeping his focus. He turned his attention to the contents of the chamber.

There was a short wooden bookshelf near the stone pedestal. He moved cautiously across the room and scanned the ancient spines. Sully touched one of the volumes, faded red, now a sickly pink, decayed and dusty. The words, like the scribbles on the walls, floor, and pedestal, were in a language he didn't understand. He left off the books and turned his attention to the rising level of rough hewed black rock next to the shelf.

Even to the untrained eye it was easy enough to tell that the rise of painted stone was an altar of some kind. Mouth dry with trepidation, Sully hesitantly climbed the three stone steps to the altar's face. On either side of the circular platform stood a dead chest level brazier, blackened charcoal crushed inside the mouth of each. They smelled of dirt and smoke, and another scent he couldn't place, like a weed fire that has been put out not too long ago, the stink haunting the air.

He walked around the altar, feeling that same strange thrumming sensation in the soles of his feet, a latent power pulsing in the handy work of stone itself. All along the outside radius of the altar, more unreadable letters had been painted, faded white, chipped and cracked with age. In the center of the stone face was a golden inlaid six-fingered hand, surrounded by various symbols such as a pentagram, circles, and esoteric slashes. Sully stared at the incredible display. The air inside the chamber was still as a tomb, but various odors wafted in the dead air. Standing in the center of the altar now, a new scent, one that raised his hackles, wafted to him. The scent of ancient spilled blood and violence. He gazed more closely at the dark spots that stained the stone. He couldn't convince himself weren't exactly what they looked like. He didn't like the way the altar made him feel, sick and angry. And that maddening sense of just-below-the-surface power pulsing through the floor was eating at his control. His breath was already quickening from the heady intoxicant that he could not see, but feel in his bones.

He had long suspected the Machens were more than just 'Southern'- as Garlen had put it. He'd always felt that there was some deeper disturbance in them that he just instinctual knew. This chamber, with its altar and crawling colors and metal inlays, was proof of that. Were they some kind of modern day witches?

Despite the things he'd done in his life, Sully didn't think of himself as a violent person. Some acts of violence were unavoidable, some were even forgivable; but some were hideous, monstrous. For whatever purpose the Machens used this place, it deserved exposure. If he did nothing else before he left this goddamned house, he promised himself, he would do just that.

Sully stepped off the altar and went back to the books. He was looking for anything that he might have as proof positive of what went on here. He scanned the books with a more critical eye this time, although most of the titles were in languages he could never hope to decipher.

He picked one book from the shelf, disturbing the years of dust and mildew gathered on its surface. Opening the thick leather cover, he scanned the first few pages. It was written in what looked like Latin, and, therefore, completely incomprehensible to him, so he put it back.

He went from book to book, pulling each out far enough to see if he recognized any of the written words. After a few minutes of searching he found a book written in English. Algernon Machen was written in faded gold old English script on the front page inside the cover.

Stewart's great grandfather.

The book smelled of cured animal hide, creaked like an ancient portal when he turned each page. The crinkled, yellow pages had a different stench, unlike any paper he'd ever smelled before. They were thick, too, almost unwieldy with weight. One didn't turn the pages so much as lift them.

He suddenly realized why the pages felt strange and almost flung the huge tome away in disgust and horror. Human skin, dried and pressed and cured. Someone had used human skin to make the pages. How many people had been flayed for this thing? Four? Six? How many pages could one get from a normal sized human being? He didn't want to count the pages; it would only escalate his loathing. It was all he could do to keep from throwing the book across the room. But, in his eyes, this book was proof enough. No matter what the text held, just the fact that it had been made of human skin would be more than enough to cause the Machens some problems once it was brought it to the attention of the authorities.

Sully took one last look around the oval chamber of horrors and decided that he had spent enough time here. He clutched to book to his chest and hurried from the blasphemous chamber.

He did not see the narrow camera eye in the high left corner of the room as it followed his departure.

CHAPTER -15-

Sheriff Lincoln looked at the gathered State lawmen and felt about as happy as a squirrel in a goddamned blender. The evening was closing in and the temperature had dipped down into the low fifties. A slight misty shower that felt more like spit than rain had started an hour before and the cold spray wasn't helping his balls feel any warmer.

Before him stood the twelve assorted uniforms sent over by the State Patrol, all dripping wet and freezing like himself, their silent attention on Sergeant Michael Samuels, head of the search party. Samuels was a large black man. Not the kind of large that his Mama would have called 'husky'. No, Samuels was fat. He had three rolls of fat muscle at his neckline, sticking above the too-tight, sweat-stained collar of his all weather jacket. Lincoln knew that because he was standing right behind the big sonuvabitch.

But obesity wasn't something he could afford to be a hypocrite about- not when he weighed close to three hundred himself. What he really didn't like about the fat bastard was his strutting arrogance, the condescending tone when he deigned to consult Lincoln in his own goddamned jurisdiction.

Of course, that was when the fat blow hard wasn't pacing back and forth before the twelve shivering men, hands behind his back like a Hollywood version of a military drill-sergeant, his voice booming ineffectively into the staunch, impenetrable bleakness of his surroundings.

Right now, the fat man was standing still, and Lincoln was looking down at the Sergeant's boots. They were shiny, polished black. Brand new, looked like. He thought he maybe should tell the old boy what those boots were going to look like in an hour out in those wetlands. But, then again, why bother? It was fine with Lincoln if the shiny new boots fell off his fat feet. Especially since the big man was already trying to throw his considerable weight around. Since his arrival, Samuels had been tossing off orders to everyone within yelling distance. Get those lights over there! Quiet those dogs down! You guys get in your vests! The fact that he was dealing with trained men who knew what needed to be done didn't seem to enter his mind or keep his loud mouth shut.

Until this asshole had come along about half an hour ago, Lincoln had already gotten the men split into teams of four, ready to start the search without Samuels. That was probably what had gotten under the cocky bastard's skin, the fact the local 'hick' Sheriff had usurped his dubious authority. Of course, if Lincoln had wanted to butt heads with the old boy, he wasn't without a few heavy hitters in his court, and thought he might have enough pull with the higher ups in the State Patrol that he could've taken the fat man down a peg or two.

But somewhere along the third or fourth yelling tirade, Lincoln decided it would be better if Algernon Wood did the humbling. Samuels had no idea what he was about to walk into; this place didn't forgive arrogance or stupidity. Sure as he was standing here freezing his nuts off, the forest was going to teach this old boy a thing or two before they called it quits, by God.

Off to the side of the parked cars, a pack of deputized hunting dogs yowled and panted in excitement, held in place by their handlers- a handful of Ellison locals Lincoln had cajoled into joining the search party. Next to the small group of huddled civilians, and their canine charges, stood Lincoln's only deputy, Francis Quail. Francis was staring off into the woods like a deer in headlights, face pale, hands clenching nervously. Boy was probably wondering how the hell he'd been snookered into this goddamned 'snipe-hunt'.

Lincoln could sympathize; he felt pretty much the same. The only thing they were likely to find tonight was cold, sore feet, mud puddles and lots of darkness…lots and lots of darkness. The search should have started early afternoon, but since he'd called in the State boys on it, he had no choice but to let them call the shots.

He turned around to see Bugsy Miller and Coon Lincoln (his cousin; and, boy, they had stopped handing out brains on his Daddy's side of the family on the day of Coon's birth) holding the dogs back and taking turns sneaking whiskey from an old coffee thermos behind Francis' back. Much longer and those two would be drunker than hell before they even got this wagon train on the move.

But that was okay; he could understand that, too. Hell, Coon worked better when he was a little 'on the way' anyway. He just wished this jackass would get this thing going before he got a little too 'on the way'.

Hands on his prodigious hips, Samuels shouted, "We're going to break up into teams of two, giving us a total of eight teams for the search. We'll spread out 60 yards apart, with flashlights and hounds."

That got Lincoln's attention; he shook his head in disbelief. Eight teams of two? 60 yards apart? Was he out of his mind? That was about the damn stupidest thing he'd heard all night. Next to him, he could see Bugsy and Coon already shaking their heads. Coon turned to Francis and started a quiet but vehement argument with the pale-faced deputy. Lincoln could already hear Coon's argument: No way were they going to bring their dogs out there under those circumstances.

In the crowd of State boys he could see some familiar faces, men who'd been in these woods before on other fruitless searches, and they weren't going to go for Samuels plan, either.

Samuels, completely unaware of the quiet murmurs of discontent in the crowd, continued to shout. "Radio contact will be established every fifteen minutes."

Lincoln sighed and figured he should let the man know. He tapped his round, meaty shoulder. "Listen," he said, trying to keep his good ole boy grin as easy and non-threatening as possible; last thing he needed was for this bastard to feel like he was getting his toes stepped on. "I ain't trying to tell you how to do your job—"

Samuels barely flicked him a look. "Then, don't." Then he turned away, cutting Lincoln off.

The big Sheriff ground his molars, feeling the muscles in his square jaw clench so hard his face hurt.

But he replaced the skin-tight grin and tapped Samuels' shoulder again. The man turned once more, aggravation plain on his bulbous face.

Lincoln reached down and grabbed Samuels' thick wrist in an iron grip. He squeezed until he felt flabby muscle meet unyielding bone. It was what his drill instructor in the Marines had called 'the sweet spot', a nerve, when pressed just right, that sent paralyzing pain shooting through the victim's neck and back. The beauty of the hold was that it left no marks. Drill instructors loved it.

Lincoln gave it an extra squeeze, just to test his hold, not because it felt good to see the big man's arrogant face suddenly drain of color. Face pasty and loose looking, Samuels' body went rigid, his eyes widened with shock. Lincoln stepped close, genial smile still plastered to his mouth, and pushed up hard against the big man, as if they were consulting one another. No one was the wiser that Samuels was about to pass out from the pain. Lincoln looked into the two pools of agony before him. "Now listen to me real careful, friend," he said. "I'm gonna say this once, and then we're gonna let this go. Them boys with the dogs ain't gonna go in them woods like you want them to. Not like that."

Samuels' eyes swiveled to take in the huddled men and their bristling dogs; he wasn't able to turn his head. Lincoln nodded amiably at the curious stares the men shot their way. "Best thing, Sergeant, is to have big teams. Better to keep those dogs close to each other. You see, you don't know them woods, son. Them woods'll eat you up." He gave the nerve another slight increase in pressure; Samuels' face twisted in uncontrollable response. "And I ain't aiming to get myself killed out here tonight. And neither do these here boys who been good enough to come out for this little shindig."

Another squeeze. Samuels' forehead dewed with sweat; his eyes rolled around.

"Now you make a big thing out of this, son, and I'll make sure they stick you out running a fruit check station on the state border. Cause you might think I'm some little yokel sheriff stuck out here in the boonies, but I know me a whole peck of people who'd do just about anything I asked them to, if things got real ugly."

Lincoln looked over Samuels's shoulder at the assembled State boys and gave them a reassuring smile. Some of the deputies were starting to get a little nervous.

"Now we understand each other, son?"

Without waiting for an answer, Lincoln stepped back, releasing his meaty wrist.

Samuels mewled in relief, stumbled a step or two, and then recovered. Shoulders stooped with the pain, he glared at Lincoln. The Sheriff could see red murder in the man's eyes. He flicked his gaze down to Samuels' sidearm, waiting to see if he would go for his gun, all the while sucking blandly on a bad tooth.

Seconds passed, then Samuels took a deep breath, and stepped away. Rubbing his swollen wrist, he turned back to the assembled officers. The deputies visibly relaxed as he proceeded to explain, that after a brief consultation with Sheriff Lincoln, it had been decided to instead use four teams, not eight, and they would stay thirty yards apart, instead of sixty.

Within ten minutes the teams had been reassigned, radio signals confirmed, and the dogs split evenly between sniffer teams. Lincoln grabbed two shirts from his prowler, shirts belonging to the two missing teens, and stuck them under the noses of each dog. The hounds began to bark and jump around, tails churning the air like fur-covered exclamations. With a shout, the men and the dogs headed into Algernon Wood.

An hour into the search and Lincoln reaffirmed what he already had known: Those two boys were gone for good. Lost in the great unknown of Algernon Wood. The dogs roamed far into the pines, led their masters sloshing through vast stretches of muddy, grasping wetlands, through vicious tangles of thorny underbrush, but they found nothing. There was no scent for them to follow; they were casting about for any scent, and moving in circles, chasing bear and raccoon.

Almost three miles from where they'd left the cars behind, Lincoln's team pushed through a particularly nasty deadfall of rotting pines and thorny bush, trying to consider an easy way to get around the hump of ancient fallen trees.

That was when he heard the first horrible screams coming in over the handheld holstered at his hip. "We lost 'em," someone yelled, breaking up the line like fractured glass. Lincoln could hear the man's hysterical echoes reverberate through the skeletal and gnarled trees. It had come from the right, two teams over from his present position. Light beams tumbled over one another in that direction, like darting, scared birds. He could see men scrambling through the underbrush. Running away?

Around him, his own team stood wide-eyed and silent, watching the bouncing lights. No one made a move to help. They were too scared. All the old timers stories came screaming back like vengeful banshees, reminding the shivering men why the Indians had stayed away from these woods.

Coon started yelling at his three hounds. They were fighting to run towards the screams. Their mournful bays sent shivers of ice up Lincoln's spine. He didn't like the sound. No, sir, not at all.

The radios exploded again with angry, frightened voices, everyone trying to talk at once, logic and control forgotten. Lincoln made a grab for his radio, so he could try and get them under control again. Coon sidled up next to him, the dogs tugging at him so fiercely Lincoln expected his cousin's arm to snap right off any second. He could see undisguised fear in Coon's alcohol addled eyes. "What's happenin,' Link?"

Before Lincoln could reply, gunfire erupted in the distance, ripping apart the wet night with brief staccato white flashes.

He couldn't make out anything was being said over the radio now. It was completely useless with garbled, frightened cross chatter; but he could sure as hell hear the terrified screams of the men down the line. The screams were getting closer; the chaos was approaching.

"Oh, shit," he muttered, the acidic taste of fear in his mouth like cold metal. He grabbed Coon's collar, hauled the man and his dogs along behind him for the first few feet. He turned to his men: "Come on! Get your asses in gear!"

He pushed through underbrush, thin branches slashing at him with all the zeal of maniacs with razors, stumbled over roots that his light found too late, bounced off tree trunks the size of elephant torso's, and saw the other team ahead of him making their way toward the violence too.

Bear. It had to be a bear. Panther maybe.

But he knew better. No panther would have hung around with all the dogs running through here.

God, damn, it! Who the hell was in charge of that team? He should have those guys under control by now.

Then he remembered. Sergeant Samuels. The big man's team.

Lincoln caught up to the other team, pushed past their leader, and screamed to them to hurry the fuck up.

He was only ten yards away from the center of the chaos when the gunfire stopped.

But the screams continued.

Dogs and men yelped and screeched with equal terrified intensity. Whatever was going down was bad. The lights were no longer bouncing around like insane will-o-the-wisps. Now they were too low to be held by anyone still standing.

Coon swept past Lincoln, dragged along by his three baying hound dogs, a helpless conspirator of their headlong race into the maelstrom. The three dogs from the second group followed suit and broke from their keeper as well. They joined Coon's pack, racing towards the screams ahead of their masters. Lincoln could only stare in horrified realization as the barking, screaming band crashed through the woods. He thrust his flashlight beam at their position, revealed Coon's disappearing back. Then he was out of the radius of his light. Gone. The dogs' frantic barks faded, as well.

Lincoln felt his extra pounds more in those next few seconds than ever before. His breath was like a burning, dry gas instead of air, as he continued to stumble along, trying to push himself to faster speeds.

A root humped from the wet ground and caught his feet. Lincoln fell forward, sprawling on his red, wet face. His light sprang from his grip, skittered forward, lodged between two low-lying branches. A sharp pain stabbed his ribcage, reminding him that his gun was still in its holster.

Behind him, the rest of his team finally caught up and passed him.

"Wait!" he screamed. No one listened to him.

From the darkness ahead, the dog pack began to yowl. The attack was brief. It finished with one last rising cry of agony and then the forest was silent again

Where the hell was Coon?

The trapped beam of his flashlight revealed the backsides of the men hurrying into the dark. He levered himself up and fumbled to retrieve his light from a tangle of tree branches. Cursing under his breath, he limped after the others.

A few feet on he found Coon lying on the ground, his bottom lip bloodied from some unknown bush slash. He was crying, pulling himself along the muddy ground, away from the others. Lincoln fell near him, feeling for any broken bones, looking for any injury more serious than a split lip. He could find nothing. His cousin began to thrash against his hold. "Let me go," Coon begged. "Help me save them. Please."

At first, Lincoln thought he was talking about the men who were still rushing headlong into danger. Then he realized his cousin meant his dogs.

"My boys! Link, my boys!"

Lincoln held fast. Now that Coon had gathered his strength, he was like a slithering eel under Lincoln's weight. "Coon, listen," he said. "We got to get out of here. Them dogs are gone."

"No," he blubbered. "Boys! Come back to Daddy!"

More screams rent the darkness. Lincoln felt his blood go cold with the sound of it. Strange shadows danced in the light play before him. A huddled inhuman shape moved among the men. Massive, so huge that he could not credit his own eyes. It moved with a spider's grace, a panther's speed, and a bear's ferocity. Long murderous limbs thrashed the bodies. Armed men and raged filled dogs fell before the thing like leaves from a dead tree.

He lifted up Coon's squirming frame, twisted them both back in the direction they had come. Within a few yards, they met the last of the search party, four frightened men looking as if they had unknowingly stepped into hell. It took only the sound of guns firing and the horrible night rending screams of their fellow officers to stop them in their tracks.

"Everybody get the hell out of here," Lincoln commanded. He waited for someone to argue with him, to tell him that they couldn't just leave those men behind, but there were no dissenters among them. They turned on their collective heels and ran. Lincoln swallowed down his own guilt and continued to drag a sobbing Coon behind him.

Somehow he managed to find the old fire line the Forest Division had ripped into the forest floor several years back, and he directed everyone to follow it. It was a little overgrown, but easier running than the deep wood they'd come in through. They were able to make it out in a quarter of the time it had taken to get in.

When he saw the whirling red and blue bubble lights of his car in the dark ahead, he didn't think he'd ever been so happy to see anything in his life. Sweating and scared, he called encouragement out to the others. Flashlights gouged out the night's belly, revealing the last fifty feet of wood between the stumbling, cursing group of men and the relative safety of the road. Beside him, Coon moaned.

Once they reached the cars, two of the surviving State Troopers got in their cars and hauled ass. Another man stumbled to his car and immediately began calling on his radio for backup. His voice was high, filled with panic, and his frantic explanation and curses echoed in the night. Lincoln had no one to call for backup. Francis was still out there somewhere, probably dead.

The State boys would send more men. By then it would be morning, and the shit was really going to hit the fan in Ellison. They would search the woods, and he had no doubt that they would find some remains- torn bits of clothing, ripped body parts too destroyed to allow identification. But the rest would simple be gone. The State head honchos would come to him for answers— answers he wouldn't be able to give them. No one was going to believe the truth. A plausible lie would always win the day over an impossible truth. And since this was his jurisdiction, this shit fest was going to be dumped squarely in his lap. He was going to eat it for this cluster fuck.

Sorry, Daddy. I let you down.

His father has been Sheriff before him. He'd been a damned fine one.

With a tired resignation, Lincoln got in his car to sit and wait. Coon, wild-eyed and shivering, knocked on his frosty window. Lincoln signaled for him to go around to the passenger's side of the patrol car. Coon slid in, his wet clothes scrapping on the seat. Whatever alcohol the man had so liberally imbibed earlier had been long burned from his system by terror. His hands shook as he ran them through his wet and wild tangle of hair.

Lincoln leaned forward across Coon and opened the glove compartment, retrieved a half-full bottle of bourbon, unscrewed the lid. He handed it to Coon and waited for him to take a few deep fortifying swallows. When he thought his cousin had had enough, he pulled it from his grip before he could finish the bottle and took a swallow for himself. The liquor burned like smooth fire all the way down to his toes. He closed his eyes and let the warmth suffuse his blood.

"Sorry about your dogs, Coon."

Coon looked out the rain-beaded glass, tears brimming in his eyes. "They was good 'uns, Link. Raised 'em from pups."

"Yeah," Lincoln said. "I know." His bleary attention went to the State patrol car in front of him. Two yelling, scared deputies were about to start swinging at one another, until another deputy jumped in the middle and broke it up with an angry shout. He wondered what had gotten it started. Probably nothing more than a case of 'combat nerves'. It was common for people who had just lived through a death-defying situation to have strong, irrepressible feelings of anger, confusion, and fear, feelings that sometimes were released in violent ways.

Lincoln figured this whole thing was going to be blamed on a panther or a bear. No one would mention neither of those predatory species had been seen in these parts in a damn long time. Everyone was going to lie to one another and eventually go on with their lives, as if this night had never happened. And the survivors would pretend that what they'd seen tonight in those woods was imagination and fear and dark.

That was the way it always happened in Ellison. No outsider would dare admit that something strange and deadly might be happening in these woods. And no one in town wanted to talk about it. He would be expected to go along with the official version and not make any waves with the press.

But Lincoln was tired of turning the other way.

Maybe it's time to go have a talk with the real residents of Algernon Wood. The flesh and blood ones. Maybe it's time to get some real answers for once.

Coon was crying again, his thin shoulders shaking. Lincoln tapped his cousin's hand with the bottle and gave it back to him. Coon needed it more than he did right now. Lincoln laid his head back and let sleep take him while he waited for backup.

CHAPTER -16-

The cloistered, candle lit bedroom smelled of blood, the stifling air heavy with barely contained violence. It was a sinister primordial stink Stewart Machen knew well enough. Birth was not an easy thing; within its creative turmoil there had always been the dichotomy of the stink of decay to match. In his youth, it had seemed less like a stink than a welcome and heady scent heralding great things to come for the family, a spawning of one of the mysterious things of shadow and light that had been the birthright of all the Machen women since the time of Algernon. Now the accompanying stench made Stewart slightly queasy if he breathed of it for too long at a time. And after an hour of watching his mother, the room seemed to be constricting around him like a slimy humid fist.

He glanced at the shadows dancing in a dream like procession on the wall and wondered how much longer she was going to drag out the ritual. He just wanted to be finished with it. Why she had to keep popping these fucking things out once a month was beyond him. It seemed to him, with age, his mother had grown more attached to the servants—or perhaps it was only the agonizing birth ritual she'd come to enjoy, the pain of their rapid gestation, and slow oozing release from her wasted womb. Perhaps because this was the closest thing to the human act of giving birth she'd ever be allowed to experience again. At her age she still had all the basic weaknesses of her sex; she still saw herself as creator, giver of life.

His mother screamed as her belly distended, crowned. Her naked withered frame glistened with sweat and embryonic fluids. Her spoken words warped and broke against the agony of birth.

Her son felt no pity for her, as he watched her ancient body bend and twist unnaturally across the tousled bed. If she were more careful with the servants, she wouldn't need to keep doing this. But she was always finding new ways to test the things, to see just how much they could stand before dissipating like smoke from a chimney. Even these demonic creations could stand only so much maltreatment before they simply gave up the ghost. Good thing the creatures were not made of more stern stuff, he thought with sardonic humor, or else the skeletons would cover this place like an open tomb.

Charlotte twisted on the stained canopy bed. The bedclothes were scattered all about, most lying off of the bed, stained with her excrement and urine, and that peculiar vomitous fluid she always excreted when giving birth to her servants. She groaned incomprehensibly, muttered something in a half heard language, and trashed against the terrible tides churning within her body. From between her legs, a glistening head appeared, black, malformed and smoking with brimstone and ash. The thing was puling even as it grappled with her inner thighs to snake itself from her body. Despite its kitten like wails, its face was a blank slate, no mouth, eyes or nose. As it slithered out and flopped to the soaked bed sheets, Stewart grimaced at its writhing body. It waved its stubby fingerless and toeless limbs in a pantomime of life. Already that sickly light was pulsing in its center as it expanded, drawing sustenance from whatever hell she had conjured it.

Charlotte cried out as her womb emptied, sobs wracking her body. She tensed, arched her crooked back from the sodden, red stained bed again as another soulless one bubbled up within her belly. Stewart moved back from the bed in disgust. Her belly drew tight all the criss-crossing scars along her skin. She screamed again, still uttering the words of power, still smiling in her agony and joy. Her body flopped back down, arched again in that timeless rhythm, pumping up and down like a fleshy jackhammer. Her thin legs shook as the thing battered against the gate of her flesh for release.

She moaned in an almost sexual ecstasy, tearing at the sodden red sheets, pushing herself up on the balls of her feet in a red faced sudden tensing of every muscle in her emaciated frame.

The stink increased—like spoiled bloody meat.

A wet sound trashed between Charlotte's legs and a familiar orange glow emanated from the round suppurating pink, gray hair shrouded hole. Another of the things writhed free from its wet bleeding exit, flopped next to its kin on the bed. Within the mewling beast's trembling chest a weak orange light began to pulse in time with its brother.

Stewart turned away in disgust. There had been a time when he had taken as much pleasure from the birth of the creatures as his mother. They were quite useful in their own way and made for welcome divergences when times were lean for entertainment.

The things stood up to quite a bit of punishment and play, and knew exactly what you liked and how hard you liked it. But as he grew older, he found himself getting bored with their nebulous flesh and needed real flesh to do his bidding. Which had been the bane of all the Machen males. All but Conley. The boy had never been able to properly appreciate the uses of the flesh. Or the value of blood, for that matter.

Then he heard something that jarred his very soul. It was the alarm bell for the chamber below the house. Someone was trying to get inside the room.

Stewart left his mother to her own writhing devices and went to a small bank of monitors near the desk on the other side of the room. With the click of a switch, he saw the reason for the alarm. Sully was trying to get inside the chamber. And from the looks of things, doing a good job of it. He'd already removed the security keypad's faceplate and the door was open.

Handy bastard, but this was definitely going to put a crimp in his dealings with Garlen. Now that Sully had seen what the chamber held, he was going to have to disappear. He couldn't be allowed to leave the house. There were too many decades of careful manipulation and secret planning to allow for someone like that nosy fuck to ruin it all.

Stewart changed the view on the camera, to capture the inside of the chamber. He watched Sully inspect the room, saw his confusion and eventual dawning horror at what the place represented. He went to the bookcase and rifled through Stewart's most prized possessions, his books of power.

"No, no, no," he muttered as he saw Sully grab the one volume from its shelves that he could allow anyone to read. It was his great grandfather's diary, a written history of the pact. He watched Sully depart the secreted chamber with a cold sense of inevitability. He had always disliked Garlen Winters' bodyguard, had never trusted his watchful eyes and emotionless gaze. Now he'd proven himself a thief as well.

From across the room Charlotte called out for him in a wheezing, phlegm-filled voice, but Stewart ignored her and continued his unknown observance of the big bodyguard. A vein pulsed in his throat with rage. He stabbed the monitor control and the screens died. If only he had the power to remotely do the same to that bastard, Sully. But he knew there was no place Sully could hide inside Machen mansion that he could not find him and retrieve his property.

He left the dead bank of monitors behind and went to the bed where Charlotte was fondling and licking her newborn monsters of smoke and shadow. The things rubbed against her in sexless ecstasy.

"I've got something I must do, mother," he said past rage clenched teeth.

But Charlotte was too lost in her play with the creatures to pay him any heed as he hurried from the room and into the dim hallways of the mansion.

CHAPTER -17-

Jeb awoke to the sound of dogs baying somewhere beyond the swamp. He was alone again. His Daddy had left sometime around sundown, gone into town to get "supplies"—another way of saying he wouldn't be back until sunup. Daddy's idea of supplies usually meant sucking down whiskey and suds down at the local bar, passing out somewhere along the way.

He wished he'd come home with real supplies this time. Jeb hadn't eaten a proper meal since the say before and the rain had kept the traps bare. He was so hungry, he'd even tried to cook some palmetto root for supper. But the roots were bitter and he'd vomited up the soapy strands of his improvised meal within an hour.

Jeb sat up in the moonlight filtering through the shack's dilapidated walls. It cast its wan light across the dirty floor at the foot of his bed: a simple wooden frame covered by a thin and worn mattress. He watched the dappled shadows of the leaves outside play along the floor, his mind trying to wrap around the sound of so many dogs barking at once. It was an unusual thing to hear in Algernon Wood, especially this close to the swampy parts. Not too many reasons he could think of for folks around here to take their hounds out in those woods at night.

Somebody must be missing again. Somebody that wasn't no swamp rat. The Sheriff would never risk losing man or beast in Algernon Wood unless it was somebody important.

Maybe it was the President of the United States out there in those woods alone, he thought excitedly. Or, even better, one of the Machens. Why, if it was one of the seldom seen Machens out there, and he could find them, bring them back, maybe they would be so happy they would give him and his Daddy some money. Then they could get a real house, so they wouldn't have to live in this shack anymore. Maybe there would even be enough money so they could bury Mama in a real cemetery.

Jeb drifted now, excited by his scenario, lost in the pretend glories of finding Mr. Machen, who would, of course, be scared and shaking, and Jeb would certainly have to keep calming him down as he coerced him gently back to civilization once more. And, of course, Mr. Machen would faint before he could get him to their shack, and Jeb would have to use all his strength to pull the older man inside. Gasping with exhaustion, he would fall to the floor just as the Sheriff and a bunch of reporters with flashing cameras came bursting in to see old Mr. Machen bent over a hardly comatose Jeb, promising him anything, anything at all, if he would only live to receive his just reward.

A sound woke him from his dream. Something big was snuffling around the shack wall near his bed. He could hear its weight scrubbing against the wall, could feel its size pressing toward him, separated only by a thin barrier of half-rotting wood and tarpaper. When he heard the familiar sound of quiet snorting, he knew the 'monster' for what it was, and felt silly that he had let a wild boar rooting for food scare him so much.

Jeb tried to go back to sleep but found himself wide-awake, too itchy to get back to sleep again. His hunger had come awake with him and now it refused to be quelled again. He wanted to be out in the night now, to feel the chill swamp breeze cooling his skin, and taste the dankness at the back of his throat. Maybe he could find some berries to eat. Maybe he'd even give the palmetto roots another shot.

He lay there for a few moments, until the sound of the searching pig moved on, then rose from his bed and dressed. Tucking the bottoms of the pants in an old pair of his Daddy's mud boots, he went outside.

The night sounds that had been so loud from inside the shack were deafening now. He couldn't have heard himself shout with as much racket as there was tonight. The way the frogs were going on probably meant that there was rain due again, either tonight or early tomorrow morning. One look at the night sky peeking through the thickness of the black canopy overhead told him he was safe for a little while yet, though. The moon was bright and clear, no obfuscating clouds yet.

The swamp waters shimmered dank silver beneath his feet as he made his way to the boards spanning the swamp surrounding the shack. He walked carefully along the sagging rotting planks, like a captive on a privateer, until he had the sensation of being utterly swallowed up by the swamp. When he looked back, he could see the small light of the shack like a distant star shining in deep space. He closed his eyes and let the night embrace him. It was as if he could hear sound in his closed and familiar world. Even the most mundane noises took on new depth this evening. It was as if his senses had been heightened somehow.

To his left, a good distance away, he heard a gator grunt and hiss, maybe a warning to a curious scavenger. In the woods to his right, a raccoon chattered over a meal. Further on, in the trees before him, an owl queried the night endlessly.

Who? Who?

The night did not answer.

Jeb went from one sound to another, allowing himself to be dragged along by the intoxicating feeling of connection. His usual fears of the swamp, and the secrets held in its depths, did not slow his breathless progress. Soon, much to his surprised trepidation, he found himself much further away from the shack than he had intended. This time, when he looked back, the light was no longer visible through the tree trunks. And the sounds that had seemed so wonderful strange a moment before now took on new, more sinister, import. The night sounds closed in around him, as if the clangor had become a solid wall cutting him off from civilization.

The boy cursed himself for a fool. He had gotten himself out in the middle of the swamp, and, while he was able to find his way with ease during the daylight hours, night was an altogether different story. There was no familiarity to the thick faceless trunks walling him in, no trail leading from one copse to the other that he could see. All was shadow and moonlight.

Then, to make his bad situation worse, the bright moon that had been his only saving grace in the darkness slithered behind a torn stretch of black clouds, and the shadows closed in around him.

Trying in vain to keep his knees from shaking, Jeb turned to follow his path back. He knew he should be able to see his footprints leading back to where he had left the plank footpath. All he had to do was walk slowly and carefully back the way he had come until he found the trail. But as he peered at the sodden ground, he discovered his folly. The recent rain had turned the ground into a vast sponge that had soaked up too much water. His steps had been forgotten, soaked into the hungry memory of water and mud. There were no imprints for him to follow.

Now true panic began to settle in. Jeb had heard stories from the old folks about how people got lost in the swamp, never to be seen again. No one, not even someone like himself who had been born and raised in the swamp, was immune to the rules of living within its ancient borders. It was dangerous and it didn't tolerate fools. Going off in any direction at this point might only compound his precarious position. He had to be careful.

He supposed he could just stand here until morning. Surely, he could not be very far away from the shack. Perhaps with sunlight the shack would be easier to see.

Jeb looked around, spying for some kind of place to sit until sunrise. He found a massive ancient willow tree. It stretched as high as any of the surrounding oaks and pines. Its gray twisted branches intertwined into locked puzzles of wood and leaf, tore at the sky with grasping fingers. Long beards of Spanish moss hung down from its heights and dragged the ground in ghost like pale curtains. Jeb avoided touching them for fear of chiggers. Once they got under your skin, there wasn't anything short of an alcohol bath that'd get rid of them. He sat down, feeling the cold wet ground soaking through his pants, and leaned his back against the thick trunk.

Jeb closed his eyes and tried to recapture that sense of vital connection that had led him astray. If he had to be stuck out here at least he could investigate the strange feeling again, maybe mentally walk around it a little until he figured out why he had been inflicted (or blessed?) by it this night.

He grasped for it with all his senses, stretched his nose, his ears, his very soul towards that remembered sensation. But, try as he might, a repeat of the wonderful event eluded him. He could still hear the night creatures going about their timeless appointed errands of survival, could smell the sweet familiar dankness of the waters around him, but as strong as each sound and smell was to his searching mind, none of them got close to that previous sensation of belonging to something larger than himself.

His stomach gurgled in rebellious, remembered hunger.

Then the night went quiet

He shifted nervously against the trees smooth bark, watchful, half afraid he would see something staring back him from the obscuring layers of shadow.

A rotten meat stink wafted from the night, subsuming him. Jeb held back a gag of revulsion, afraid to give away his position to whatever belonged to that terrible stench.

The night seemed to hold its collective breath. Just like before. When he'd seen the Black Beast.

The moon escaped the cloud cover in time to blanket the wood in silver light.

Something limp and heavy flew from the trees before him. Jeb yelped as a half eaten deer landed at his feet. Something had torn apart its lower half; what remained were the head, broken antlers and glistening dead black eyes, bloodied muzzle, and the upper torso; ropy intestines oozed body fluids.

Jeb looked from the deer to the trees from where it had been thrown. Two glittering eyes watched him. He heard a grunt and a snuffle. Then the eyes disappeared. Soon, the night sounds returned.

Jeb touched the cold deer corpse at his feet, petting the velveteen fur with something approaching awe.

It had given him a gift. But why? What did it want in return?

His fingers made their way to the soft raw meat at the deer's neck. Blood oozed at his touch. Jeb could smell the meat now and his stomach ached to taste it.

He wanted to wait until morning when he could make it back to the shack so he could properly cook the gift, but his hunger won out. He grabbed a knot of meat from the deer's shattered upper ribcage and tore it away with a soft grunt of anticipation. He brought the raw bleeding offering to his mouth and bit into it. It was stringy, but tasted like heaven at the moment. Jeb gobbled down the uncooked meat with animal sounds of delight and contentment. After a few more handfuls, his hunger abated and he was reminded of what he was doing, eating raw meat. The fine taste from moments before faded and he stopped, wiping blood from his hands and face. He expected the deer meat to go the way of the palmetto roots from earlier in the evening, but the food stayed down and he sat back.

His thoughts wandered, concerned but gratified by the strange and unexpected offering. After a time, his attention went back to earlier concerns about the sensation of being connected into the vast mainframe of the swamp.

Jeb fell asleep with his mind still searching for reasons why he had been shown such a delight to have it snatched away again so cruelly. Fast asleep, he never heard the echoing, distant sounds of violence as Sheriff Lincoln's search party met their fate.

Night in Algernon Wood moved along its usual ancient pace, uncaring of life and death.

CHAPTER -18-

Clutching the book under his arm, he hurried from the place, making sure that the heavy iron door clang shut and locked behind him. Back up the bare wooden steps, and, soon, he left behind the crumbling stone and bare light bulbs, and found the upper floors of the mansion. In the twisting and reaching hallways and stairways, twice he paused when he saw a glowing orange light pulsing in the darkness ahead. But both times the light faded and finally disappeared after a few moments of tense waiting.

The whole time, he could feel the terrible weight of the book in his arms.

It took him about an hour to find his room again. He slunk inside, went to check on Garlen, who was still snoring in the big canopied bed. As much as he wanted to wake his employer, make him share this terrible discovery with him, he wanted more to look over his evidence first. Now that he was in the relative sane light of the upper floors again, he needed to calm himself and step back to take a logical approach as to what should be done next. Contact the authorities, yes. But who first? And there was Mary and Timmy to consider before he did anything else.

Sully emptied his pockets, laid his gun and flashlight on the dresser, then went to the bathroom and switched on the light. At the sink he washed his face and hands of dust and cobwebs that he'd accumulated during his travels, and then he sat down on the closed lid of the toilet to see what the book held.

Sullly sat on the closed toilet, his head in his hands, the book in his lap. His eyes were red and felt like sandpaper against the inside of his lids. Now that he had gotten back to a sanctuary of sorts, his exhaustion was getting the best of him. But the heavy ancient book held answers he desperately needed. As tired as he was, there was inside him also a sense of urgency about what the book contained. A glance at his watch told him it was only two hours until sunrise. Plenty of time to see what Stewart Machen felt he had to hide from the rest of the world.

In the enclosed space of the bathroom, the ancient mustiness of tome wafted in the humid air. Sweat rolled down his brow, dripped to the tile floor.

He opened the book. The leathery covers creaked and crackled, excreting ancient dust on his shaking hands. The first few pages were filled with figures that meant nothing to Sully, and looked more like financial records of some kind. He scanned further until he found the diary entries he'd seen before. The small evenly spaced lines were written in a tight, scratchy hand, skittering along the yellowed pages like running spiders.

Sully read the first entry:

August 20th

This forest is strange, somehow seemingly darker than any other I've ever seen. It is the first thing I noticed upon my arrival in this lost forest of the Georgia outback. At night, it as if the real world, the world to which I once belonged, has disappeared. We are the first white men to step foot in this place; I am sure of it.

I have come to survey and raze this hidden land in the name of commerce. It is here that I hope to start my fortune. For I cannot hope to receive any fortune from my father. He has disowned me, thrown me from the house. From his heart. He has found out about the women and does not understand. The 'hideous acts of depravations' as he terms the experiments, he has thankfully kept secret from my dear mother. My 'indiscretions' would dishonor the family, and cause her no end of grief. I think he'd be surprised at what mother could, and, indeed, has endured without his knowledge. After all, she has needs, physical needs that father has not been able to perform for some time now. The dear girl had sought comfort in the arms of those that she finds familiar and safe."

August 21st

"Today I met the troop of sixteen men with which I am for some time to share my camp, a disgusting lot- every one of them thoroughly filthy. They stink like animals. The half-grunted conversations I hear remind more of pigs than men. Exceedingly violent men, given to drunken brawling, and the pulling of hidden knives to settle a disagreement. It sickens me, being around such vileness. My father wished to punish me, wished to send me to Hell, as he said. He has succeeded."

Sully skipped ahead, ignoring entries about logging, geometry, and day-to-day trivia, until his scanning eyes found an interesting entry:

September 5th

"Something odd has happened this night.

As we sat round the campfire outside our communal sleeping quarters, several quiet shapes stole upon us from out of the dark forest. Norton, who was sitting across from me, grew quiet and watchful and called our attention to the fact of their presence as he leaned forward in the guise of getting more coffee. The word passed quickly in whispers from one man to the next until everyone was on alert. These shadow shapes crouched within the bush and watched us for some time.

Wilton made it known by hand and facial signals that he was all for rushing the shapes and attacking them. But, luckily, we were able to talk him out of such a foolhardy maneuver. Instead, everyone seemed to follow my lead, and we waited for what would happen next.

As the fire died down, I threw a log on, sending fireflies into the night air. At the sudden flare, our lurkers slunk back into the forest beyond, leaving us unmolested. After we were sure of their departure, we doused the fire and retired to the cabin, barring the door behind us."

Nothing more for a few more days. Sully wiped sweat from his brow and flipped the heavy pages.

September 12th

"Lost a man today. Norton. He was last seen in the East quadrant this morning, marking trees for cutting, as per his assignment. Sometime after noon, another logger, Markos, half a mile from Norton's position, heard a terrific scream. He raced to Norton's aid only to find him gone. No trace of him,

nothing left but his tools scattered about the base of a giant oak tree. Markos hurried back to camp and three of us followed him back, armed and cautious. But there was not a drop of blood, nor strip of cloth, to indicate our companion's fate. My suspicions is that he was waylaid by a passing bear, or, perhaps, a panther- two species of carnivore that must be prevalent in this part of the wood, for we have found numerous skeletal remains belonging to both.

I suppose Norton's strange disappearance might be attributed to our visitors from last week, stolen away for some savage purpose of their own. I have heard that the Indians have been known to eat the flesh of humans. But why would they attack now, and in broad daylight, when they could have done us all in the other night before we were even aware of their presence?"

September 12th-night

"The Seminoles have returned. I am writing this entry by the sheltered light of a single dim candle sitting beside my bed, so as not to disturb the others. They have had an exciting night and need their sleep. It was hard enough to keep them from rushing the near-silent shadows lurking in the bush all around us, especially Wilton. After Norton's disappearance, these men firmly believe in an eye for an eye. Some of us, too few of us to my liking, were able to convince them, otherwise. But I do not know how much longer our talk will stop them if there is another disappearance.

Instead, they trade stories tonight, and tell of evil spirits the savages can call forth and control. I do not know if I believe in such demons or not. But I do know that I would prefer not to have to make such a choice in this forbidden black wood."

September 13th

"Two more men have disappeared this day. This time there were no screams. I cannot be sure that they met with violence. It's entirely possible that they left on their own recognizance."

September 18th

"Several of the men reported hearing strange noises outside our cabin last night. When asked to describe them, they claim the sounds were of something shambling back and forth outside the bunker walls. I'm not sure if I believe or not, but am considering posting a guard."

September 23rd

"Supplies are getting low. I sent a six-man team this morning to get more. They would not agree to go without at least that many. I have outfitted them with our small buggy, Jehovah, our mule, guns and ammo aplenty. They have been warned that if any living thing approaches them, especially the savages, for I am still unconvinced that they play no little part in these worries somehow, they are to shoot to kill."

September 28th

"The wagon has not returned."

September 29th

"Still no sign of the wagon or the men that I sent out several days before. It is the general consensus among the remainder

of us- eight now!- they may have run into problems with the wagon, the mule, or both. No one says what lies heavy in all our hearts. They have been swallowed up by this damnable forest like the others."

October 2nd

"Even the stouthearted individuals among us now agree it's likely the six man team have met with a bad end. Scalped and eaten by the savages, perhaps.

Work has stopped altogether for these past several days. I cannot convince any man of the group to go beyond a few hundred yards from the camp. Certainly not outside of shouting distance.

What are we to do now? We have very little supplies. Even for the small remainder of our party. They will not last out to the end of the week."

October 2nd-night

"The Seminoles came once more tonight. One of the dark skinned bastards came forward. Dressed in a rough looking animal skin that hung to his knees, face shiny with sweat and grime, and his dark eyes reflecting the light of our fire, he tossed a pile of white man's clothing into our midst. The shirt and pants were bloody and torn, ripped to bits as if by a large beast. They had belonged to Fletcher, one of the men who'd been part of the supply run."

October 3rd

"The thing came back last night. And now I know that I do not dream. In the night, another man has disappeared

with no trace. We leave this day. We will follow the logging trail through the wood, in the hopes of getting away before night falls again. We start at first light."

October 3rd-afternoon

"Several hours into our escape, we have found the wagon. It was deserted. No bodies anywhere. The mule is gone, too. Snyder took two of the men and searched the immediate area, but all they found was a rusted pistol, the cylinder half-empty.

I only wish that I could now convince myself that something so mundane as the Seminoles are to blame for their disappearance.

I ordered the search quickly ended. We have too little time before nightfall, less than eight hours."

October 3rd-early evening

"Disaster has struck our party again! We have been slowed to a crawl. In our hurry to leave this place behind, one of the men, Hooper, has broken his leg. What will become of us now?"

October 3rd-near sunset

"Snyder has solved our problem. With night approaching, and fearful of finding ourselves trapped in this forest primeval after dark, Synder has shot Hooper in the head. The others gave him dire looks, but Snyder dared any man to do anything about it. It did solve our problem quite succinctly, but the truth is not any easier to like. A couple of the men wanted to give poor, dead Hooper a Christian burial,

but Snyder told them he would shoot the first man to pick up a shovel.

In the end we left him slumped against a pine tree trunk and hurried away.

I expect trouble from the men, later. They hate Synder and I wouldn't be surprised if one of them tries to kill him for his actions this day, no matter how necessary for our survival."

October 3rd-night

"Night has fallen and we are still encamped in this damnable wood. The darkness surrounds us like a living beast. My heart sounds too loud in this place, my breath like a clarion. We have several miles to find civilization again. I am afraid that this may be the last entry. I can only hope that someone might find these words and take warning against exploration of the dark corners of the world."

October 4th-early morning

"The night brought horror upon horror. If I live to be a hundred, which I highly suspect will not be the case, for I doubt I shall see another sunset, I will never forget the things I saw last night. I am the only one left now. I have levered myself into the bole of a gigantic tree, as far back as the tree will allow me to squeeze into its hollowed out body. I await my end."

Sully skipped the next few pages, for they rambled on without sense or meaning. He stopped when he found a coherent entry. There was no date.

Evening

"I have been told that it's been days since I left the safety of my hiding place to search for water. I recall staggering out of the tight hole, and then falling a great distance with nothing to catch me for miles around.

The savages have brought me back to their village, which is some distance from the abandoned logging camp. They are slowly nursing me back to health. We don't talk much, using hand signals whenever the need arises to communicate in our limited fashion. Their village is surprisingly well ordered, clean, and quiet. They subsists mainly on fruits and vegetables, some deer meat. Their homes, and even their clothes, are constructed from the hides of animals they've eaten. No part of the animal is wasted.

They are friendly enough, but seem to fear me. Some of the older men visit me and gesticulate wildly as they try to tell me something. But I can only nod and smile, for I do not understand their heathen language. Eventually they lose their patience and leave me alone again.

They allow me out now. I walk among them, watching the daily rituals they must perform to fill their heathen bellies, to make things run smoothly for the tribe. When I limp towards the surrounding woods to see if anything lies beyond this camp, one of them always tries to gesture me back to the center of the cluttered domiciles. I allow myself to be led back, wondering why they will not let me near the woods.

Not that I want to go out into their bleak depths.

That thing is still out there somewhere; I can feel it waiting and watching even now. I have no need to test its power again.

The women stay well clear of me. Which is a shame, because as my strength grows, so does my secret need. Perhaps it is the presence of the fairer sex again, or perhaps it was facing my own death, whichever, it has caused a reawakening of the heat inside of me that screams for release. I can scarce control it. Something is happening to me and I don't know how to explain it. My taste for experimentation is a beast within me. There is so much more I can do. I must find some way to get at one of them, preferably one of the little ones. That way there won't be such a fight to get her alone, to do what I need to do. I've been sharpening my knife on and off for days, readying myself if the opportunity presents itself."

Morning, date unknown

"It came to me last night and spoke. But not in words. It showed me through a series of glorious sensations what it could give me if only I would agree to its infernal soul contract, a hideous agreement. Suffice it to say this Black Beast requires a servant and it has promised me much to do its bidding. It knows things about me that no living person could ever know. It knows all about my fun with the wayward girls in Atlanta. It knows all about my need to experiment upon the flesh of the whores. It knows every cut I ever made into the living flesh on one of my subjects.

Surely, this thing is the devil. And what it purposes is the devil's work, indeed. But it is either me or them."

Evening, same day

"The deed is done. I belong to this creature, body and soul. But I still live. They are gone and I live.

Last night the thing came for the savages and took every last one of them. With the exception, as per our agreement, of one little girl of about ten years of age. I was its way and guide for the death of the savages. Now it shows me how it is going to give me life. A long and fruitful life. All I need to do is find a wife and get her with child. With my fortune that will not be a problem. I can now buy a wife, if needs be. When the child comes along, there is the rest of the soul contract to be fulfilled.

The Black Beast has given me the ritual words and signs needed for fulfillment of the rest of our agreement. These precious things must be passed from one male Machen to the next, to forever be remembered. All Machens belong to it now. The Black Beast owns my soul.

There is one catch to this infernal contract.."

Sully gasped in shock. He reread the entry, unsure of its import. The words became clear as the dawning realization hit home.

"...to break it means death for another Machen of the male sex."

Sully shut the leather bound journal with a sick taste in his mouth.

If any of this was even half true…

No, he couldn't bring himself to believe that someone in their right mind would do the things required by this imaginary creature called the Black Beast. The man who had written this was surely insane. That could be the only explanation.

He hefted the book in his hands, feeling a sick repugnance.

Garlen needed to see this. Mary, too. Her son was a Machen male. Her husband's death had broken this supposed contract with the imaginary devil of the woods the Machens believed in. That put boy in great danger. Conley Machen had broken the contract and now another Machen male had to be used as a replacement.

Sully didn't have to believe in any of it to see that Stewart was insane enough to use his own grandson as a sacrifice to this thing- whatever the hell it was. Why else did he have all that shit in the hidden and secured room? He was planning to use Timmy to keep his family's end of the contract with some imaginary monster.

Sully stood and stretched. He'd been sitting for a couple of hours now and his legs were half asleep. The electric tingle of awakening nerves skittered up his calves and ankles. As he reached for the door, behind him a panel slid away and a shadow stepped forward. The shadow moved swiftly; a hypodermic needle appeared from its sleeve. It jabbed Sully in the neck. The big man had time to grunt in surprise, and half turn before the drug hit his system like a wave of darkness. He staggered, trying to catch hold of the dimming shape before him. But his body gave out and he slumped to the floor.

The shape grabbed his ankles and dragged him through the hidden doorway. The panel slid quietly back into place and the figures disappeared.

CHAPTER -19-

Lincoln stopped the patrol car in front of the massive Machen Mansion. His body felt every knock he'd taken last night and sleep beckoned him. But he knew there were questions that needed answers and the only place to find them was inside this house.

He made his weary way up the front steps and rang the doorbell. When the door was finally opened, it was Charlotte Machen's pale mushroom face that frowned up at him. Lincoln greeted her with a nervous smirk. She did not smile back, only looked at him like a disapproving mother staring down an insolent child. Her eyes told him how she felt about the local bumpkin sheriff dirtying her doorstep. Lincoln swallowed his anger and said, "Sorry to bother you this early, Mrs. Machen, but I need to talk with Mr. Machen. He around?"

Her lips pinched into a severe line of disapproval. "Stewart is not available right now. May I deliver a message?"

So she thought she was going to shoo him away like a dirty-footed child?

Lincoln shook his head. "No, ma'am. I'm afraid that ain't gonna be good enough. I need to know where he is and how to get in touch with him right now." His face was red and hot, but he could barely look her in the eye. Some things were hard to get over; like his deference to the Machens. They both knew he had every right to ask where Mr. Machen was, but she wanted to play Southern matriarchal games with him. "Please," he added almost as an afterthought, hoping to temper the demand.

Charlotte's eyes widened and her stooped shoulders shifted, as if she were unconsciously making her small body a barrier against his entrance into the house. "As you well know, Sheriff," she said his authoritarian title as if it was shit in her mouth. "I can't do that." Her thin lips quivered with Machen outrage at his presumption.

Lincoln felt his own temper rising at her finality.

By God, he was going to get inside and right now. Who the hell did this old bag of bones think she was? He was the, by God, Sheriff here. Not her. Not the, by God, almighty Machens.

Lincoln shoved his foot inside the door, so she couldn't close it.

She looked at his foot. "How dare you? Why, I'll—"

"All I need to do is speak with Mr. Machen."

"I already told you, you ass-" she began, but Lincoln held up a hand and shoved his florid face nearer. "You want to watch your mouth right now, old woman. I am not in the mood to cow tow to the high and almighty fucking Machens this morning. I will come back here with a court order, if I need to. It might take me some time to get one, but I promise you, not everyone in the world gives a fuck about your money. Now do you want me to set the wheels in motion?"

Charlotte's mouth hung open in shock.

"I am not leaving this house until I see him. And I don't really have to be so nice about it either. I can go through this place room by room until I find him. Am I making myself clear?"

Charlotte shook with rage now. Her hands clenched and unclenched spastically at her withered hips. Lincoln thought she looked half ready to claw his eyes out. Not that he was too worried about a woman who probably weighed less a hundred and ten pounds, but he took a precautionary step back, just in case.

"That won't be necessary, Sheriff."

Lincoln looked past Charlotte to see Stewart Machen coming down a long sweeping staircase. He exchanged one last glare with Charlotte. "Mr. Machen," he said in a strained attempt at ease. "You might let your mother know it's against the law to lie to an officer of the law about someone's whereabouts when questioned."

"I'm sorry, Sheriff," Stewart said, flashing a toothy smile. "Mother gets a little too protective at times." He leaned close, whispered loudly enough his mother could hear every word. "She's getting along in years and loses control of her emotions sometimes."

Charlotte Machen's eyes narrowed as she gave her son a fierce glance.

Lincoln didn't like Stewart Machen's attempt to smile his mother's way out of the scene, but he only gave a noncommittal grunt, decided to let it go. This time. No need to push too hard for now. But things were going to change in Ellison. Starting today there would be no mistake who was the law here.

Lincoln nodded at the old woman and gave

her a half smile. "Nothing to make a scene over, Mr. Machen." She did not return the smile. She looked like a wolf bitch about to leap for his throat. He ignored her. "Is there some place we can talk in private?"

"Of course." Stewart motioned him to a hallway to the left of the staircase. Lincoln followed the old man's brisk stride, ignoring the heat of the old woman's stare at his back. The darkness swallowed them. All he could see for a few seconds was the old man's back, dimming and getting dimmer, as if they had descended into a tunnel instead of a hallway.

Christ. As rich as these assholes were, you'd think that they could turn on a goddamn light or two around here.

If he stumbled over a piece of iron antique furniture and hurt himself, he was gonna sue the britches off these shit heels.

A door opened, but it was only one kind of darkness to another, and Stewart disappeared inside. Lincoln hurried to catch up, feeling an unaccountable sense of fear at the nebulous power this murk had over his sight.

He stepped past the door and it closed behind with a quiet 'snick'. A small click sound, and the room rose up out of the dim yellow light. Lincoln looked over the contents of room. Next to a small table, the source of the dull light- a yellow beaded glass lamp. Antique weapons hung on the walls: swords, guns, and gleaming bayonets. Most of them looked to have come from the Civil War. A number of torn uniforms bedecked the room as well. Some had black stained bullet holes peppering the disintegrating fabric. There were also a number of gold buttons and tattered officer's braids behind a glass display case.

Seeing the treasures the room had to offer, Lincoln couldn't help but feel a little disgust for the old man. All this shit was just toys for a rich man who had too much money and too little imagination to know how to spend it. Pure old junk.

Lincoln found a chair next to a display of knives and scabbards, and eased his tired bulk into its less than comfortable wooden straightness. He felt as if he were about ready to collapse. He needed a couple of hours of sleep. But first he needed to get some information out of this old man. Then he could finally find a bed somewhere and get some shuteye. At least until the pissed off state boys found him. They weren't going to be none too happy about his having left the scene the way he had. But he figured there wasn't much he could do for them boys no how. They was all dead. No amount of pissed off state troopers was going to change that fact, by God.

Stewart went to a small cabinet next to a stand of rifles and bayonets and leaned over the open doors. Lincoln could see several decanters of golden and brown liquors. When he offered Lincoln a drink, he did not refuse. He accepted bourbon and sipped at the smooth elixir, letting the burn of the drink ride down his gullet.

Wasn't no reason why he couldn't drink the old bastard's alcohol. Besides, he needed a little something right now. And how often did a poor man get to taste only the best. For the Machens, he had no doubt that was the only thing they had.

Two swallows and he felt his fatigue settle a little lower on his slumped shoulders.

While Stewart mixed himself a drink, Lincoln said, "I lost about a dozen or so men last night out on your property, Mr. Machen." He watched the old man's face, but it was as impassive as a still lake of cold water on a winter night.

"Are they lost? Or are they dead?"

Lincoln frowned at the ludicrous question. The old man knew as well as he did in Algernon Wood there was no such thing as getting lost. "They're dead all right," he replied, taking another sip of bourbon. "Something was out in them woods with us last night. Whatever it was killed those men. We'll send another search party in a little while, but we both know what we're going to find. Nothing."

Stewart turned to watch Lincoln from the reflection of one of his cases.

He sipped more of his drink, glad to let it chase away his fears of the old bastard. Maybe if he drank enough he could tell the stupid old fuck what he thought of the Machens and the way they had treated his old man. God, he felt so tired…

"But you already know that, don'chu' you, Mizzer Machen," he repeated.

Now why had he done that? And had he slurred that last part? Why did his tongue feel so thick and heavy suddenly? And his arms and legs suddenly limbs felt useless too. What was going on here?

His eyes suddenly felt loose as marbles rolling around in his head. Lincoln shifted a heavy stare to the half full glass in his hand. His hand opened and the giant, too heavy glass fell to the floor. Golden rivers of alcohol spilled across the carpet.

"Ngghun mumm," he muttered.

The old man still had his back to him and began to softly whisper to himself. Lincoln could barely catch the words, but what he heard made no sense. It was too singsong, a hymnal cadence, a ceremonial noise. Hearing it, Lincoln wanted to cry, to sleep, to vomit, all at once, and he had no control to do any of them. His body was a slab of dead meat. He could feel his heart thumping slowly in his chest.

As his eyes began to slip closed, Stewart Machen turned, a sneering shark smile on his shriveled lips. The old man came toward him, pouring out streamers of psychedelic colors with every movement. A million years later, Stewart reached him. Lincoln's breath came in shallow snorts.

Machen's hand came slowly forward from the next galaxy. Thin, cold fingers brushed along his slack jaw. Lincoln forced his eyes open. Stewart Machen held one of the bayonets from the display case. The dull light played along its deadly edge; it glittered like ice in his glazed eyes. Crouching next to him, Stewart's lips touched his ear, like two cold oysters lying against his dumb flesh. But he was no longer uttering those gut crunching words, and for that, at least, Lincoln was grateful.

"Sorry, Sheriff," Stewart said, "it would be best if you disappeared after last night. I need to throw a little confusion into the mix, and you being gone will give the state goons someone to look for. Everyone will assume that you had something to do with it. And why not? Little towns like this are always full of secret murderers, aren't they?"

Lincoln felt those spidery fingers entangle themselves in his hair. The old man lifted his heavy head, exposing his throat.

Lincoln was helpless to prevent what he knew was coming next.

The ceiling shadows danced above him. Something loomed black in those shadows. Something cold touched his exposed throat, something sharp.

He felt a sharp stinging sensation across the flesh of his throat. Then he was gurgling on something hot and wet. The taste of blood on his clumsy tongue and knew it was his own. He wanted to grab his throat, hold the sliced flesh together, but his hands remained useless and numb.

Stewart watched the last light of life flicker from the Sheriff's eyes, then pushed the dead body to the blood stained floor. With seemingly no effort, the old man hefted Lincoln's three hundred plus pounds by the ankles and pulled him to the door, opened it, and dragged him out. In the hall outside the room, Stewart felt along the wall opposite the doorway. Within the gold and red filigree design, he triggered a release stud, and silently, a secreted door slid back to reveal a gloom filled mouth and steps leading down. He dragged the Sheriff's cumbersome weight inside. The door closed behind him, only a blood trail to mark his passage.

CHAPTER -20-

Awareness came back to Sully in sensory phases. First there was the pain in his head: A throbbing brand of icy fire. The steady drip...drip...drip of water from some unseen distance. Then came the smell. A familiar blood scent. Metal and stone. Past violence.

He knew where he was before he even opened his bleary eyes, back in the chamber where he'd stolen the diary only hours before. He was alone. Except for his small groans against the pain in his head, and the dripping of the water, the room was silent. Someone had done a bang up job of trussing him. His hands and feet were numb from the tightness of the thin, dirty rope.

How long? An hour? A day?

There was no way to know how long he'd been out. He was half sitting against the circular wall, facing the door that he'd come through before.

Sully gave his head an experimental shake and the room spun few seconds; nausea crawled up the back of his throat. Swallowing the desire to vomit, he tested the ropes. After a hard pull, he found them more than adequate to keep him form escape. The knots cut deep into his flesh, cutting off his blood supply; white and purple colored reams of his skin gleamed through the ropes. Much longer and he'd have to worry about serious blood constriction problems in his extremities. After a certain point, amputation was the only cure. But somehow he didn't figure whoever had brought him here was too worried his losing an arm or a foot.

Because he knew there was nothing else could do, Sully leaned against the wall and tried to think how he'd screwed up, trying to will the drug out of his system. Figuring out the identity of his captor was no great feat of deduction. Sully was sure Stewart Machen was responsible. Of course, he'd underestimated the man's madness- even after seeing this chamber and after reading the family diary. It was easy to see in hindsight that he'd probably been watched the whole time, Stewart possibly alarmed by some kind of silent trigger when he'd opened the door. The old man had something dastardly planned for him. Why else bother to keep him alive? He could've easily finished the job while he was out.

Time passed, and he caught himself slipping in and out of consciousness several times. But whenever he was able to keep from passing out, Sully tried to slowly twist his legs and arms around so that the knots moved past his discolored areas. It didn't do much good; he still couldn't feel much in his legs, but his hands were beginning to burn in a more painful way- a good sign he'd managed to get some much needed blood flowing back into them again.

Sully was methodically tensing and untensing his calf muscles, beginning to feel some pain in his lower legs of increased blood flow, when Stewart Machen came through the door. He was dragging a large man's body behind him. Sully recognized the discolored uniform. It was the big Sheriff he and the others had talked with before. The man's face was pale and lifeless, his eyes dead slits. His throat had been laid open by a neat rent across the wattle of flabby flesh. Dark arterial blood covered the dead man's lower torso.

Stewart pulled his burden to drop him at Sully's feet. The dead man's heels hit the floor with an empty thud.

"I brought you a little company," Stewart said. "But I'm afraid the conversation won't be too lively."

Sully looked from the body to Stewart. "You are one crazy old fuck. You know that?" Sully saw a sudden flash of rage in the old man's eyes, but then the easy handsome smile was back again. Stewart shook his head, clucking his tongue as if Sully had been a rude child. He was trying hard to convince Sully he was only amused. But he could tell the insult had hit pay dirt. Sully would remember that.

With rising hope, he let his gaze slip down the Sheriff's belt. But, of course, they were empty. How he could have gotten to a gun, if one had been there, wasn't something he'd considered. The empty holster made it useless speculation anyway.

"Of course, I know you found my diary," he turned to motion at the chamber, "and this room. So I'm afraid, Mr. Borland, you have to die."

Sully sighed, looked up at the ceiling with an air of insouciance, and shrugged. "You know, Machen, you're either the most evil motherfucker or the most bug fuck crazy son of a bitch I've ever had the displeasure to meet. I just can't decide."

Stewart leaned over Sully, a confused look in his eyes belying the amused smile on his face. "You're rather insolent for someone who's about to die soon,"

Stewart said. "I suppose I should be grateful for your boorish behavior. Better than begging for your life, young man. Shows real character to take it like this."

Sully knew his little speech was meant to rattle him, show him who was in control. But Sully had seen the flare of anger twice now, at his being called crazy. It was a weakness he hoped to exploit in his favor. "Do your worst, you fucking looney tune asshole."

For a moment, he saw anger so great- so overwhelming- in the old man's eyes Sully knew he'd hit the right button now. He laughed at Stewart's open mouth and his flaring nostrils. But to his disappointed surprise, Stewart began to laugh with him, huge guffaws that resounded across the stone walls of the chamber. Sully decided he didn't like the old man laughing with him.

"You know," Sully said, past forced chuckles. "If I get out of this alive I'm going to make you hurt real bad, you nutcase son of a bitch."

But his words did not have the intended effect. The rage was gone, replaced now by a steady eye and a firm hand. The old man had turned the table on him, laughing at the threats. Tears of mirth rolled from his eyes. Sully felt panic now, that he'd made the situation deadlier. He felt his chest tightening with increased terror. He was going to die. And there was no way for him to stop it.

But Sully refused to show his fear. Instead, he gave an unconcerned sneer, watched the old man's movements carefully. He might get a second and nothing more to strike. *If only he could get some more feeling in his legs...*

Stewart quieted his laughter to a snicker. "But you're not going to live through this, my boy. There won't be any last minute rescue for the damsel and themore.

"Kill you?" Stewart said. "Not by my hand, my boy. I have grander aspirations for your death than a simple judicious bullet to the head. Or a quick slit to the throat." He pointed at the Sheriff's corpse. "No, Mr. Borland, I've got more in store for you yet."

With that, Stewart tapped his foot somewhere behind the pedestal and Sully heard the sound of grinding, stone on stone. A round portal set in the wall behind the altar slid aside, and the pedestal moved back to allow room for it to open. The dank stink of the swamp overwhelmed the room. Inside the portal, there was a profound darkness; Sully could hear lapping water.

Stewart left the altar and walked back to the corpse. He hefted the Sheriff's weight by his thick leather belt, and muscles standing out on his lean frame, the old man pulled him to the low portal opening. With a slight grunt, he heaved his carcass through it. There was a muted splash.

Red faced from his exertions, Stewart made his way back to Sully. From his pant pocket, he pulled a pistol, aimed it at Sully's chest as he approached. It was the Sheriff's gun, the one he'd boasted about to Timmy the morning before.

Sully stared the old man in the eye, refusing to look away from his approaching doom. Despite his claim against a bullet to the head, the gun's barrel still looked bigger than portal to the unknown at the moment.

But Stewart didn't shoot him. From his other pant pocket he retrieved a folding knife, and using his straight white teeth, he hinged out a silver flash of blade. He leaned forward, keeping out of range of Sully's teeth, and sawed away his bonds. "It'll be more fun this way," he said.

"What the hell are you talking about?" Sully asked.

But Stewart only gave him an enigmatic smile.

The ropes fell away with a whisper and Sully's near-paralyzed body lay akimbo on the cold floor. He began to demand an answer, his panic seeping to the surface of his controlled emotions. Then the pain hit him and his mind could fathom nothing else.

Burning cold. Pulsing needles of heat. Then numbness, followed by too much feeling, as the creeping blood began once more to circulate through his writhing body. Sully gritted his teeth against anguished groans. Past the pain, Sully's mind easily devised a hundred different ways he could take the old bastard out right now, but he couldn't move any more than he could with the ropes around him.

Stewart kept the gun trained on him. "When you're able, I want you to go to the portal and jump in, Mr. Borland."

"Fuck you," Sully managed to gasp past the agony. His head swam with darkness again, threatening to sink him into a faint once more. If that happened, he knew he was good as tossed in that fucking portal! He fought against the surging waves of inner darkness, clenched his jaws against the burning agony in his arms and legs. *He had to keep conscious! Had to think of something to save himself! To save the others!*

"A smart man like yourself, would do as I say," Stewart said. "At least in there you have a chance to survive. A very, very slim one." His tone hardened, devoid of amusement. "And if you don't do as I say, I'll put a fucking bullet in your head and throw you in anyway."

"Bullshit," Sully snarled between gritted teeth. "You won't do that, Machen. For some reason you want me alive when I go in there. You've got something planned." He jerked his head towards the dark mouth of the portal. "What's in there? Gators? Snakes?"

Stewart's cold smile sent chills up Sully's convulsing spine. "Much worse," he said. "But you'll know that soon enough." He gave a savage kick to child."

He turned away from Sully, made his way up the altar steps in the middle of the raised stone dais. As he continued, he spoke louder, so that Sully could hear him from across the room. "You've read the diary, of course, so you must know what has to happen for me to continue to survive." He struck a match and began to light the braziers to either side of the pedestal standing before the hewn rock altar.

Sully felt a rush of rage at knowing what Machen intended for Timmy; he didn't even want to give thought to what he might intend for the boy's mother. "Yeah, I read it. So is everyone in your family a fucking nutcase? Your great grandfather sure as hell was."

Stewart nodded without looking at him. "Oh, he had his proclivities, to be sure, Mr. Borland. But crazy? No, he knew things about what lies behind this veil we call life, things that would drive a normal man insane. He was a visionary. A prophet."

Sully snorted derisively. "He was fucked in the head. Just like you." He felt like he was standing before a badger's lair, poking and prodding the beast within, trying to get it to attack.

But Stewart seemed to have grown bored with the conversation. "People like you, Mr. Borland, are merely pawn on the chessboard of life, fodder to be used by great men like myself. Your opinion is of no consequence at all." It had been said with such disdain, that Sully knew he'd lost the advantage he sought. The old man's anger could not be used to make him do something stupid Sully might use to his advantage. And, ultimately, there was no argument with a mad man.

"If you're going to kill me, get on with it," he said.

"In such a hurry?" Stewart asked, with a bemused smile.

"I'm in no hurry to die, but the thought of having to hear you go on about how great your nut bag family is in the universal scheme of things is just too much to bear. At this point, I'd rather have a bullet in my head."

That earned a smirk from the old man, nothingSully's rubs. "Get up."

After a few seconds more, Stewart lost patience and grabbed Sully's right leg, began to drag him toward the portal. How in the hell had he gotten so strong, Sully wondered. The old fuck must be seventy something, but he was pulling his two hundred and fifty plus pounds along as if he were a bag of crisp fall leaves.

Sully's shoulder jarred painfully against the stone lip of the portal and he felt Stewart's hands under his arms as he lifted him. Sully groaned in frustration and snapped his teeth towards the old man's face, but he wasn't near enough. Up he went, inexorable up and up. His arms flailed uselessly as he felt the cold stone of the portal, then there was emptiness.

He fell backwards. The mouth of the portal, the dim light of the chamber beyond rose away from him as he descended.

Sully managed to turn his body turned as he hit the cold stinking water like a sack of iron. Down he went. He tried to kick, but his legs were still useless flesh beneath him and he continued to sink into the cloying black water. He thrashed with his weak arms at the churning waters. But it only slowed his progress, did not stop him from falling deeper.

The faint light that colored the water suddenly disappeared and he was in darkness; the portal had been closed. He was trapped, helpless against whatever Stewart Machen had planned for him. Worse, there was no one to warn the others about the Machens.

CHAPTER -21-

For hours, in the slow, gray light of morning, she had lain next to Timmy, waiting for the fear of what she had seen to pass, trying in vain to convince herself that the thing she had seen in the hallway was a nightmare only- her imagination gone crazy in this damnable house. But with the light streaming in through the window, she felt the need to open the door and face the hallway again. Perhaps make a quick detour for downstairs to find Sully and Garlen. She needed someone to tell her how crazy it was, that she had only imagined the creature, the voices...and Conley's impossible entreaties.

She sat up in bed; sweat damp covers pressed anxiously against her chest, her heartbeat like a heavy-footed marcher against her breast. Next to her, Timmy stirred, then settled once more into unaware sleep.

She forced herself from the dubious safety of the bed, made her way cross the chill wood of the floor. Her ear pressed against the door, breath quivering unsteadily in her throat, she listened.

Nothing.

She opened the door. The hall was murky but empty. She pulled her shirt closer to her chin and closed the door behind her, made a hurried path to the stairs, the only thing she could, with reasonable certainty, find in this place. Downstairs, she found no one stirring yet. She found the hallway leading to Sully and Garlen's rooms. She knocked on Sully's first, but there was no answer. She knocked harder this time. Still no one replied.

"Mary?" Garlen's uncertain voice said from the door next to Sully's room. She gasped in relief. The door opened to a pale and shaky Garlen sitting upright in his wheelchair. His face was pinched with concern. He peered past her, as if half expecting to see someone besides her in the corridor. When he saw only her, his face fell into new misery.

"What's wrong, Garlen?"

Garlen motioned for her to enter his room. He closed the door behind her. "I know it's none of my business," he said. "But have you seen Sully this morning?"

"No, I haven't seen him since last night. What's wrong?" she asked again, a chill scurrying up her spine. The old man looked scared, and that made her even more frightened than before.

"Neither have I," he said. He shook his head and rubbed his pale face. Mary could see a gray pepper of stubble on his thin cheeks.

"Have you looked outside?"

He shook his head and looked down meaningfully at his chair. Mary stifled a foolish grin at her stupid question. "Not yet, my dear. I was hoping that you'd seen him. It's so unlike Sully to disappear without telling me where he's going." She saw tears glisten at the corners of his eyes. "He wouldn't miss our morning conversations. It's important to both of us. He's like a son to me after all these years." He looked at her with his swimming eyes. "I think something's happened to him, Mary."

"Let me get dressed and we'll go out and search for him." She paused. "Have you spoken with Stewart or Charlotte about this yet?"

He shook his head again. "I wanted to make sure you hadn't seen him yet. I keep hoping he'll show up. Oh, what could have happened to him?"

"Calm down," she said, even though she felt anything but calm herself. "We'll find him. I promise."

"Sully helps me get around in this horrible contraption," he said. "He's quite strong." A tear rolled unheeded down his wrinkled cheeks. "I think something bad has happened to him while I was sleeping like a lazy old fool." He smashed an ineffectual fist into the chair arm. He shook his head. "I found one of his guns lying on the dresser this morning." He drew a dull black handgun from the pocket of his jacket and showed her. "It was loaded. He told me he was going to look around last night, but I didn't know he was going to be carrying this cannon around with him. Sully would never have carried around a gun unless he thought something was wrong." Garlen gazed up at her miserably. "You don't know Sully the way I know him. He...." The old man's face melted in agony, his memories searching a long closed vault once more. The gunshots...the pain...the blood...Sully pulling him from the car, feeling nothing below his legs, seeing his life ripped apart by bullets. Bullets that had been meant for him! He shook his head again. "He would do anything to avoid tragedy again."

Mary waited for him to continue, but Garlen had apparently said as much as he intended about his relationship with Sully. Mary had guessed some kind of tragedy held them together, but could only guess at the extent.

"I'll be right back," she said. "Stay here."

She tried to hide her own growing fear for Sully, a mysterious man she'd found herself thinking about more and more with every passing day, and hurried back upstairs. After a few wrong turns, she finally found their bedroom and got dressed.

Mary checked Timmy, who was still out. She decided to get this Sully thing cleared up before waking him. Besides, there might be a confrontation between she and the grandparents this morning; she was definitely telling them they were leaving today. She didn't think he needed to see that.

As she passed the window, she caught sight of the police car in the front drive. Her heart skipped a beat. Was it here because something had happened to Sully? But then she remembered the two missing teenagers and realized it was more likely the Sheriff was here to speak with the Machens about them.

She could barely make out someone sitting behind the wheel of the car as it started to move down the drive. But whoever was driving wasn't going towards the exit. Instead, the car wheeled towards a long, squat unattached building that was big enough to be a miniature house in itself. She assumed it was a garage.

As the car turned at an angle, Mary could clearly see Stewart behind the wheel. Mary felt a cold chill scurry down her spine. Why would he be driving the car? Where was the Sheriff? Surely this family's medieval fiefdom-like power didn't extend to allowing them to drive around county owned cars.

They found Charlotte in the dining room, a place where she seemed to spend a great deal of her time, in deep repose. Her face was gray clay, devoid of all emotion, as she stared into a distance only she could see.

She'd already shared what she'd seen with Garlen and now both of them were determined to get answers form their hosts, no matter what it took to do so. She pushed Garlen before her to the table and cleared of her throat to inform the old woman that she was no longer alone. Startled out of her private thoughts, and realizing that she was no longer alone, Mary watched as the old woman put on what Mary had come to think of as Charlotte's "sweet-old-harmless-woman" mask. But they had caught her unaware and Mary meant to make the most of this element of surprise. She meant to have answers to her questions this time. Even before that pasted smile was on Charlotte's lips, Mary went headlong into her examination. "Why was Stewart driving the police car to the garage, Charlotte?" she demanded.

The old woman frowned. She hadn't been expecting this. There was an uneasy pause, and an uncertain silence filled the room. Mary could see her searching for some convincing lie. But Garlen didn't give her time. "Where the hell is Sully?" he asked in a stern and trembling voice. He leaned forward in his chair as if he meant to dive for her if the answer was not what he sought.

"Garlen..." Charlotte said in a startled tone, clutching at her throat as if hearing the curse word had pained her.

Mary was too scared, and too tired, to go for the her act. She followed up Garlen's attack. "Answer the question, Charlotte," she said. "And where the hell is my car?"

"I don't know what's gotten into the both of you, but this is no way to treat someone who's taken you into their heart and home." She continued to hold that breathless, shocked pose.

"Bullshit!" Garlen snapped angrily. "Something's going on here, and we want to know what."

And then she saw, that slow dissolving of the mask. Charlotte's features twitched with unsuppressed anger, her eyes flared with hatred, lips turned into a sneer of malevolent glee. When next she spoke, the breathless old lady was no longer to be heard. Her voice was hard now and full of spite. "Oh, you'll both know soon enough, you goddamned gimp son of a bitch," she said. Her yellow teeth were set into a death head's grin of rage. In her hand she suddenly clenched a butter knife. She turned her baleful stare on Mary. "And you," she growled like an animal. "You'll never see your fucking car again. You fucking whore! Don't think I don't know what you've got planned with my son. I've seen the way he looks at you. Time to get rid of the old woman who has kept him straight all this time. Don't' think I'm so fucking stupid that I don't see what's happening around me."

Mary and Garlen drew back, uncertain in the face of her venom. This was like another entity, twisting her face, altering her voice. But Mary was sure she had finally found the true Charlotte Machen. This malevolent spirit had been hiding just below the congeniality all the time. Even though she always suspected that things were not how they seemed here in Machan Mansion, she hadn't expected such a blast of sneering resentment from the old woman. The inference of this display was like a maelstrom raging within her and she had to have time to think- to reassess what this meant.

She grasped Garlen's chair, intent on pulling them both from the room, away from the heaving and twitching creature before them, holding a butter knife with every intention of using it. Then a familiar voice sounded from behind.

"Oh, dear," Stewart said. "I see we have come to the impasse that I've dreaded all along."

Mary whirled to see Stewart standing in the doorway behind them. Angry words and demands for answers were already on her lips, denunciations for Charlotte's behavior, demands for her missing car, for Sully. All of them died in her gaping mouth at the sight of the gun in Stewart's hand.

She and Garlen were both stunned into silence. Seeing their surprised dismay, Stewart began to laugh, eyes full of a nasty jeering triumph.

Mary felt more than saw a movement next to her. She tried to turn, but it was too late. There was a sharp stinging sensation between her shoulder blades. Half turning, half falling, Mary saw Charlotte standing over her, a glistening hypodermic needle in her hand, a sneer upon her wrinkled lips. Garlen's frightened screams followed her down into darkness.

CHAPTER -22-

Timmy awoke to find his grandmother smiling down at him. His mother's side of the bed was empty, only rumpled sheets, twisted blankets and indented pillows as proof that she had been there at all.

"Where's Mama?" he said, blinking the residual blur of sleep from his eyes.

"Good morning," Charlotte said, ignoring his question.

He looked toward the open bathroom door, could clearly see his mother wasn't in there. Where was she? She wouldn't have left him without telling him where she was going, even if he had been sound asleep. He returned his bleary gaze to Charlotte, still awaiting an explanation. Her mouth bent into a frown. It was only for a moment, but to Timmy it was a telling moment.

"Oh, she's going to be back anytime now," his grandmother said. "She and your grandfather went for a little ride on the horses."

Timmy knew she lying. Mama didn't like horses. In fact, she was scared of them. Once, long ago, before Daddy had gone away, they had all gone for horse rides at the circus. Mama had screamed when the horse trotted, screamed when the horse didn't run, she even screamed when the horse just threw its head. Timmy remembered how shaky she had been after that. He and Daddy had kidded her about it, but Timmy could tell she had really been scared.

His eyes narrowed and he pulled the musty blanket close to his chest, unconsciously seeking protection from its thin fabric. His grandmother was lying, but why?

"How about some breakfast?" the old woman said, reaching to pull aside the bed sheets for his exit.

She kept that sweet, wrinkled grin on him until he felt his strange sense of danger seeping away. He was hungry...and he shouldn't get scared just because Mama wasn't right next to him, he told himself. It was a little kid thing to do. He shouldn't act like a baby. Besides, while he was eating, he could look outside for Mama. If she were really riding a horse like grandmother said, then he'd probably be able to see her. If he saw her, he'd stop being scared.

"Come on." Charlotte held out her arms, ready to receive him. "Aren't you hungry?"

Hesitating, Timmy finally nodded.

"I remember when I was your age. It seemed like I was hungry all the time," she said. She pulled him from the bed. His feet recoiled at the feeling of the chill wooden floor. "I grew up poor white trash. Just like you and your Mama."

Timmy glared at her, angry. He had heard the kids at school calling him and Mama poor white trash, and even if he didn't know what it meant, the negative connotation was well understood. Just like right now, it was clear to his ears. "We ain't no poor white trash," he told Charlotte, voice shaky but resolute.

Charlotte gave him a small placating smile, shook her head, as if he were just being silly by denying it. Timmy managed to stare her down for a few more moments; but his natural deference to adults made him finally look away. Still, he was angry that she had called them that bad name. "Let's get you some food," she said.

Timmy followed her because he didn't know what else to do. But he promised himself Mama would know what his grandmother had said about them. Mama would make her take it back.

On their way downstairs, Timmy felt a sort of heaviness to the air, like when Christmas was about to happen- only this felt like that in a bad way. The house was quiet, except for the sound of their footsteps on the soft carpet. It was a brooding silence that frightened him even more. The house felt dead somehow, as if the whole place, the crushing red and gold walls, the heavily curtained windows, and the leering dark portraits on the way down the staircase, were all listening, waiting for something to happen.

In the dining room, as the other times that he and Mama had come down for breakfast, the long, shiny table was covered with bowls and plates of food. His stomach growled with hunger at the sight. Still feeling upset with the old woman, he took a seat near the door, hoping she wouldn't ask him why he was sitting so far away from her seat near the middle of the spread. She didn't seem to notice because all she said was 'help yourself, dear'.

He lifted a lid and meaty steam billowed forth, masking his face in the heat and the smell of bacon. He used his fingers to pull two crisp slices from the pile, before he noticed the shiny silver serving fork sitting beside the plate. He murmured an apology, but

Charlotte didn't seem to worry about his using his fingers instead of the proper utensil. She only smiled benignly at him as he began to munch on his bacon strips. She shuffled to the coffee server and started pouring something. Timmy took the opportunity of her back being to him to peer hopefully out the side window. He didn't see Mama or his grandfather anywhere out there. Just more trees and grass and some dark clouds scudding across the sky. Another storm.

While he was busy looking for any sign of them, Charlotte finished at the coffee cart and moved to stand before him. Timmy drew back with a startled gasp, dropping his bacon on the carpet. He expected to be yelled at for it, especially since there was now a dollop of cooling bacon fat soaking into the shag rug. But the old woman kept smiling at him, hovering over him. Timmy couldn't help but think of all the scary stories he read in the big book of fairy tales, the ones like Hansel and Gretel and Snow White. In those stories there was always an old woman who was always smiling at the innocent young princess, or the gullible, trusting child. They always wore a smile on the outside, but there was always something beneath that old woman smile. Just like right now, the way grandmother was smiling down at him. It wasn't a nice smile. He felt like she was hiding what she really wanted beneath it. He swallowed his chewed up bacon with difficulty. "Is Mama going to have breakfast, too?"

His grandmother's hands were behind her back, holding something from his view.

"She's already had breakfast with your grandfather and I. You were such a sleepy-head you missed it."

Timmy knew she was lying again, but could not understand why.

She drew her hands from her back, displaying a large sweat beaded glass of chocolate milk. Grinning, Charlotte showed several small yellow teeth peeking from between thin wrinkled lips. She set the glass before him on the table. "This is for you, my dear."

He looked at the glass and back at her, seeing the red, red apple from Snow White in his head. He swallowed the dryness in his throat. "Mama says I shouldn't have sweets for breakfast," he told Charlotte, thankful for once about a stupid rule. He shrugged as if he were helpless to disobey the rule. She stared at him in grim silence. "Sorry," he added, feeling the weight of the old woman's gaze. He suddenly didn't want to be near her or the chocolate milk.

"Well," Charlotte replied in a mock whisper. "We'll just make sure we don't say anything to her about it." She reached forward and pushed the glass closer.

He tried not to let his fear show, gave her a heavy sigh of mock disappointment. "No, thank you. I better not. Mama'll be mad at me."

Charlotte's smile fell away. "I said we wouldn't say anything, Timmy. Now drink the chocolate milk. It's very rude to not accept a gift someone has gone through a great deal of trouble to give you."

His fear plain now, he gazed up her with wide frightened eyes. Shaking his head, he pushed away from the glass.

"Honestly," Charlotte muttered. "Just like you're hard-headed father, boy." She shoved the glass again, this time more violently, not seeming to care that she managed to spill most of the dark liquid on the white tablecloth. "I said drink it."

"No!" Timmy yelled. "Where's my mama?"

He started from the chair, intent on getting away. But Charlotte's thin hand flashed out and grabbed his shoulder in an iron claw. She shoved him hard, slamming him back into the chair. He fell into it, legs weak with terror. Before he could gather himself for another attempt at escape, Charlotte, red-faced and spittle dripping from her pressed lips, straddled the chair so that she had a thin quivering leg on either side of him, locking her ankles around the chair legs.

Timmy gave a muted scream of terror. Charlotte slapped him, stunning the scream out of him. His face went numb from the hit. Before he could begin to cry from the pain, from the terrible surprise of it all, she pinched his nose between two cold fingers. When Timmy opened his mouth to scream again Charlotte poured the viscous, sickly sweet chocolate milk down his convulsing throat. It went past his tongue, down his gullet. He swallowed to keep from choking. Some of it splashed across his face and chest as he struggled and twisted to get away from the gagging concoction.

Charlotte boxed his head again with a back handed slap, hard enough to make his ears ring, enough to double his vision for a second or two. He could see her grinning down at him, an insane, wild haired woman, face red with exertion, thin arms ropy with strings of muscles, fingers clenched like nails in the dough of his face.

The glass swam before him again. She yelled, "Drink it, you little fucker!" A wash of her hot, venomous spittle splattered against his burning cheeks. She held his nose together and poured more of the drink down his mouth. He had no choice: he had to swallow to keep from choking on it.

Finally, the glass was empty and Charlotte released his nose. She stepped away from the chair, gasping for air, still cackling at him like some insane witch from a horrible fairytale. She threw the glass to the ground with triumph, smashing it, backing away, letting him slide down in the chair.

Now was the time to get away, he told himself. While she's out of breath and moving away from me. He thought about pushing away from the soft comfort of the chair, but no matter how much he tried, his hands and feet refused to move. It was as if he was swimming and couldn't make his way to the surface again. But the worst part of it was that he didn't seem to be able to care that he couldn't move. His head felt too big for his body; his eyes swam like loose marbles in their sockets; a creeping numbness stole up his rubber feeling body, from his churning gut to the tips of fingers he could no longer feel. He felt a long string of spit dribble from his lips, down his chin, down his chest.

Someone came into his limited view. He recognized his grandfather through the drug haze, standing over him. The old man reached forward from a million miles away, taking light years to touch his face. Timmy felt his head being turned first one way, then the other, as if it were a disconnected part of him. The warm tickle of his grandfather's breath was on his face. The old man's face grew into a monstrosity, filling the whole world with wrinkles and wattles. "Are you sure that you didn't give him too much?" His grandfather's voice was like a boom. "We can't have him this way for the ceremony, as you well know, mother."

The two shapes swam around him, totally unconnected to his world. Night swallowed his vision, as he felt himself falling from the soft chair.

"You worry too much, Stewart," was the last thing he heard as he surrendered to the liquid warm darkness.

CHAPTER 23-

He was there again. Standing, like always, forty yards from the limousine. He could see Garlen's silhouette through the shade of the darkened back passenger window, the jutting jaw of his profile, as he talked in his usual animated way with his wife and son. Even through the obfuscation of the car window Sully could see him laughing, a happy, content laughter- the blissful laughter of a man who has everything.

It took less than five seconds to kill that laugh for good.

And Sully stood there, watched it happen, as always. Unable to act, frozen by the timeline vision, like a fly stuck in amber, knowing he would always be too late to stop the black sedan racing towards Garlen's parked limousine. In the early evening light, he could see a purpose to the speeding car's direction, a silver shark moving in for the kill. Even as Sully reached for his gun, he knew it was too late.

A metallic stitch-spray of bullets ripped across the side of the limo, tore into the unarmored frame, sending a violent shower of shattered glass and steamy fluids everywhere. The driver was dead in an instant, his brains splattered in a crimson and gray wash across the starred and ruined windshield.

And he stood there watching it all over again. Unable to change any of it.

Forty-seven bullets later, when it was all done, and the dead had been counted, he and Garlen would wonder how Bird's small frame could ever hold fourteen bullets. The boy's small, precious body, so alive and full of promise moments before, had been torn apart by the gunfire. Garlen's wife had fared no better. Ten bullets; three in her head, demolishing her face beyond repair.

Ironically, Garlen, the target of the assassination attempt, had received only one bullet. But it had been enough. His life was changed forever by that single bullet. Spine shattered, his wife and child dead.

And Sully had stood there like an impotent excuse for a knight in shining armor, watched that goddamned black car coming at them. Too stunned to move. Too sure of his own measures against the threats of the enemy that he couldn't fathom that he had missed an angle somewhere.

Some fucking bodyguard.

Let the fucking darkness take me. Let it end all this misery. I can't take this anymore. It was my goddamned duty to protect them and I let them die.

The scene receded, like a movie playing in a tunnel, and his own inner dark engulfed him once more.

Sully's body continued to fall into the cold dark water like a stone. The cold, a sharp pain in ever pore of his exposed skin, stung like needles into his arms and face. He was in a universe of forever blackness, a chill world of the infinite.

It could end here. I could let the darkness finally win.

Death would be a relief now. What was he leaving behind, after all?

The cold caressed him with a lover's sure fingers,

promising forgiveness and an end to the pain, and the forlorn disappointment with his useless existence.

But a niggling thought kept scratching at the back of his relief at ending it all; a desperate inner voice reminded him there was more at stake here than his own end. Stewart wasn't only killing him by this insane turn in darkness. There were others. Without him to warn them, they'd die.

The boy will die. She will die. Garlen will probably die, too.

Nagging thoughts of duty he couldn't shunt aside.

Sully's lungs began to burn. A great pressure heaved within him to draw breath again. An instinct for survival began to beat a wild tattoo in his chest, past his desire to give up.

He couldn't let them die. He had to stop the Machens. He knew what would happen to the kid if he didn't at least try to live.

Heavy numb arms and legs began to move without his knowledge. He could not feel the motions as he began to rise in a slow ascent to the surface. He was still too numb, too cold.

His face broke the cold barrier of water and he drew in the cold air in gasping breaths. His frantic noises threw back loud echoes along unseen walls.

Blinking water from his eyes, he found not even an intimation of light anywhere. He continued to flounder in the stench-ridden water, feeling gossamer filaments of slime clinging to his legs and arms. With numb shaking hands he reached up to find a curving and slime slick surface a few feet above his head. A ceiling of some sort. His feet had yet to touch bottom. With his hands, he managed to ascertain that the curved walls disappeared into the water to either side.

He had no idea where the doorway which he had been thrown through could be, only that it was out of reach above him somewhere, so he stabilized himself and let the slight current of the water carry him blindly along. Logic dictated if water flowed it had to end somewhere and anywhere was better than here.

Something floating in the water bumped into him. His first panicked thought was that it was an alligator. He waited to feel savage teeth tearing into him, but when nothing happened, he felt along the sodden, cold thing and discovered what felt like thin seaweed waving in water. He let his shaking hands move further along the thing and found a knobby bulb that felt much too fleshy to belong to a log. Sully ran his palm across the protrusion and realized with disgust that it was a nose. He snatched his hand back with an alarmed yelp.

He had found Sheriff Lincoln.

But the corpse wasn't moving with the current. Something was holding it in place.

He hung on to a belt loop, and fighting against nausea, reached underneath the dead man's body. With questing fingers, brushing cold flesh, he found the man's empty gun belt. It had snagged onto some unseen thing beneath it. Fumbling at the belt, he fought the insistent pull of the current, and managed to dislodge the man's body from its impediment. He found himself clinging to the floating corpse, carried along with it.

Despite the morbidity of the situation, Sully couldn't help but feel a perverse kind of joy at having found the dead man in all this darkness. Maybe there was a chance Machen had left something on his person Sully could use as a weapon.

And he hadn't forgotten the old bastard's dire words indicating that he was being given over to something in this watery graveyard. There was still that unknown danger to be faced yet.

Keeping a firm hold on the soggy leather gun belt, Sully began a search of every pocket he could find, clumsily turning the body first one way, then the other, until he was satisfied that he'd found all there was to find. What he managed to find wasn't exactly a treasure trove. He turned up a handful of change, a money clip with a thin fold of wet bills, a half sodden pack of spearmint chewing gum, four shells for a nonexistent gun, a plastic ballpoint pen, and a small penknife. The money he let fall away in the water, as well as the shells and the gum- none of which he had any use for in his present situation. He hung on to the ballpoint pen and the penknife.

As he finished rifling through the dead sheriff's possessions Sully felt an increase in the strength of the current. It was hard to tell how fast he was going, but the violent churning of the water around him, and a slight dank breeze against his face, told him that he was definitely picking up speed. Lincoln's bloated body began to twist and turn in the excited current. Sully had to finally let him go, treading water to keep from being dragged along in the big man's wake.

What could be motivating the body of liquid? A pump of some kind? Gravity?

There was a dim light ahead, an illumination portending an end to this infernal watery prison.

Sully smiled.

Maybe he'd get out of this alive, after all.

He let the current carry him again, eager to find the source of light, a possible escape route.

Ahead of him, something unseen hit the water. It was heavy enough to cause waves to wash across Sully's face. Something large slithered in front of him. He felt the weight of the thing's sudden approach. An animal snort of curiosity echoed in the tunnel.

Sully fought the current, treading water. He peered into the dimness before him. Fear blossomed in his gut.

What the hell was that?

The meager light reflected off of something grotesquely disproportioned, something hulking and dark moving in the current before him. It was shrouded in shifting shadow play from the water crescents reflected on the slime-ridden ceiling and the backlight of the tunnel's eventual end. He couldn't make out its features. It could have been human, but on a scale out of focus with reality.

Sully kicked a hasty retreat backwards as Lincoln's body rose from the water. The unknown thing had the corpse suspended before its face, inspecting the dead Sheriff's stilled features. It gave a grunt that almost sounded questioning, as if it were unsure what to make of this unexpected gift in the water. It snuffled, tasting the scent of death. Then the tunnel went quiet except for drops of dank water falling back to the inscrutable black churn below. Sully held his breath, trying to make out the dark shape.

The hulking monster heaved Lincoln's body away, dissatisfied with the cold bag of flesh. Sully tried to backpedal in the water, almost sensing what was to come next.

Two shining eyes glowed like black ice from the scintillating darkness ahead. The thing began snuffling again, coming in Sully's direction. It had picked up on his scent, a living thing that it could rend and destroy. It pulled its massive body through the water with ease, against the tugging, pulling current as if wading through a stiff breeze.

In a panic, he pushed harder against the flow in an effort to put more distance between him and the thing- a distance that the thing was closing very quickly.

Sully knew he was losing, so he did the only thing he could think to do. He went underwater. Something like a sword blade sliced through the water after him and he felt a stinging pain rip across his left shoulder. He couldn't stifle his scream and he blew out most of his air in a wash of discarded bubbles. Another tearing pain followed across the other shoulder. The pain was agony and he almost froze in the black depths, unable to remember how to escape the pain. Stinking water invaded his open mouth; he choked on it; his ears and nose filled with it. Strands of clinging filth swam around him. Those twin centers of pain felt like he had been shot. He was numb with the immensity of the pain. All he could do was fall to the bottom.

Violent explosions of water. A force ripped past his head, narrowly missing him. He sought the deeper depths of the tunnel, found the slime slick bottom, and fought his still buoyant body to stay down. Through the turbulent, murky water, he saw the scant light silhouetting the monster above him. It was tearing at the water with its claws in an effort to find him.

But his air was running out. He couldn't stay down forever; he'd have to go back to the surface soon.

The creature stopped raking at the water and it grew still.

Sully felt a weight of horror descend on him as he realized the thing had figured out his situation. It stayed poised above him, waiting for him to come up for air.

Sully's shoulders burned and spasmed with pain. It was becoming an effort to hold himself in place at the bottom of the tunnel's curved, slime-slick floor.

Something huge splashed into the water above him; Lincoln's desiccated and torn corpse sunk past him, rested in a tangled mess at his feet. Whatever the thing was, it meant business.

His lungs burned for air now, his throat convulsed for it, dark spots danced before his eyes. He couldn't stay down much longer. Lincoln's half-eaten face stared up at him, waiting for him to make a decision; crooked yellow teeth smiled from the red wound slash of the man's mouth. Bits of white flesh danced like morbid seaweed at the gaping wound of the throat.

Lungs on fire, Sully kicked up, hands held in defense in front of his face, and broke the surface, slime dripping from his face and neck. He took a sweet breath of air. A few feet away, a surprised snort sounded and the thing made a move to snatch him. Something clubbed at him and he threw up his arm to intercept it. A burning line of pain slashed his waving left arm, as he felt something vital snap. Without thinking, like a beast driven by pure instinct to get away from the pain, Sully dove back for the depths again.

It was the only thing that saved him from death, as the creature began to throw back huge chunks of water to get at him. In its violence, the churning effect obscured Sully's struggle to escape. He sank to the bottom, jostling against Lincoln's body.

His shallow breath of air wasn't going to last forever. And he knew he wasn't going to make it past that thing again.

Sully kicked away from Lincoln, pulled his weakened body through the dark slime in an effort put more distance between him and the thing. Every feeble effort to fight the density of the liquid medium took more air from his body, more energy. His lungs were already burning again and dark spots returned to cloud his vision. He had to do something. But he knew if he went up again the creature would be ready for him this time. The thing would decapitate him in a flash.

What could he fight it with? The penknife wasn't going to do him much good against whatever it was. And what good was a ballpoint pen against it? For Christ's sake, it wasn't even solid.

It was...hollow.

Sully tore frantically at his shirt pocket and retrieved the pen. With shaking hands, he unscrewed the cylinder and shook out the ink cartridge, kicked slowly towards the surface. He treaded to keep himself below the surface, head throbbing with the need for air. He shoved one end of the pen out of the water, put the other end in his mouth.

Here goes nothing.

Hands numb with lack of oxygen, Sully took a deep pull on the pen and swallowed a mouthful of rank water and gagged. But his need to breathe outweighed his desire to vomit up the disgusting liquid, so he drew more air. He was rewarded this time with a thin stream of sweet oxygen.

But it wasn't enough. He had let himself go too long with nothing and now his body wasn't going to be fobbed off with such a stingy amount. He needed to get a large breath and now, or he was dead either way.

He shoved himself out of the water and gulped deeply. Something stung his forehead and warm blood spurted across his face. An angry howl echoed off the walls as he pushed himself down again. Sully made himself hold in the scream this time; he needed all the air he could get, and writhed away, sank below the frothing surface.

He was losing blood. A couple more hits and he wouldn't have to worry about air anymore. He would bleed to death, instead.

Sully gave the pen trick another try, kicking a little closer in the direction of the light. Before he tried to draw air, he blew the water from the barrel this time, remembering the rank taste of the toxic brew from before. He was able to pull enough air through the thin tube to keep from drowning.

But he needed a plan. He couldn't just stay here and breath through a ballpoint pen for the rest of his life. He had to stop the Machens.

The creature was waiting for him, probably wondering why he hadn't come back up for air yet. Sully figured the thing would get tired of waiting soon and come for him. Why it had not so far was a mystery. Unless it liked to play with its food first. Of course, he might be attributing a lot more intelligence to the thing than it deserved. Although if this were the same beast he'd read about in the Machen diary, then this was no dumb creature. It was intelligent, cunning, a forest demon that used its victims for its own ends.

Sully took one more deep pull for air and pushed back to the bottom. He pulled himself towards the light and soon found that the current was inexorably drawn towards a grate sunk in the floor of the tunnel ahead of him. As he got closer, the pull increased in strength, and he could see clumps of slime and detritus, rotted sticks, leaves, and small white things that Sully was sure had to be human teeth, snagged and clung to the thick metal bars. But some of it was being pulled down even as he watched. This was where the light was coming from. A diffuse light, as if it were being filtered past some obstruction.

Lungs screaming for air again, Sully grabbed the grate's slippery slime covered bars and gave it a tug. It didn't budge. He waved away some of the filth and saw why. There were several large screws holding the thing in place. He sure as hell wasn't going to pull the thing off.

Needing air again, he slowly surfaced, allowing the tip of the hollow pen to extend from the water. The shape of the beast leered above, waiting. He blew the water from the barrel and pulled in a thin welcome stream of air.

Suddenly, the creature lunged, thrusting Sully's latent image in the water below it. Something hit the pen and it flew from his grasp, falling away in the dank water beyond his sight. He quickly pushed away from the surface, as the thing thrashed at the dark waters, seeking its prey.

Sully knew all of his tricks were at an end. He had only one thing left to try and that was to pry that bastard grill off the floor and see where it led.

He kicked back to the bottom. Blinking past the roiling, undulating strings of scum, he pulled the penknife from his pocket. If the knife didn't work, he was in deep shit. The small amount of air in his exhausted lungs was all he was going to have to do the job, too. There would be no more surfacing, not as a living being anyway.

He set to it, frantically sweeping away the debris. Laying the blade at a side angle, he set the knife too far down its length and it snapped as soon as he put pressure on it. Half of its length floated to settle into the leafy sediment near the grillwork.

Angry and feeling like an idiot, he dug in again, trying to maintain his precarious position by kicking forward, while also trying to put his body torque into turning the screw. It wasn't moving at all, and he knew why. He just couldn't get the leverage he needed to do it. He couldn't kick and pull at the same time; his body was full of air and was trying to surface all the while. That life saving deep breath was also keeping him from performing his task.

He used precious time and air to kick back to Lincoln's body. He snatched the man's belt from his waist, pulling it from the rolling corpse, all the while waiting for the monster to make another try for him. With the belt in hand, he swam back to the grill, and hooked the belt's buckle in one of the grill tines. He tugged to test the hold.

Now he could keep from floating to the top and still work to save his ass.

Wrapping the soggy leather around his left hand, he went back to work on the screws with his right.

The first one was the bastard of the bunch. He wasted way more time and air than he could afford just to turn the stubborn screw through one complete revolution. Finally, with a rusty protest, the screw came loose, sailed out like it was on an oiled track. The next two screws came loose easily and he was feeling as if he might just make it, a grin of triumph splitting his face.

Then he started in on the final screw. It wouldn't budge. No matter how hard he turned, the son of a bitch just wouldn't give. The knife kept slipping from his shaking hand and his lungs convulsed for much needed oxygen.

The creature's shadow fell across him. Its great hands began to churn the water looking for him.

Panic squeezing his soul Sully turned his attention back to the last screw. He twisted and tugged, but the broken penknife kept slipping free of the screw.

Something that wasn't swamp waste touched his shoulder curiously.

It was the creature searching for him.

He threw aside the useless knife. Grabbing the slippery leather belt with both hands, Sully pulled for all he was worth. His back arched; his stomach trembled with the effort. He blew out his remaining air in a pale tumult of angry bubbles as he screamed out his rage and frustration.

One of the thing's questing limbs played along his left cheek and another lighted on his right shoulder. It was getting ready to snag him.

He wanted to sob in frustration. Held back from freedom by one stubborn goddamned screw.

He had one last mighty tug left in him.

Even now black stars danced in his vision.

Sully bent forward, feeling the scrapping of the thing's searching limbs along his body. He pulled with everything he had left.

The belt held…held…then popped loose.

The buckle went sailing past his face.

He slumped forward, ready to take in a mouthful of the disgusting water, maybe drown himself before the thing could get to him.

Then he saw that the grill had come loose. The whole thing had shifted in its setting, debris slushed down the offered egress.

The creature made a grab for him, snagged his torn shirt and pulled at him. Sully felt himself rising helplessly in its insistent grasp.

He pulled the front of his shirt and tore it. The material parted from the strain in an almost thankful surrender, slipped from his body, the eager paws pulling it quickly through the dank water, up to the hungry beast above.

Sully had no time left to waste. He was going to black out soon.

He pushed at the grill's incredible weight, shoving it aside so that he could squirm past its frame. Cold slime and rotting debris washed along his naked torso, until he was sucked down in a tumult of filthy water and bubbles.

Sully prayed to see the slimy tunnel's end and the light at the other end.

CHAPTER -24-

During Mary's brief moments of wakefulness she saw him come into the dim chamber, naked and sweating. His muscles stood out on his shining tanned body like knots of steel. On a younger man it would have been esthetically appealing, even sensual. But on Stewart Machen's aged frame it was grotesque, an anomaly of solidity within ancient rugose flesh.

She watched him, a distant observer in this nauseous dream state. She sensed his fitful movements- from the strange stone altar in the middle of the chamber, to the burning braziers, back to the bookcase- were important to her immediate safety in some way. But her level of awareness he intended her harm did not match her drugged level of anxiety. No matter how her primal core screamed for her return to the surface of this deep ocean sensation of falling away reality, she could not do so.

Once, Stewart moved close, leaning into her face, lifting one eyelid, then the next, and his animal musk pungency slipped past her drifting drug fall. It awakened her enough to attempt speech, at least she thought she remembered trying, tried to beg him to stop whatever it was he planned. Stewart ignored her pathetic pleas. With a savage grin, he grabbed a handful of hair, jerked her face up to his, then let her heavy head fall again. She felt indignant, but unable to voice her outrage at his manhandling, she gave up and drifted again.

Now, her senses were coming back. Her face felt too big, puffy and swollen. She ran her thick tongue across her lower lip and tasted blood. What did he do to her?

Through slitted eyes, she watched him move to a small huddle of clothing a few feet away. He bent over and spoke in a low, reassuring voice to the clothing. It wasn't until the bundle moved did she realize it was Timmy lying on the floor. His head lolled from side to side as he tried to focus on the old man. Like her, he had obviously been drugged as well.

She had to help Timmy. She had to stop that bastard from harming her son.

Mary tried to move, but after a few seconds of limbo, she slumped forward, head down. A slobbering moan of protest was all she could manage. Whatever they had shot into her was keeping her submerged beneath its effects. She was trapped inside her own body, a captive to whatever the sick bastards had planned for her and her son.

Her heavy head rolled to the right to see Garlen slumped against the wall not far from her. His breathing was deep and even, a sign that he was still out. Several wraps of dirty rope bound him.

She heard a door close with a heavy metallic click, and despite her efforts to fight it, the inner darkness swarmed up again, taking her under.

Some unknown time later, Mary woke again.

This time, the effects of the drug had weakened. She was able to move her head back and forth. Slowly, but she could move.

Stewart was nowhere to be seen.

With her return to stability came also the pain associated with her captivity. Her face was swollen. She used her tongue to probe the degree of damage to her face. Bottom lip split, crusty blood caked to her mouth. Her feet and hands were bound.

The ropes reminded her of Garlen. She turned to see his position hadn't changed. He was still slumped on his side, looking more dead than alive. He didn't look good either. His face was swollen from some beating he'd received, clothes disheveled and torn. Beneath the dry blood splattering his face, Mary could see his pallor was pale and sallow. His thinning tufts of hair stuck out all over his head. He looked like a drunk in the tank after a long, lost weekend. Mary felt sorrow for his reduction to such a state. Sorrow and a burning anger. Her hatred was like a roaring fire within, spreading through the forest of her drug-induced haze, burning it away like thin, dry branches.

She tested her voice: "Garlen". Weak and hollow, but she heard herself.

But Garlen hadn't; he remained still. Then his eyes fluttered open, a scared, animal confusion in his stare.

"Garlen," she called to him as loudly as she dared. "It's me. Mary. Can you hear me?"

"S-sully," the old man moaned. "Is that you, Sully? I don't feel so good. Can you help me into my chair? I believe I'm sick. My head, oh, my head…"

She shouted to him again, in an effort to make him realize what was happening, but his eyes blinked like a stunned cow a few times, and then fell shut again.

He was soon breathing with a nasty sounding unnatural hitch.

Whatever she was going to do, she was on her own.

Timmy still lay in a crumpled heap near the stained black stone altar. She could make out several painted symbols along its surface. From above, a brightly concentrated light shown down on a podium jutting from its center. A large ancient looking book lay open upon it. The sight of her unconscious son lying so close to the altar made her even more afraid. She twisted against the thick ropes that bound her, but only managed to dig them deeper into her shivering, aching flesh.

There came a loud click from the door across the room. Mary immediately feigned unconsciousness. Through the cautious slits of her eyelids, she saw Stewart enter, still naked and sweating. He walked across the room with a bounce in his step and bent over Timmy, checking his pulse. Satisfied, he left the boy, and then moved to Garlen. He looked down at the old man with a sneering scowl. After a moment, he shoved at his body with the heel of a bare foot. Garlen groaned in pain. Stewart left Garlen and came in her direction. His lascivious grin made her quiver inside. His eyes roamed across her flesh as if he were a starving man inspecting a side of beef. She squeezed her eyes shut, afraid to give herself away.

The old man stooped down next to her, and again that pungent animal musk clogged her throat. She could feel the heat of his body, could feel his hot, stinking pungent breath against her cheek. His hands fumble roughly along her body. She couldn't repress a tremor of revulsion as he rubbed her breasts beneath the painful layers of rope and torn clothing. His fingers dug at her trembling flesh, squeezed her right nipple in a harsh pinch. Mary held her breath against the pain, refusing to cry out. Stewart released her burning swelling nipple. She relaxed, sure he had tired of the cruel game of pain and degradation, but he wasn't done yet.

His open hand smashed her face. The gasp of pained surprise escaped without thought, as she was sent sprawling on her side. Her head smacked against the floor with a thunderous thud. Darkness swarmed up, threatened to take her again. She was only able to hang on to consciousness by sheer willpower.

"Who do you think you're fooling, you stupid bitch," Stewart said with a cruel chuckle. "Open your fucking eyes so I can see how scared you are."

Mary opened her eyes, managed to focus past the stinging pain in her face, her stare full of hatred. Her head ached where she'd hit the hard stone floor, and the ropes dug deeper trenches into her flesh. Fresh blood dribbled from her nose, ran in a warm, thick rivulet down her pale cheek. "Why are you doing this?" she asked.

He tried to grab her cheeks, but she twisted away. With the ferocity of a monstrous child, Stewart seized her hair and forced her to look up at him. With his other hand he dabbed a finger in the small river of blood on her cheek, then brought the crimson soaked digit to his lips and sucked her blood from it. His face wore a mask of pleasure that made her cringe inside. He was insane beyond any of her wildest imaginings. How could you hope to reason with such a crazy person? How could she hope to save Timmy from this kind of insanity?

Her eyes flicked at a movement over the old man's naked shoulder.

Timmy was moving like a stunned bird. He was alive.

Quickly, she looked back at Stewart, afraid he might turn to see the boy moving, and what he would do if he did. As much as she wanted to make sure her son was okay, not bleeding or dying, she made herself stare at Stewart, so that his attention would stay on her.

"I'm doing this for something you white-trash scum could never understand," Stewart answered. He hadn't spoken for so long, that she'd almost forgotten the question she'd asked him a few moments before. "I'm doing this for the family. A heritage is important, my dear." He caressed her cheek. "Now, I'm here to offer you a last chance, Mary, to be part of it all. I've needed a wife for some time now. I think we could make a go of it." He ran his hand through her sweat soaked hair. "What do you say?"

Her eyes flicked past him. Timmy was sitting up, wiping his face, and shaking his head. She looked back at Stewart. "What are you going to do with Timmy?"

His frown was the telling gesture. "I'm going to kill him, my dear," he said. "He'll be a sacrifice tonight to something wonderful, a creature older than mankind. His death will mean my life, and the continuing life of all male Machens."

She shook her head. Hearing it put in to words-even though she had already guessed his intent was malevolent- made the whole horrible experience somehow more real. Knowing for certain what he meant for her son broke the last vestiges of the drug's effects, and that burning anger, the knowledge that she was helpless to stop him from carrying out his mad plan, boiled and roiled in her stomach like lava. Tears pooled at the corners of her eyes. But she would not beg for herself, and begging for Timmy would be wasted on this man.

Seeing eyes harden, he reached forward again. She spat a mouthful of blood in his face. Amused, he touched the warm dribble and smiled down at her. "That's too bad," he said. He paused to inspect the bloody spit on the tip of his finger. "However, I will enjoy watching the Black Beast tear you and Garlen apart. It will be most enjoyable indeed, my dear." With a casual flick of his arm, he slapped her again. Her head bounced off the stone. Dark stars danced in her eyes; she gasped for air past the surprised pain. She watched Stewart walk away through the haze of burning agony. Past him, Timmy was lying down again.

Had he passed out again? Was he dead?

Stewart passed him by, back to the altar. Climbing the steps, he turned to the podium and all she could see was his back now. She could hear him turning thick pages in the book in front of him, mumbling to himself, words she couldn't identify, like the sibilant whisper of the things she'd seen in the halls above.

She sobbed, hot, stinging tears full of hopelessness.

What could she do, bound like a pig ready for slaughter? There was no escape for any of them now.

Then Timmy moved again. He raised his head and watched Stewart's back for a moment before turning to look at Mary. Their eyes met; she could see tears glistening on his cheeks. But there was resolve in his pinched and pained features. She wanted to shout out to him, tell him to get away, run, but there was nowhere to run in this chamber. The door was sealed shut.

Timmy pulled his legs under himself and began to crawl towards something on the ground. He reached forward and cautiously drew the thing towards him. She caught the silvery glint of reflected light from the knife. The blade was as long as a small sword, with a deadly evil glitter to its single sharpened edge. Timmy continued to watch Stewart as the old man perused the giant tome before him.

Timmy began a slow crawl up the stone steps of the altar.

Oh, my God, she thought hysterically. *No, Timmy! Run!*

Stewart set the book on the floor and got down on his knees. His voice rose like a chant in a church, a singsong cadence, that reminded Mary of monks reading evening vespers.

When Stewart moved, Timmy waited at the top of the steps, tense and shaking. The knife caught the bright overhead light. The silver light washed across her son's pale face.

Mary's breath caught in her throat; her heart thumped like a drum of doom. She was trapped, watching her son risk his life, and there wasn't a damn thing she could do to help or stop him.

After a moment, Timmy moved forward again, like a thin, pale spider, making his slow way across the cold stone altar, until he was less than a foot from Stewart's muscled back. Stewart's voice rose as the knife rose.

Please, God, don't let him turn around, Mary prayed. She was so scared for Timmy she couldn't even draw a breath. She tugged at her bindings in vain.

There was that single moment when the knife sat like a sharp star in the air, then, with a furious and terrified grunt, Timmy brought the weapon down, his full weight behind its deadly thrust. Even from across the room, Mary could hear the horrible sound as the metal sunk into Stewart's exposed flesh, tearing past muscle and bone, until it stopped at half its murderous length, sticking out of Stewart like a misplaced horn. Stewart gave a rising moan of surprised agony and fell face first under the attack.

Timmy pushed away from the old man's writhing body; Mary could hear him crying; she twisted in her impossible ropes again, but they did not give.

Stewart reached back, trying to pull the quivering knife from his back. Small rivulets of blood, dark and viscid, seeped from the great tearing wound. He grunted like a trapped animal, arms twisting in every direction in an effort to get to the knife. He sobbed and called out in nonsensical curses and pleadings, but couldn't reach the knife. His pitched forward, gasping for air. His body gave one last great heave, and then his arms fell away with solid thumps to his side. Then he was still, slumped on the stone altar, an unintentional sacrifice to his own madness. Timmy was a sobbing huddle next to the dead man, watching his grandfather give up the last breath of his life. The body seemed to sink into itself, deprived of its soul.

Mary writhed in frustration, trying to get to her son, to comfort him, to dry his tears, and to tell him that it was okay that he done the terrible thing that had to be done...

But she couldn't get out of these goddamned ropes.

The handle of the knife drew her attention.

"Timmy," she called. "Can you get the knife? You need to cut me out of these ropes."

The boy raised his head and looked at her. His whole body was racked by his sobs. "I can't," he said. "No...no...no..." He turned a terrified expression to Stewart's splayed form.

"Timmy, you've got to do it," she said. "Garlen's hurt, baby. We've got to get him to a doctor. You've got to get that knife. Please."

But he continued to stare at Stewart, shaking his head. He was falling away from her, withdrawing from the horror of what he'd done. Soon, he might not respond at all. She hated the dead man on the altar for what he had done to her, but what he had done to her little boy's mind was unforgivably. She prayed he rotted in Hell.

Closing her eyes, she grimaced in disgust at what she knew she had to do. Even before she uttered the desperate words, she felt horrible. "Please do this for Mama, baby. If you love me, you'll do it."

"No, Mama, no...I can't..." His body pulled into itself; the terror was too much. His face wrenched up in terrible emotional pain, as he sobbed in great heaves. He scooted farther away from the old man.

"Timmy!" She made herself harden at his pain; she had to. "You've got to get that damn knife. Garlen will die, if we don't help him."

After a few moments, Timmy brushed his tears away with an angry swipe of his arm. He sniffed back more tears and moved in a slow crawl towards Stewart's still body. He hesitated a few times, reaching forward, then pulling back, afraid to touch his grandfather's dead body. Then looking at his mother one last time, he grabbed the knife hilt with a trembling hand. His fingers wrapped around it

Stewart gave an animal howl and twisted around to grab Timmy by the throat. Blood dribbled in a thin line from one side of his mouth. His face was a grotesque mask of delirium and pain, the insane grin of a lunatic that has seen a glimpse of what lies on the other side of that final darkness and knows that it is waiting for him.

Timmy gurgled in terror, as he tried to escape the man's iron grip. Stewart heaved himself up, crying out in agony. Timmy's kicking feet left the ground, as Stewart lifted him over his shoulder, intent upon smashing him against the stone floor.

Timmy saw the knife quiver in the grip of Stewart's rock hard muscles. He desperately fumbled for it, fingers slipping on the gore soaked hilt. He gripped the bloody handle in both hands and gave it a frantic twist. The blade scraped bone and suddenly he was falling to the floor. But, in his panic, Timmy did not release the knife hilt. With unconscious tenacity, he hung on, and the blade sliced down Stewart's back like a fishing line through water, opening him up from shoulders to buttocks. A great gaping red eye opened as Timmy plummeted to the hard stone floor.

The old man turned in a stumbling gait, his mouth open in a silent scream of final terror. He looked down at Timmy, almost comical in his surprise at having been killed by a boy less than half his size. His last words were nothing more than a whisper, "What have you done?" Then his eyes rolled to the back of his head and he fell face first to the stone floor with a final thud. Gouts of Machen blood burst from the large, gaping wound and splashed the altar and Timmy. The blood river ran from one step to the next, painting the symbols in crimson, seeping into the indentions and deep slashes, in short, creating a circle of blood from one end of the altar to the other. After a few moments, the lines of blood met, rolled together like liquid lovers, and the circuit closed.

The room was silent except for Timmy's rapid gasps for air and Mary's moaning cries for her son. The heavy silence was replaced by a grating of stone against stone.

Mary and Timmy looked at one another across the expanse of the room. The chamber rocked under them, as if some unheard explosion had gone off in the earth. A rain of pebbles fell, rattled and bounced on the floor. They both looked at the rock ceiling above them. The small quaver deepened, became a lower, more intense, rumble of violence. More sediment rained down; more pebbles clattered to the floor.

"Timmy," Mary said as calmly as possible. "Get the knife. Now."

CHAPTER -25-

Charlotte was getting ready to have tea when she felt the first unhappy shudders in the mansion's vast, old frame. There was a sense of doom-laden inevitability to the small quakes being transmitted through the walls and floor, as if she had expected this moment all along.

She set aside her teacup and heaved her aged body from the comfortable chair. Wincing, she moved slowly. Her lower body still ached from last night's ritual birthing. She loved the feeling of creation and destruction as she shoved those dark orphic forms from her cunt, but the pain was sometimes too much to bear, transcendent, almost euphoric, in its intensity. Of course, what she did with her newborns later that made it all worthwhile.

Charlotte made her way to a cabinet sitting like a soldier in the corner of the dimly lighted room and opened the top door. It squealed on unused hinges. Behind a set of antique Civil War thimbles, she found what she sought, a small handgun. It hadn't been used in some time, so she hoped its presence would be enough. Charlotte gave the load a quick check, and saw that it was loaded and ready, even if she wasn't.

She despised having to go into that damned ceremonial chamber. The place was like a dungeon and it smelled bad, and that putrid swamp running beneath its stones made her uneasy. She considered sending a few servants down in her stead. But for all their entertainment value, she knew they possessed no reasoning power and would be as helpless as babes if a situation had arisen that required quick decisive action.

No, it would be best if she went below to find out the matter for herself.

The house gave another lurch, much greater this time, and dust rained down from a light fixture overhead.

Charlotte frowned. This might be more serious than she first considered.

And there was something else, some sound she couldn't quite place. A low throbbing that she felt in her bones more than she heard with her ear. It made her skin itch and crawl as if she had stumbled into a flea nest. Little pinpricks of discomfort raced along her body, quickening her aged pulse. She shook off the building sensation and hurried for the secret door behind the middle bookcase in her son's study. The dank tunnel passage, with the small dim lights on the walls, would lead her down to the ceremonial chamber quickly enough.

The throbbing was at first only uncomfortable, but to her dismay, soon turned painful, and oddly enough, more a mental pain than a physical one. Nonetheless, she felt her heart begin to beat faster in panic. This had never happened before, this shaking of the foundations, this discomfiting throb in her bones. It could only mean one thing: Stewart had somehow botched the ceremony.

But the ceremony wasn't to have started for another four hours yet. There were quite a number of pages that had to be read aloud. She knew it was too soon for Timmy to be conscious and sentient; he had to be aware of what was happening to him or else the ceremony was no good. The pain and the terror were the Black Beast's demanded price. The Machen blood was almost like an afterthought. Or at least that was what Stewart had always told her.

The house's violent shudders did not instill confidence in his astuteness.

The throbbing pulse of the disintegrating house was like a like a tickle of pain in the back of her throat, a wiggle of itch in her ear. It was disorienting as she made her way down the tight stinking tunnel.

Maybe it wouldn't be such a bad idea to have some help below if things had been so badly botched.

Charlotte closed her eyes and gave a hurried mental command. Soon, an orange, glowing light subsumed the passage. One of the faceless servants floated from the ethereal darkness to join her. She could see by its wavering light that the quavering of the house was agitating the creature as well. Its light ebbed and brightened with the subtle bone-deep throb of the house. "We've work to do," she told the specter. "Come with me." Master and unholy servant descended into the stinking darkness together.

By the servant's spectral illumination, Charlotte made her way down into the belly of the mansion. Slinking through the tight, winding passage, to finally land at a set of worn wooden steps. The steps led even further into the rotten core of Machen Mansion. Along the way the house shook and groaned all around her like an old man caught in a fit of nightmare ague. Clouds of century-thick dust fell in lazy curtains, ancient long vacated cobwebs ripped into shreds across her face, as she hurried through the dimly lighted darkness. A profusion of spiders, roaches, and silverfish ran for more solid ground- driven by instinct to leave the place. Some of the secreted ways of Machen mansion hadn't been used for decades. Next to her, the shadow servant whispered fearfully, its soul-light quivering in sympathy with the trembling domicile.

At the bottom of the steep, rail less stairway, she found the door to the ceremonial chamber locked, as usual. Charlotte punched in the number combination on the keypad with a shaking hand. She gave a mental command that the servant should wait here. Its power might make matters worse. Whatever was tearing the place apart was bad enough.

And as if her thoughts were the catalyst, the throbbing sound grew more powerful. She could feel it at the back of her throat.

The door swung open and she peered inside.

Charlotte cried out in misery at the sight of Stewart lying upon the altar, bloodied and still. Across the room, Timmy was sawing away with Stewart's ceremonial dagger at the thick cords of ropes that bound his mother. Garlen was slumped over into unconsciousness, his ropes already parted, lying like dead snakes all around him. She stepped inside. "Put down that knife, you little bastard."

Timmy jumped at the sound of Charlotte's strident command as if he'd been shocked, frozen in mid-cut. Mary's gaze shifted to the gun. Charlotte shifted the gun to her, motioning the boy away. "Do as I tell you or I'll shoot your mother, boy."

For a moment Timmy stood, indecisive, the knife still poised above the last few coils of rope holding his mother imprisoned. Then his shoulders sagged and his face crumpled in defeat; the knife clattered to the floor.

Charlotte smiled like a hungry vulture.

Mary sobbed.

Feeling in control of the situation again, she made her way to the two of them, shaking her head sadly. She looked in disgust at Stewart's body. Her swimming, hard eyes found Timmy. "You...you...have no idea what you've done. Hundreds of years of power lost in mere moments of white-trash ignorance." She moved to look at Garlen's pale still form; she gave him a savage kick to his undefended ribcage. His body rolled over lifelessly. Then she turned her attention to her living captives. "The blood you spilled wasn't ordinary blood. It was Machen blood. And in Hell that means a lot. There was a pact many years ago with something unholy, boy. Killing Stewart ended it." She glanced at the trembling roof in darkness above, at the shifting shelves, the tumbling books, and the slightly askew podium. "It's must begin anew. Someone must be the conduit." Charlotte moved towards the boy.

"My God," Mary cried out. "You can't be serious. He's just a little boy, Charlotte." She writhed for escape, but the remaining ropes still clung tenaciously to her upper body, preventing her from extricating herself.

Charlotte ignored her, moved closer to Timmy. The boy stumbled back, eyes wide with terror.

"The blood has already been spilled by your hand, boy," she said. "Come take what's yours." She held out her hand, gave him a yellow skeletal grin.

Around them the vibrations, and the headache-inducing throb, escalated into new levels of violence, turning the room into a shaking world of dust and crumbling stone and falling books. On the altar, the cooling blood seeped into the ancient cracks and grooves of the stone. And it could be felt, this satisfying of a venerable pact between what was and what should not be; like an electrical thrumming beneath the toothache throb, something had been done that could not be taken back, an ironclad contract more solid than death.

Something beyond the sealed round portal on the other side of the altar began to beat in a harried rhythm of demand. Something unnamable sought ingress.

Charlotte moved like a striking snake, snatched Timmy from his mother's side. The boy yelped in surprise. Reaching down, she retrieved the ceremonial dagger, and dragged him backward to the altar, the gun pressed against his temple. She looked between the running blood on the stone, and then over her shoulder at the quivering portal door, an expectant smile plastered cross her thin cruel lips.

Machen blood was only the first part of the bargain.

The next was the most crucial. The gift of Machen flesh.

Timmy had conveniently taken care of that for her as well. Charlotte spared a glance at her son's cooling body.

She had to open the door. Charlotte made sure of her grip on the boy's arm, twisting it to show she meant business, and then set aside the gun. It was best not to approach the Black Beast with a weapon in hand. It might be misconstrued. The beast was cunning and seemed to understand the bargain, but wasn't to be trusted to know every nuance of human action. Her own father had lost an arm in that manner when he'd mistakenly approached the beast with a sword in his hand. It was a mistake that no Machen had repeated since.

After the ceremony there would be the boy with which to be dealt. Would she be able to control him? If not by his own choice, there were ways of making him do what she wanted. The mother might come in handy, if the boy thought there was a chance of keeping her alive. And she intended to have the power under her control, a power that the beast would only allow a male Machen. She would reach new heights with it that Stewart could never have imagined. She knew there must be ways to carry the power beyond this damned swamp and she intended to find them all.

The din increased. The floor vibrated at a steady rate now, thrumming like a snoring giant beneath her feet. The portal shuddered under the great strength of the beast on the other side.

Charlotte tugged the boy behind her, as she reached for the portal release mechanism.

She hit the handle.

The door began to swing open.

CHAPTER -26-

Sully was freezing. He hadn't been in this much pain since his military days. His arm was numb from the fracture he had suffered and his shoulders were riddled with deep, slicing cuts from the Beast's earlier attacks. He didn't know how much blood he'd lost, but knew it wasn't doing him much good in his present condition. He felt all but done in. The only thing keeping him upright and moving was the soul-deep need to get back to the house and save the others.

But he had no idea where the house was- let alone how to get there.

After his escape from the tunnel, he had slid for what seemed like forever through the tight, twisting pipe. With startling abruptness, the slime-covered chute spit him into a vast swamp. He'd barely missing several ancient cypress stumps protruding from the inscrutable dark waters. He'd risen, gasping for air, from the dank waters, his only thought getting as much distance between him and the Black Beast as possible. And he'd taken off in a stumbling, confused gait, pulling his weak, shaking legs over fallen, half-submerged tree roots, pushing through moss swollen limbs, past thick stands of mud caked bush.

And now he had stopped to check his surroundings in this primordial swamp. He didn't know how long he had been in the tunnel, but it must have been longer than he thought, because the sun was going down and the surrounding wood was getting darker and less hospitable by the moment. It looked like something pulled from history's predawn. Twisted trees, cypress, pines, and oaks, arched into the darkening skies, ripping at the underbelly of the rolling storm clouds. The smell was death and life, congealed by eons of slow decay and rebirth from that decay. Strands of Spanish moss flipped and curled in the wind. Constant animal calls echoed through the deep forest, creating layers of depths unseen. He turned from side to side, trying to decide which way to move next.

He was lost. There was no way to sugarcoat it.

The dark, unfamiliar territory, and the fact that every stand of trees looked exactly like the one before it, had all combined to keep him off balance.

Turning until he caught the dim glow of the setting sun, he tried to remember which side of the house the sun had set on last night. It had been shining past the iron front gate, so if he moved toward the sun, there was a chance he might find the house. Slim, but better than standing around bleeding to death, surely.

It could be miles. Sully didn't know how much more he could keep pushing himself. He was tough as nails, prided himself on that fact, but every man had his limits. He was slowly bleeding to death, dead on his feet with exhaustion. Some men might lie down and die right here, give up to the darkness. But there was some unexplainable element to men like Sully, something that would not allow surrender. He had to keep going. With the sun going down quickly, he couldn't help but feel things were coming to a head back in that horrible house. Night surely meant

Stewart's dark plans were close to fruition. After all, night was the time of evil things.

He stopped for a moment to catch his breath, holding up his tired body against a moss covered tree root. For a moment he wasn't sure he felt it, but he held his breath, watched the water at his feet. A tremor set the pool in motion.

Sully started to move away, but the ground lurched violently beneath him and he had to grip the slimy tree to keep from pitching forward. The waters bubbled next to him. Black liquid burst in stinking sympathy with the mysterious movement.

He looked ahead, at a point beyond the thickness of the swamp forest. It wasn't hard to figure out that this had something to do with the Machens. The insistent need to hurry pushed him onward again. He shoved away from the tree, stumbling forward. A bone deep throb began to cycle through his body. His fillings sang in sympathy with the constant droning keen. Instead of causing him despair, this new pain acted as an brace and smiled, knowing it could only mean he was getting closer.

As he passed by a copse of trees he felt as if he might have passed a million times, when a young boy's voice came from them. "Hey, mister," the boy said, as he stepped from behind the trees. "Whachu doin out here?"

Sully staggered to the nearest tree trunk and held himself up. He tried to speak, but only a croaking sound came out. He raised a shaking arm to point in the direction of where he was sure the house should be.

The boy watched the gesture and frowned in confusion. Then his eyes widened with understanding. "Hey! You came here in that big ole helly-copter, huh? I saw it flying over the other day."

Sully nodded, trying to catch his breath. Every moment was one less moment he had in which to stop the Machens. He had to get moving again.

The kid hesitated and then moved closer. "You lost? Tryin' to get back to the Machen place?"

Sully spit a wad of copper tasting blood to the side. "Yeah," he answered. "I gotta get there fast."

The boy looked around him for a second, peering into the trees beyond, scanning the dark. An indecisive moment passed, and then he nodded. "I can show you the way, mister," he said.

"Yes. Please, let's hurry." He shoved upright, felt the world sin a bit, then level out once more. The bone deep thrumming noise caused his head to ache even more. He grunted against the pain and waved the boy on.

"I guess you feel it, too, huh?" he asked. "Feels like a toothache or something."

"Worse," Sully responded.

The sure-footed boy led him through the dank swamp landscape, finding an unerring pathway through the trees and undergrowth, avoiding the swampy deeps, and putting them on high ground when possible. Sully admired his surety. The boy knew every inch, or so it seemed to him. He was a ragged boy, skinny, pale and malnourished. His clothes were full of holes and his shoes looked ready to give up the ghost and fall off his feet in pieces.

They came upon an area where there was more water than land and he started off in a tangential direction to avoid it. Sully gauged how far they'd need to go around. "I'm not afraid to walk through a little water, kid."

The boy half turned, eyes serious. "You sure better be. Gators round here just as soon eat you as a possum, mister."

After that, Sully kept quiet and didn't question him again. He battled against the growing sensation he was already too late.

The storm built above them, shoving the swamp trees against one another, drawing haunting sounds of wood against wood. The limbs and the moss combined to make a shifting landscape.

It seemed like miles before Sully finally saw light shining through tangled vines and scraggly limbs. The illumination could have only one source: the Machen mansion. Sully hurried them on, the light his beacon, his mind swimming with blood loss and fever. The boy showed him a path to the security. Sully pulled himself up the cold metal tines and turned to the boy on the other side. "You should probably leave now," he said, wiping cold sweat from his face. "I appreciate your help. If there's anyway I can, later, I'll come thank you again." The boy stared at him in silence. Sully waved him away weakly and started a weaving run for the house.

The boy watched the big man running for the house. He hesitated for a moment, glancing over his shoulder. But there was only the wind tossed wood behind him.

Finally, he followed Sully's example and started to scale the security fence.

There was a chill in Sully's bones that had nothing to do with the temperature of the night. Some of his cuts had stopped bleeding, clotted on their own, but the deeper ones, the ones that caused him the most concern continued to slowly seep his life away. Sweat had dried in a plastic coating across his naked chest, hair plastered to his skull like a web. The throbbing had gained in strength and venom; his chest ached with its deep ruuummm…ruuummm-ing.

The mansion loomed up before him. The long expanse of lawn had taken on the aspect of a field of blood.

The ground gave another of those great vomit lurches. Sully stumbled to his knees and groaned. He felt ready to collapse. His body shook all over.

Get up, dammit! Forget the pain and doubt. You've got to save them.

Mary's face swam before his eyes like a ghost, followed by Timmy and Garlen. He had to stop the evil from consuming them. He couldn't let it happen all over again.

Sully forced himself up, knees like wobbly balloons under his mass. He moved forward, and finally staggered against the door to the house. He shoved against the door, feeling his muscles tense like iron under his injuries and exhaustion. There was a low squeal of resistance, and then the frame split, ancient wood finally giving way. The door collapsed inward with a loud crash.

The ground shook again. Dust showered him. Some fragile object inside the house fell and broke somewhere beyond. He stumbled over the broken door, peered in the dimness. A darkened chandelier tinkled overhead, as if to warn him that the universe was falling apart. Sully shook his head of useless visions and kept making one foot move in front of the other.

He needed to find a weapon.

Standing uncertainly, he remembered the old man had mentioned guns to Timmy the night before. He searched several rooms, unsure of where Machen kept his weapons. Luck was with him when he accidentally found a hunting room. Stuffed animal heads glared in frozen menace as he hurried to a rifle cabinet.

It was locked.

Sully punched his elbow through the thin glass, reached in and grabbed a double barrel shotgun. The gun felt wonderfully heavy in his shaking arms, the side-by-side barrels as thick as three of his fingers put together. He figured whatever he might confront in this chamber of horrors the shotgun should do the trick.

Ammo was stored conveniently in a drawer below the weapons. With a grim smile, Sully picked a handful of the thick red shells, stuffed as many as he could fit into the pockets of his blue jeans.

He felt better already.

He spied a liquor cabinet across the room. The cabinet wasn't locked, but he used the butt-end of the shotgun on it anyway. Glass and wood crumpled beneath his assault. He snatched a bottle of yellow colored liquor. With trembling fingers he unscrewed the cap and gulped down three large mouthfuls of the burning liquor. It hit his stomach like lava and warmed him like a stoked fire. The pain ebbed under the hot flood of liquor and he thanked whatever gods created the beautiful stuff. The remainder he doused along his body, scrubbing at the various cuts and nicks he'd received in the last few hours. The burning sensation helped clear some of his mental cobwebs away. He tore a strip of red velvet lining from inside the cabinet and made a makeshift tourniquet for the deepest of the cuts along his right arm. The fracture was still numb, but eh could feel the pain coming on in slow waves.

Satisfied with his work, he sped from the room, eager to find Mary, Garlen, and Timmy. But, mostly, he wanted to put both barrels of the shotgun against Stewart Machen's head and pull the double action trigger. Sully wasn't a violent man. Not to say that he had not done violence in his life. There was a time and place for it that no talk could ever get you out of. The dark side of human nature, the violent side, was in everyone. This day he had been pushed to the limit. Now it was kill or be killed.

Around him, the house continued to shake itself to pieces; heavier objects could be heard tumbling in upper levels, crashing to the floor. The irritating subconscious toothache throb had escalated, making the small hairs on his arms and legs stand up, as if he were walking inside a giant dynamo.

He made his way to a set of stairs, hoping that his memory wasn't playing tricks on him, as he left the landing and ran down a familiar looking hallway. His and Garlen's room had to be down here somewhere.

The house gave another violent shudder, throwing him off balance. Sully fell, the gun slipping from his grasp, skittering across the eye-searing carpet.

He heard a tearing sound above. Looking up he saw the roof was coming apart. Bits of it fell around him. He fumbled to his feet and grabbed the shotgun.

He found the bedroom, recognizing Garlen's suitcase as he passed the room by. The old man's wheelchair was gone. The bedclothes were still rumpled. The room had a distressing deadness about it. He went to his own room, to the bathroom, the place where he'd been abducted in the wee hours of the morning.

Tapping the walls behind the toilet, he found a nice hollow sound to the left. Hefting the shotgun, he pulled the triggers. The explosion was like a small bomb in the bathroom's tight quarters and the wall disintegrated under the double punch of the high power ammo. Sully coughed against the smoke, his ears ringing under the noisy onslaught. Using the butt-end of his weapon, he cleared away more of the debris so that he could crawl through the hole. Beyond was a tight, black trembling passage to greet him. He cracked the gun open and ejected the two spent shells. Digging more from his pockets, he loaded again.

Despite the blinding darkness, Sully pushed quickly down the passageway. He made two false turns, coming to a halt at dead ends, before he found a set of steps leading down.

This must be it. Into the belly of the beast, then.

Down the teetering steps, only a cold stone wall to either side, Sully kept the shotgun pointed into the shadows ahead, his heart thundering in counterpoint to the thrum of the house. Step after step, and the case twisted round like a dragon eating its own tail.

He stepped off the last stair, the key padded security door before him.

From the gathering of black near the corner lurched a thin blank faced creature; a dull orange glow pulsed in its chest. The thing's wavering, insubstantial arms stretched forward to embrace Sully. He tried to get his gun up as the living shadow swarmed over him. Seeming to be made of equal parts smoke and ether, nonetheless Sully felt its reality as it bounced him back to land against the unforgiving stone wall behind him.

Air burst out in a single gasping stunned shout.

Before he could move, the glowing creature was on him again. Snaking smoky fingers reached for his throat. Cold black swallowed him as the thing pulled him for a final embrace.

His hand convulsed in panic.

The shotgun went off, pointblank in the middle of the mercurial ghost creature. Its body blew away to nothing under the double assault, dissipated into useless smoke. Sully watched in stunned amazement as its last vestige, the dim orange light, weakened until it was no more than a blown out match head, and then the creature was gone.

In shock, he wrenched himself up, still staring in unbelieving terror at the now blank space before him. With shaking hands, Sully reloaded the shotgun, the constant thrum inside of his head like a steel wool pad on soft wood.

His vision was beginning to waver again. His body was reaching its limit, despite the tourniquet, despite the numbing effects of the alcohol. Whatever he was going to do, he'd best be about it before his inner night took him down.

With that dire thought, Sully pushed through the partially open door and into the chamber.

CHAPTER -27-

When Sully entered the shivering ceremonial chamber, he realized what he'd taken as his own thundering heartbeat was something pounding to get in from the other side of the portal where Stewart Machen had tossed him. It didn't take a huge jump in logic to guess what was doing the pounding.

He took in the room and its occupants with relief. They were still alive.

Charlotte and Timmy stood near the shivering portal door. The old woman had a menacing hold on the boy's arm. Sully saw she was reaching forward to open the portal.

Stewart lay on the raised dais, his naked body, still and bloodied.

Writhing on the floor beyond the altar was Mary, bound by rope, her face ashen and tear stained. Her pleas to Charlotte were lost under the groans of the dying structure, diluted by the throbbing of the altar. Light from above flickered brightly then dimmed as the room shook.

The sight of Garlen lying on his side, pale faced and still, made his heart skip a beat with terror.

Grimly, Sully hobbled in. Charlotte Machen had her back to him. He leveled the shotgun at her. "Stop, Charlotte," he said. "Don't open that door." And the act of speaking seemed to drain him. His voice sounded weak, even to him. He could feel himself wavering on his feet. He was sallow and shaky, growing weaker by the moment. Silently, he cursed his body's weakness. The room was beginning to spin around him, reality unhinging, a counterpoint to the seeming destruction of the chamber. But he had to hold on for just a little longer. He had to get the boy away from her. Had to keep the door closed.

Surprised, Charlotte turned to him, a diabolical smile on her wrinkled countenance. "I knew Stewart was wrong about you, boy," she said. "You are a scrapper, aren't you? That was one of Stewart's biggest faults. He was always underestimating people."

"Let the boy go," Sully said. He blinked cold sweat from his eyes. The room tilted, but he resisted the impulse to sway with it, unsure if it was the room actually moving or if it was in his head.

Charlotte glanced at the pistol near her foot and then the double barrel; she let go of Timmy's arm. "Doesn't matter," she said. "It's already started." She backed away, hands held out before her.

Timmy hurried to his mother's side. Sully saw the kid wasting no time, as he began tugging at the last few coils of rope holding her prisoner, urged on by Mary's strident sobs. The solid tattoo against the portal door continued, its violence growing with every passing second. Sully took a step towards the old woman, motioning her away from the portal. He did not want the beast getting inside. Even with this monstrosity of a gun he didn't feel quite up to tackling the thing. The speed with which it had moved in the tunnel earlier was terrifying. And he wasn't at what he could call peak condition at the moment. He knew he wasn't going to get much further on what he had left.Charlotte was still watching him, a sneer on her thin lips. Now that he was confronted with option, Sully wasn't sure he could actually kill the old woman. Seeing Stewart's dead body lying akimbo across the altar had drained much of his need for vengeance. All he wanted to do was get everyone the hell out of Machen mansion. Hurry Garlen to a hospital…if it wasn't too late.

But Charlotte wasn't done with him yet. Her eyes narrowed as she took in his unsteady legs and shaking grip on the shotgun as it dipped lower against his will. "You're almost gone, aren't you, boy? I doubt you even have enough strength left to pull the trigger."

"Don't try me, you old bag," he warned, feeling his legs shaking under him. The room tilted again. He swayed with it this time, but caught himself before he could fall.

She snorted in disdain. She ignored the gun and turned away from him, reached for the portal release again.

"Goddamn it, I'm not kidding. I'll kill you if I have to." His eyes wobbled in his head, unable to track properly. He wasn't even sure he was pointing at Charlotte any longer, because he suddenly saw three of her. A profound darkness began to crowd at the edges of his distorted vision.

He knew he'd waited too long. The decision had been taken from him. His body had nothing left. The blood loss and the exhaustion had come to collect their due.

And Charlotte knew it at the same time he did. She lurched for the release handle.

Sully pulled the triggers. The twin blasts knocked him off his feet. He heard the old woman's insane laughter follow him down into the dark. It was not a comforting companion.

Timmy almost had the last few coils of rope from her when Sully pulled the triggers. Mary whirled to see with a sinking heart that the shots had missed, blasting, instead, the tumbled podium.

"Oh Sully..." she whispered in despair, bowing her head in defeat.

Timmy pulled harder at the rough ropes. Fingers torn and bleeding from the strain, they kept slipping from the coils. Frustrated tears clouded his vision.

Charlotte was still cackling.

The portal shuddered with the force of the thing on the other side.

A horrible roar of impatience echoed beyond the pulsing metal.

Mary could see Charlotte pulling at the portal release. The thing would soon be among them.

A loud crashing shot sounded over the toothache noise and the constant pounding.

A large red blossom appeared in Charlotte's back. She gasped in surprise, a rage filled denial on her lips, and half turned.

Confused, Mary and Timmy followed her gaze to see a pallid Garlen, still lying on the ground, his legs thrown out uselessly behind him. He held Charlotte's pistol in both hands, the weapon weaving back and forth.

Charlotte gasped, trying to pull air into her collapsed lung; her face turned a deep shade of purple, but the insane grin was still there. She staggered towards the handle, and defied death long enough to fall towards it. Catching the lever in quivering hands, she pulled it down with her dying body.

For a moment, even the crumbling house grew quiet.

Then the door shuddered open. The mouth gaped open, exposing deep night.

The insistent banging stopped.

They watched the empty dark of the door with wide and frightened eyes.

Something grunted, then there was silence again.

"Oh jesus...oh god...Timmy, hurry up," Mary begged. He ripped the rope from her arms. Hands free, she tore the last two coils from her legs.

Across the room, Garlen collapsed again, the fallen gun still smoking, lying next to his sprawled hands.

Timmy stared at the gun and then the open portal. He scurried to his feet and ran for the gun.

"Wait, Timmy," Mary called.

Sliding down next to Garlen, he fumbled for the gun. He pointed it at the darkness of the portal.

Overhead, the light blinked spastically in its death shivers. The ceiling crumbled more and more by the moment. Small chunks of rock smashed like gunshots to the stone floor.

Something shone in that darkness. Two eyes peered back at him.

Mary watched the portal in terror. She could feel something waiting. "Come here," she whispered to Timmy. "Hurry. Give me the gun."

Timmy looked at her, eyes wide and blinking, and then hurried to her side. He handed over the gun in a clumsy two-handed way, clung to her side in a desperate grip. She took the pistol. Wiping tears from her face, she steadied the gun.

At the portal, something snorted and sighed. A deep growl sounded from the dark. Then two enormous paws grasped the edges of the portal mouth and the creature began to pull itself from the tunnel.

She moaned as the massive creature filled the hole with its gigantic form. Dark haired, red eyed, and scaled in places, the humanoid monster sniffed the air hungrily. All eight feet of it finally dropped from the portal mouth, landed with a solid smack to the stone floor of the chamber.

Mary kept the gun on it, ready to fire at the least sign that it intended them harm. But the thing only spared mother and son a slow dumb-animal gaze, and then looked down at Charlotte's dead body lying next to it. Tucking the pistol down her jeans, Mary grabbed Timmy's hand, began to guide them along the wall.

The Black Beast squatted over Charlotte, bent forward and ran a long reptilian tongue along her still form. It grunted and pushed at the dead woman, prodding her to move. After a moment, it settled down and wasted no time in beginning its meal.

She wanted to run while the thing was busy with its horrible feast, but one try to put her weight on her legs told her she was not running anywhere. Her legs tingled painfully now that the blood was rushing back to its rightful place. She could move but not too fast. Her mind turned to the others and how she was going to get them out of here. She and Timmy might be able to drag Garlen out together, but Sully must weigh close to two hundred and fifty pounds. How was she going to get him out?

Mary turned away in horror as the thing began to pull at Charlotte's dead flesh, tearing the old woman apart in large bloody chunks, stuffing the pieces in its large oval mouth. She pulled Timmy behind her limping form towards Garlen. The thing didn't seem to notice or care that they were moving, only continued its eating of Charlotte Machen in rapid, but economical, motions. There wasn't much left of her now- a pink gore covered skeleton in a pool of spreading blood and missed chunks on the floor.

She motioned for Timmy to grab Garlen's arm and they hauled him towards the still open doorway of the chamber. She wanted to check for a pulse, but seeing the thing would soon be done with Charlotte, she decided to wait.

Sully was ashen and filthy, looking more dead than alive. But she saw with a grateful tremble in her stomach that his chest still rose and fell in even breaths. So much blood, but when she touched his face it was warm and alive.

Timmy handed her the shotgun. She held it close to her chest, unsure if she could use it, yet feeling an odd comfort in its solid balanced weight. "Hurry up, honey," she said. "Grab his other leg." She indicated Sully's leg, motioning at him impatiently. But Timmy was staring wide-eyed past her shoulder, and the question of whether she could use the shotgun or not was taken from her hands, as she turned to see that the creature had finished its grisly meal and was making its way toward them. Mary dropped her hold on Sully's leg and aimed the shotgun.

"Kill it, Mama," Timmy said, his voice rising in panic.

The thing was taking its time, rummaging through the broken debris of the altar and watching them at the same time. Mary and Timmy froze. The creature snuffled at their scents and grunted. Its dead black eyes watched Mary.

She pulled the twin triggers. And heard two dry useless clicks from the weapon. The shells were spent. She had not reloaded.

Mary popped the weapon open and clumsily pulled the two shells from their breeches. She looked around for ammunition. Then she saw Sully's bulging jean pockets. She pushed Timmy behind her and dug for shells. As large as they would have looked to her in any other circumstance, right now the damn things looked too small, too inept, to hurt something as monstrous as the thing before her. She shoved them into the breech uncertainly and snapped the weapon closed. She hefted its weight to her shoulder, aimed at the thing's head.

With a savage mewl the Black Beast lunged forward.

Mary fired. The shotgun punched her shoulder, throwing most of the shot over her intended target. The beast scrambled to a hasty stop and peered down at her. It looked from the shotgun and back at her, paced back and forth, like a predator who does not quite know how to handle a new enemy.

"Timmy, I want you to run as quick as you can."

She tried to keep her voice calm, despite her terror and tears. "Get out. Go stay by Garlen."

"No, Mama, no" Timmy whined. "I want to stay with you."

She gave her son a stern stare and shook her head. "Get out. Please, Timmy."

"I won't leave you," Timmy said; a firmness in his tone that made her angry and scared for him all at once. She started to admonish him, beg him even, to get out, but she never had the chance.

The beast made its move. This time it came at them in a low loping run. Mary had no time to react, and no shells loaded to do so if she could.

Mary felt herself lifted from the ground by the monster's thick arms. Two sudden slashes of pain lanced her arms, as black claws tore through her clothes and into her trembling flesh. The unexpected attack sent the empty shotgun flying from her grasp and it clattered away.

The thing drew her close to its terrible face. Two red eyes blazed hate at her. Distantly she heard Timmy screaming for her, but the pain drove rational thought from her head like a hammer driving nails through cardboard.

The Black Beast smelled of swamps and beetles and rot. Its red eyes shone like evil fires in the thick black fur and deep wrinkles of its hideous face. A twin row of yellow, blood stained teeth sneered at her gasping pain. The teeth moved apart, ready to rend her as they had Charlotte Machen. She was about to be torn apart in front of her son.

The house gave another lurch, spitting up

stone and wood, rocking the floor under her. Mary felt nothing but the pain and the desperate desire for life, as the stone pitched and shook itself to finality. "Put her down, you fuck," Sully demanded.

Her pain filled gaze found his, and she saw him barely standing, bracing his legs in a wide stance. His eyes were slits of pain and concentration.

Something hot and bright flashed past her, followed by an ear-shattering explosion. The beast squealed like a scalded rat and the twin points of steel pain released her and she tumbled to the floor in a heap of pained flesh. She groaned, vaguely felt her son's arms encircle her, as he dragged her away from the monster.

Sully sank to one knee, head hung in exhaustion. He lifted his ashen features and sneered at the squealing beast. Blood poured from its chest. Two black holes smoked and bleed where the twin shots had taken it. Weakly, he held the shotgun cradled in his trembling arms. "I've had just about enough of this voodoo bullshit," he said through gritted, blood stained teeth.

The thing roared in defiance, circling him, watching the gun.

Its rage poured more dust from the high ceiling; it cascaded down in a white dry rain.

Sully popped the weapon open and dug shells from his pocket. With unsteady hands he tried to load the shotgun again. One of the shells fell to the floor; the other slid into place. Sully knew he had no time to retrieve it and snapped the breech closed again. He swung the business end at the Black Beast.

It snuffled the air again and turned its gaze to Timmy.

"No, no, no," Sully cried and moved to intercept it.

The creature hurdled past Sully and snatched at Timmy. The screaming boy in its clutches, Sully couldn't chance hitting him by accident.

The beast, content with its prize, leaped for the open portal, Timmy screaming and kicking at its impossible girth. "Mama!" he cried.

Mary screamed, tried to haul herself up. The overwhelming pain in her arms was too much; muscles cramped, mutinied, threw her to the ground. "SULLY!!" she screamed, a final plea.

Sully pushed up and swayed for a second. The thing was close to the black mouth of the portal, raising its body up to go through the opening. He leaped for its bulk, snagged the slime-ridden hair and hung on like a rat, grunting at the effort it took not to fall off the huge towering monster.

The Black Beast leaped into the darkness below, carrying he and Timmy through the black.

They hit the cold, dank swamp water. Sully felt it rushing over him in undulating waves. The thing's body moved like an eel through grease.

Sully had the shotgun in one hand and a tenacious grasp on the thing's hairy body with the other. He could feel his weight dragging, knew the thing had to be aware it had a passenger.

He was lifted clear of the water and could see by the dimness of the light of the chamber above. The creature threw the boy aside, and Sully watched in horror as the little body bounced off the slimy wall. He roared in hatred at the beast towering above him, all dripping black fur and red blazing eyes, tearing claws, blood stained teeth.

He kicked away from the thing, jerked the shotgun up, and pulled the trigger.

The shot was point blank.

The elephant gun exploded, briefly lighting the tunnel, enough to allow him to see the beast take the shot full in the face. Its horrific features shredded away under the violent blast. Dark, hot fluid sprayed Sully and he fell away, slipping under the water again. The thing gurgled in agony once and fell beneath the churning black swamp waters.

When Sully broke the surface again, the creature was gone, carried away by the tunnel current. Bits of smoking furry flesh floated on the surface of the frothing water.

Sully swam with what little energy he had left to the boy. He was lying face down in the water, his little body limp. He drew Timmy into his arms and slapped his face lightly. There was no response. He wasn't breathing. Sully felt for a pulse, but he couldn't keep his hand still enough to feel anything. "Sully?"

He looked up to the glowing portal opening to see Mary peering anxiously into the hole. Her mind registered her son in his arms. Her face crumpled. It was like watching a horrible tragedy being played all over again.

Once again, he was alive and the ones he cared for were dead.

Well, he wasn't going to let this happen again. No goddamn way!

He shoved the boy towards her. "Take him! Get him out of this damn water. He's only been under for a little while. We've still got time, Mary."

Mary hung half way from the portal, grabbed Timmy by his limp shoulder, lifted his dripping form, and pulled him back into the shuddering stone room. Sully was able to find small handholds and managed to pull himself out.

Once out, he wanted to collapse on the floor, but he crawled to Mary and Timmy. She had already started clearing his breathing passages, had him turned on his side to empty anything from his mouth. Sully watched helplessly, feeling the dark take him again. The dark finally won, as he fell side ways. He heard Mary calling for her son across a vast gulf of blackness as he fell into his own blackness.

CHAPTER -28-

For Sully it was long way back from his darkness. He traveled through a limitless space of half-heard sounds and half-glimpsed images- none of which made any sense to his addled mind. He was only sure of one thing: that he was dead. He had failed the boy, Mary, and Garlen. Black, unknown space seemed a fitting hell for his failure. He did not fight it. He accepted it without question.

The only thing that kept interrupting his undisputed penance was the pain. It came in flashes of awareness, his arm and chest being hit and smashed.

Something tight holding him down.

A stinging in his arms.

Hell was fine, but why all the nonsensical pain?

When he opened his eyes again, he was just as surprised as the woman sitting next to him. Mary saw his squinting expression of confusion and burst into tears, throwing herself against his aching chest. He muttered something, a question, maybe, and then he was out again, floating in the unknown.

Sometime later, he heard someone say his name.

He forced his eyes open.

Bright daylight blasted him and he groaned. His head ached, but the pain had retreated somewhat. He was in a white room, with blue blinds. A machine beeped its hospital rhythm next to him; a band of multicolored wires ran from it and terminated along various parts of his blanket-covered body. The smell of alcohol permeated the air. A pole stood near him, holding a bag of clear fluid. He followed its drip tube to his right arm. Beyond his too bright room he could hear footsteps on tile and a muffled speaker voice calling for "Dr. Watson".

"Sully?"

He turned to see Mary looking down at him. "Where am I?" His voice sounded like a frog croaking for rain.

As answer, Mary leaned in and kissed his dry cracked lips. "You're back where you belong. You're alive. Thank you for not dying on me."

Sully gave her a confused glazed stare. "How? What happened?"

A doctor came in the room, holding a clipboard. The elderly black man smiled down at Sully with professional ease and moved around him, checking the machine and Sully, talking cheerily the whole time, not allowing any time between his words for any questions.

Then he remembered. He pushed the doctor away, reached for Mary's hand.

"Timmy!"

The startled doctor eyed Mary and collected his clipboard. When he was gone again, Mary placed both her small hands on each side of his face and smiled. "He's fine. Everything's fine."

"Garlen?"

"Fine."

The door flew open again and proof came through in the form of Timmy and Garlen. The boy was bandaged and smiling, seemingly no worse for the wear. Although his head was bandaged in a thick swath of white cloth, indicating that the wall he'd bounced off of had done some damage. He ran to Sully's side and squeezed past his mother. The doctor returned and started to hustle everyone from the room.

Garlen eased his electric chair next to him. "Just a few minutes, doctor. We promise to keep it quiet."

The elderly man looked at the collected faces: Timmy's hopeful one, Mary's blissful, Garlen's begging, the patient totally confused. He nodded and smiled. "Five minutes and that's it."

"Thanks," Garlen said.

The doctor stepped from the room and shut the door.

Sully looked at Garlen. The old man looked bad as he felt, face puffy and bruised, lips split and stitched with black nylon surgical thread. His left arm was in a white cast, and Sully could see beneath his blue hospital bathrobe that he wore a swath of bandages. Probably cracked ribs. But the old coot was still alive, thank God.

Garlen wheeled next to the bed, beside Mary and Timmy. "I never thought I'd be so happy to see your ugly mug, you bastard."

Sully grinned and laid a swollen bruised hand on his friend's shoulder.

"Hey," Mary said. "Watch how you talk about my future husband."

Sully looked at her. "Future what?"

She smoothed the blankets near his face. "You heard me, mister. The day you get released from here, we're getting hitched."

Sully shook his head. "Mary, you hardly know me. I may not be the man you think I am."

Garlen snickered, so did Timmy.

Mary leaned down and kissed his forehead. "I know enough." She drew away, frowning in mock anger. "You mean you don't want to marry me?"

Sully looked at Garlen, then at Timmy, both laughing at his stunned expression. He looked at Mary again, beautiful Mary, with her sparkling eyes, her wonderful soul, no longer sad. "Will you marry me?" he asked.

"I thought you'd never ask," she said, leaning forward to kiss him again.

It took another two days before the doctors would allow anyone but Mary to stay in his room for any amount of time. But she told him the story of their escape.

Mary had been able to get her son breathing again and they had managed to drag Sully from the room. The house was falling down around them and she thought for sure that they would all be buried underneath the rubble any minute. But Timmy led her through a series of tunnels to the outside again. Once she was sure that the tunnels would probably hold up, they hurried back to get Sully and Garlen. It took quite a bit of pulling, she told him with a grin, but they finally got all of them out of the house.

"And not a moment too soon", she said. "Because the place really started to go then." Last she saw there were several fires inside the house and smoke boiling from its lower depths. Within minutes, she heard sirens, and then there were men in suits flashing badges at her, pulling them to safety, asking her questions she couldn't answer. They were looking for Sheriff Lincoln...had she seen him? She was loaded into an ambulance with Timmy and last she saw the house was in flames, fire dancing along the roof and gambles, smoke obscuring the trees and the moon.

"I don't suppose they'll ever find him," Sully said. He told her about Lincoln and the tunnel beneath the house and how he had barely escaped with his life. Together they filled in the details of their separate ordeals. The story was not pleasant, but it was done.

"And no one found the Black Beast?"

Mary shook her head. "I tried at first to tell them but no one would believe me. Garlen said leave it be so I stopped."

Sully nodded his understanding.

What did it matter now anyway? It was gone for good. What good would it do to drag all the bad memories back to the surface again?

Then Sully remembered something else.

"What about the boy?"

Mary frowned at him in confusion. "What boy?"

"The boy who helped me find my way back to Machen mansion."

She shook her head. "You were pretty bad when you made it back in."

"There was a boy," he said. "A little swamp rat kid. He helped me get back."

Mary rubbed hair from his forehead. "There was no boy, Sully."

Sully sighed. Had he imagined the kid? If not, then what had become of him?

Mary interpreted his silence as acquiescence and told him about where she planned their honeymoon. But Sully could not help but wonder how much he had imagined and how much had been reality in the swamp.

What had happened to the boy?

EPILOGUE

The night called.

Jeb followed the familiar path through the swamp; the gibbous moon his only light. He preferred the dark. Now he had nothing to fear in the swamp, he found it much more beautiful when the trees were thin sharp shadows and the still dank waters were pure black like death itself. The gators and the panthers no longer worried him. All the creatures knew better than to harm him.

At first, the voice calling to him had scared him, left him shivering in his bed at night. But he found himself feeling sorrow for the thing's pain. The big man had hurt it bad, scarred it forever.

Even gods could feel pain, or so it seemed.

It took a few weeks of hearing the voice calling for him, making the promises over and over again, promises of riches and never being hungry again. But the best part was he got to relive that wonderful moment when he'd been one with the night, feeling the sounds, smelling the scents that only the night animals knew. Each time he felt that moment transpire inside him, he ran to the woods, eager to serve the thing that made the promises.

After sloshing through the muck and rot of several stands of watery brush, Jeb finally found the familiar copse of trees and stood beneath the towering thick arboreal guardians.

Something huge moved within their hidden depths.

He waited for the face to appear, fractured and scarred, full of hate and pain. The Black Beast looked him over again, as it did every time, as if deciding weather he was worthy of the power. Jeb straightened his shoulders, puffed out his thin chest. He wanted his friend to stay and teach him. He knew, soon, the time would come when the Black Beast would require the sacrifice. Jeb knew what the thing wanted him to do. The pictures had been bad at first, made him have nightmares, but after a while the dire images made sense.

After all, it had to be done to get the power.

He didn't think getting his daddy out here would be problem, especially if he was drunk enough.

Jeb sat down before the face and closed his eyes. The voice told him all the wonderful things he would soon be able to accomplish. If there was enough blood, there was nothing that he could desire which he could not have. And Jeb would make sure there was always enough blood, no matter what.

THE END

About the Author

Nickolas Cook lives in the Southwest desert with his wife and three pugs. His short fiction, reviews, interviews and non-fiction articles have appeared in many print and e-zines. He is also the author of *Baleful Eye* and *Paint it Black*.

More information about the author may be found by visiting his myspace site: myspace.com/nickolasecook.

Nickolas Cook is the Moderator for Shocklines Writing Group. It can be found at Shocklines.com

The Horror and Jazz-Blues Review is the official website of Nickolas Cook. It can be found at angelfire.com/jazz/nickolascook/

Also available from Dailey Swan Publishing, Inc

Revenge by JH Hardy	$12.95
Endlight Event John P Cater	$14.95
Deadline! by Paula Tutman	$15.95
In Lieu of Light by Wayne Jackson	$13.95
Dupers Fork (Prisoners of War) by Andrew Winter	$14.95
Journey Across Time by KD Richardson	$14.95
The Transyvania Connection by Garrison Walters	$15.95
The Acorn Dossier by William Beecher	$14.95
The Pub at the Center of the Universe by Dale Mettam	$14.95
Widdershins by Eve Lastrange	$13.95

www.daileyswanpublishing.com